The Starliner Murders

An Avei Themis Mystery

Kari Charsper

Starliner Press LLC

Cover design by CoverKitchen

First edition April 2025

For my mother, whose love of books sparked a lifelong passion for reading in her three daughters.

Prologue

Avei Themis lay curled up on the couch, feet twisted in a blanket. Empty alcohol units littered the coffee table. Neon lights from neighboring skyscrapers swept the darkened living room in a dizzying array of colors, creating a surreal dreamscape. Icy rain hit the windows, and a long, low rumble of thunder reverberated through the towering city.

Clad only in a thin tank top and pajama shorts, Avei shivered and pushed herself up to untangle the blanket. After a feeble attempt, she gave up and fell back, rubbing her arms. She forced her eyes to remain fixed on the hover vehicles flying on the skyway two streets over. A muffled roar signaled the departure of another passenger shuttle as it rose from the Mernin Spaceport. The sleek vehicle caught her eye as it plowed through the swirling storm clouds on its way to the spacehub.

Avei felt the hypnotic pull of the holographic monitor floating nearby, displaying an image of her smiling alongside a young man and woman. She closed her eyes tight and burrowed her head into a cushion, knowing the effort was pointless.

Why do I keep torturing myself?

With a moan, her eyes opened, and she stared at the picture, taken on one of the happiest days of her life. The trio wore black uniforms and stood in front of a mirrored tower, home to the Mernin Security Forces. Tral and Ezo towered over Avei and pointed at her right arm with three woven gold slashes on the sleeve. A heaviness settled on her chest as grief swamped her, making it difficult to breathe. Tears filled her eyes. Her two best friends were dead because of her.

As the image faded, Avei sucked in a ragged breath. The next picture materialized; this time of her and a statuesque woman, laughing under a yellow bisphina tree covered in lavender blossoms. The sisters both had their mother's purple hair and eyes, but only Anastasia had been lucky enough to inherit their mother's height. She had often teased Avei about sharing their father's petite stature, which had been supremely irritating at the time. Now Avei would give anything to hear her sister's voice, teasing or not.

The tears started afresh as she clutched the holographic locket around her neck and held it tight, wondering if she would ever feel normal again.

1

It had been three months since Avei had confronted a deranged serial killer known as Apollyona, having tracked her down to an abandoned warehouse. Avei had almost died in the ensuing fire. Now, while doctors said her physical injuries had almost healed, her emotional and spiritual wounds were another matter. The therapists implored her to forgive herself, fearing she might otherwise never recover. They called it survivor's guilt. One even referred to her emotional state as complicated grief. *Ridiculous*. Yes, she was guilty. Guilty of murdering twenty people, including her two best friends.

She knew her apartment reeked of neglect. A plate of protein noodles in rich gravy sat congealing on the dining room table. Another forgotten dinner. Takeout containers from a dozen restaurants littered the kitchen counter, their odor confirming they'd been there a while. A hardened puddle of something brown covered the floor in front of the sink. It disgusted her, but not enough to muster the energy to clean it.

Once again, she'd spent the entire day lying on the couch and had accomplished not one damn thing.

Avei's eyes drifted across the living room, which lacked any personal touches. No pictures on the wall, no knickknacks. *Pathetic.* She had bought the furnished apartment six years ago, with grand plans to spruce it up and make it her own. Given that she was currently curled up on the same scratchy couch that came with the unit, confirmed that had clearly never happened.

Avei wiped the tears from her face with the corner of her tank top. How did her home become this impersonal, transitory stop between cases?

Her mother said it was her oasis of neutrality from a life that dealt with evil and depravity every day. *Possible.*

Ezo had tried everything to get her to update her apartment and had even promised to help. Ezo was a genius with decorating and had refurbished her own place in the vibrant Jerdium style, where every color made an appearance but instead of overwhelming the senses, Ezo's home felt warm and welcoming. Avei and Tral loved her place, and it had become their second home. Ezo never minded. She loved to entertain. *Why didn't I accept her offer?*

Whenever Ezo brought up Avei's insipid decor, Tral defended her. He'd say their job kept them off the planet most of the time, so why should Avei fill her rare downtime with something as frivolous as decorating? This from a guy whose place reeked of personality. A gaming holochair consumed half his living room and a beer fridge and snack cabinet filled the other half. He had arranged everything, so he never had to leave his chair. They suspected he even slept in that chair. *Gods, I miss them so much.*

Tral was right. Mernin Security Forces' jurisdiction covered thirty-two planets, countless moons, and other less hospitable places. Wherever intelligent life flourished; be it human, alien, or hybrid, you found killers who developed a taste for taking a life. As a homicide inspector, Avei's entire focus was on serial killers and bringing them to justice on behalf of their victims. That was the reason she rarely spent more than a few days a month at home.

A small, black hover-vehicle caught her attention as it slid sideways from the skyway, turned and sped toward her building. Etched across the front was a bright neon-green MSF logo. And, just in case anyone missed it the first time, the same logo appeared on the doors, roof, back, and under the chaise.

The car stopped, hovering outside Avei's window. The glare of the headlights caused her to squint. *Damn him.*

She was miserable and furious in equal measures. Deputy Inspector Skora had no right to invade her privacy, even though she knew the reason for his visit. Of course, he wanted to see her after he'd received her resignation letter. *What did I expect?*

When the car zoomed off, Avei sat up. "Lights."

The windows frosted over as the room brightened, bathing the space in a warm glow. She kicked herself for not doing that earlier. The light revealed her vivid tattoos of alien arachnids in various shapes, sizes and colors, covering her legs and arms and peeking out from the top of her wrinkled tank top. To Avei's mind there was no such thing as too many spider tattoos.

Ragged burn scars covered the backs and palms of both hands and her left cheek. Avei had rejected the doctor's offer to remove them. When he asked her why, she didn't have an answer, and even now the reason for keeping the scars remained elusive. She tried to smooth down her short, purple hair, which stuck up in all directions. Every time she pressed it down, it bounced back.

Avei caught sight of her reflection in the darkened window and startled. She looked like one of those addicts hooked on Zenith, a new designer drug notorious for causing intense hallucinations that muddled the mind. Fantasy became reality, causing a staggering number of people across their corner of the galaxy to die, from suicide or accidental death.

Despite her current appearance, drugs had never appealed to Avei and she stayed away from them. Not so with alcohol. She cringed at the ever-present pile of empty units of alcohol on the coffee table. *Might be time to cut back.*

Avei scanned her messy home. She knew Skora would be there any moment, and she needed to do something about the mess before he arrived. She leaped up and a wave of dizziness hit. Her vision narrowed, followed by a brief bout of nausea. *Did I eat today*? When her vision cleared, the sight of the untouched food on the dining table answered her question. The doctors had warned that if she didn't eat regularly, she'd find herself back in the hospital. A clear sign her priorities needed recalibration.

Avei scooped up the alcohol containers and brought them to a small door in the wall next to the kitchen, shoving them inside. The garbage slid down to the incinerator in the basement. The food containers on the counter went next, most still full of food. Wiping her hands on her pajama shorts reminded her she also needed to change. Her face flushed red at the thought of meeting her boss in her pjs.

She dashed into her bedroom, where the unmade bed sat amidst a sea of dirty clothes. On the nightstand was a framed picture of her as a little girl, laughing as she hugged a massive Andior spider. *Magnus.* Avei averted her eyes from the picture, which represented another painful loss, and stepped between two large piles of clothes to push a button on the wall. A door slid open to reveal a row of empty hangers. How long had it been since she did the laundry? A bolt of fear went through her. Since she had been home, she had done nothing except wallow in self-pity.

With another pledge to do better, Avei bent over the clothes piled nearest to her and dug through them. A sharp pain erupted in her right abdomen from the laser wound she had suffered in the showdown with Apollyona. Hands on her knees, she sucked in deep breaths until the throbbing subsided to a manageable level. *Gods, I'm a mess.* She straightened up, a wrinkled dress gripped in her hands. She used it to blot the beads of sweat dotting her forehead. A *ding* from the front door announced Skora's arrival. Avei held out the crumpled dress and sighed. Out of time, she threw it over her head and pulled it down over her pajamas.

"It's D.I. Skora." His deep voice came through on the comm device next to the front door. "I received your resignation letter. Can we please talk?"

Avei smoothed her dress as she walked from the bedroom to the front door. Her insides roiled at the coming conversation. Notifying Skora of her retirement hadn't been an impulsive act. She had spent her entire convalescence thinking about it and written her resignation letter weeks ago. But she knew that he wouldn't let her go easily; she had one of the highest close rates on the force and he'd do almost anything to keep her on the job.

This was going to take some willpower. It wouldn't be easy walking away from a job she loved, not to mention Sezin Watson. Avei had come to count on her eccentric AI associate and it no longer seemed anything but normal that her partner in solving crime was a holographic image emitted from a floating holoball.

Sezin relished the idea of being Avei's sidekick, which was endearing but could be equally problematic. MSF technology didn't allow AIs to manifest into solid form, which prevented an AI from taking any kind of physical action when they found themselves in dangerous situations. To compensate, Sezin's over-the-top personality manifested itself in unconventional choices of attire and personas. Sezin would often try to trick an assailant by switching to their favorite avatar, a seven-foot-tall Vusian wrestler with multiple guns peppered to the exterior of their armor, and a massive rail gun named Esmeralda nestled in their giant hands. Subtle wasn't a word that could be applied to Avei's partner. *Gods, I'm going to miss Sezin.*

The inner critic she'd wrestled with over the last three months came roaring back, casting doubt on her decision to leave the Mernin Security Forces. It was a job she no longer had any business doing. A job that got twenty innocent people killed because she made a terrible mistake.

That reminder put an end to the vacillation. Avei continued to the door and reached for the switch just as Skora spoke again.

"Avei, I need your help. We've got a new serial killer using spiders to kill their victims. I tell you, it's the stuff of nightmares. Well, my nightmares, not yours. Nexus is calling the killer Zarul, after the species of spiders they used to murder their first two victims. I think they're called the zarultikna. Or zarultissa. Something like that. Maybe you've seen the news reports?"

They're called zarultalzin. Avei pulled her hand back and leaned into the door to listen.

"You have to admit the name Zarul is a marked improvement over some of the names Nexus has come up with in the past for your serial killers. They could have gone with arachnaslayer, spidassassin, or some other ridiculous name we'd be stuck with for the duration of the case. Anyway, the lunatic just killed again, using a different kind of spider and it's massive. At least ten times as big as the zarul-whatever. I had no idea they came that big. I may never sleep again. Anyway, I digress. Given your obsession with the horrid little... well, not so little... bugs, I'd love your thoughts on the situation."

Arachnids, not bugs. Avei couldn't deny she was intrigued. The zarultalzin spiders were particularly aggressive and their venom caused an agonizing death. A sense of duty flared, along with the familiar moral obligation she experienced when a serial killer was on the loose. *How many people will die after I quit?*

"I know how close you were to Tral and Ezo," Skora said, sensing he had her attention. "I don't believe they'd want you to leave the force."

Avei reared back from the door. The air was heavy with silence. A repudiation of sorts.

A heavy sigh came through the comm. "Okay Avei, I know what you're going through, and I'll give you a bit more time. I'll swing by the spaceport in a few days when you are back from medical leave. We'll talk then. In the meantime, I'm sending you what we have on Zarul. Please look at the files and let me know your thoughts. I need your expertise to work up a profile so we can catch this monster."

Avei leaned against the door and listened to his footsteps recede down the hallway. She needed to talk to her parents. Given what they'd gone through over the last few months, she owed it to them. Almost losing their last living child had taken its toll. They never talked about it, but the fear never left their faces. They would be ecstatic to see her leave the force. So *why the dread?*

She touched the locket. The one subject she had avoided thinking about when penning her resignation letter crashed to the forefront and it tore her breath away. The day she became a citizen meant ending the search for Brasnik, the serial killer who had tortured and murdered Anastasia. Bringing him to justice had driven Avei to join the Mernin Security Forces a decade ago. What she hadn't expected was how much she had fallen in love with the job. Now she was walking away. She slid down the wall, her eyes locked on the monitor as the picture of her and Anastasia reappeared.

"Lights off." The room plunged into darkness.

2

The Mernin cityscape loomed over the decrepit west side; a place where those with nothing lived in despair and hardship. Their dreams of a better life had little chance of becoming reality and, deep down, they knew it. Consequently, when death came calling in its various forms, they didn't fight it as vehemently as those who lived in the fancy buildings. This all made the west side the perfect hunting ground for a serial killer.

As far as seedy hotels go, the one that Zarul chose for their next victim took it up a notch. The hallways and rooms reeked of urine and seldom-washed bodies. The doors didn't lock, and no one cared. There was nothing of value to steal. The communal bathroom on the third floor had the only working toilet and there was always a line waiting in the hall. No one remembered the last time they had clean sheets. And yet, despite the living conditions and an indifferent staff, the hotel overflowed with guests. The occupants preferred sleeping in dry filth over the frigid, damp streets during the long monsoon season.

In the deep dark of the night, Zarul entered the hotel through a side door, carrying a large duffle bag. Having scouted the place earlier in the week, the killer made their way up the rickety stairs to the second floor and headed down the hall to room 27. A quick search of the corridor confirmed they were alone. Zarul opened the door and peered inside, the light from the corridor falling across their next victim, who lay on the bed in a state of drunken stupor. The murderer had observed the man for a week and had never seen him sober. It would make restraining him a breeze.

***

Around an hour later, the experimentation phase of the project neared completion. Excitement shot through the killer as success finally seemed certain.

A metal pole held the door closed, just in case anyone grew curious about the strange noises coming from the room. A holographic medical telemetry screen floated near the rusty bed, providing the only light in the grimy, windowless room. The only other furniture in the room was a broken metal chair leaning against the wall in the corner. The duffle bag sat open on the floor.

A shirtless man lay on the bed, his mouth gagged. Thin metal bands secured his hands and feet to the frame. Orange fluid oozed from a large bite that covered the whole left side of his neck. A single drop of blood dribbled down his left shoulder. The victim hovered between life and death. His vital signs barely registered on the telemetry.

Zarul, dressed head to toe in black, watched from the end of the bed, face distorted behind a mask that shimmered with oscillating hues of black and gray. A clear, thin band crossed their eyes, allowing them to see.

Zarul glanced at the telemetry. The man's respiration and heartbeat increased, then stabilized. "At last."

The man awakened with a start. He whimpered through the gag as his eyes darted around the room and landed on Zarul, who just stared at him. The bindings held fast as the man bucked on the bed, trying to pull his arms and legs free. His movements caused the bed frame to bang against the wall and the springs to screech.

Zarul rushed to the door and listened for approaching footsteps. Nothing. The psychopath turned back to the victim and felt a surge of pride. To borrow a phrase from old Earth, they had killed two birds with one stone. The removal of a parasite from the world and a hypothesis proved out. Time to pack up and leave.

"Now, now, none of that. I can't have you bringing attention to our little endeavor." Zarul removed a glove and tapped once on a small silver device strapped to their wrist.

A massive grenwal spider skittered out from under the bed. Its viridian-colored hourglass body was ten inches long with thick, black, eighteen-inch legs. Embedded on its back was a small silver disk. The grenwal scurried up the side of the bed and climbed onto the man's stomach, where it stilled. One-inch fangs protruded from the spider's mouth and dripped orange venom. Menace oozed from the grenwal as its eight eyes observed the man's thrashing movements.

The man shook his head and moaned. The metal dug into his wrists as he struggled to free himself. Blood welled up and flowed down his arms. The grenwal crouched down and hung on, despite the victim's best efforts.

The man's eyes pleaded with Zarul, who ignored him. Their rapt attention focused on the beautiful creature they'd unleashed on the world. A deep, satisfying thrill coursed through their body, knowing this man's life was in their hands and they got to play God. Again. The thought caused the murderer to shiver with delight.

In a weakened state, the victim's efforts sputtered out and he lay panting. Zarul watched his eyes and saw the moment the man gave up. With a satisfied sigh, the killer tapped the wrist device twice and the spider leaped to the victim's neck and hunched down. Its fangs sunk deep into his flesh.

The man's eyes rolled back and his body writhed in violent convulsions. Orange foam bubbled around the gag as the medical telemetry red-lined and the victim stilled, his body contorted.

Work done, the killer tapped once, and the spider wrenched its fangs from the man's neck, then scurried down the bed. It ran across the floor to the duffle bag and climbed in. Zarul tapped the side of the bag and the top knitted together, sealing in the grenwal.

After a quick scan of the room and the victim, Zarul pulled on their gloves then peeled a small gray device from the wall. The holographic telemetry screen disappeared and the room plunged into darkness. Using the meager light from the mask, Zarul tucked the disk into a pocket on the side of the bag and picked it up. Lifting the pole from the door, the killer exited the room without a backward glance.

3

Avei approached the Anastasia Themis Institute of Arachnology, a glass tower ten stories high and shaped like an arachnid. A living memorial to a beloved daughter and sister who had been making a name for herself in the field of venom research when Brasnik took her life.

Opening the institute had been the girls' parents' dream, and they had finally made it a reality eight years ago. The first six rounded floors represented an arachnid's abdomen. The top four floors narrowed to depict the cephalothorax, the head, and thorax. Avei loved how the unusual structure stood out amid the uniformity of the surrounding buildings. Her father, Albert Themis, had wanted to add legs, but his wife Iveila had eventually talked him out of it. *Thank the gods.*

The institute had finally achieved solvency last year. The antidotes, vaccines, and medicines they had developed from spider venom now paid for everything, allowing Albert and Iveila to provide free antidotes to poverty-stricken communities. It also eased Avei's mind. The institute had been built and funded by the payments from the books and Nexus movies about Avei's cases. All that would end now she had quit.

Avei entered the institute where she worked when she had time between cases. It kept her doctorate in arachnology current and allowed her to continue her research with the largest arachnids. She loved her job but this was her passion.

Avei kissed the locket, then her fingers, and touched the image of her sister that graced the wall in the entryway. She did this every time she entered. *I love and miss you, big sis.* Anastasia's smile was incandescent as she cradled a large rahima; a furry yellow, docile arachnid the size of a small dog. The sisters had traveled together to the rahima's home world, a small planetoid in the Kressa system, and spent a beautiful day doing what they both loved most, spending time with arachnids. Two months later, Anastasia was gone. Avei often fantasized about what her life would have been like if her sister had lived. One certainty was she would not have joined the Mernin Security Force, or apprehended sixty-two serial killers. It was hard sometimes to reconcile the life that should have been with the one she had actually lived for the last ten years.

The smell of coffee hit her when she entered the institute's lobby, jolting her out of her musings. The conversation pit consumed the right side, with comfortable furniture and a beverage bar that dispensed a variety of hot and cold beverages. Holographic images of arachnids from across the galaxy covered the walls, some so alien in appearance that one questioned if they even belonged to the Arthropod family. The small water fountain in the corner provided soothing sounds to calm the faint of heart.

A large holographic display filled the space behind two female security officers. It touted the institute's achievements. The women, one human and one alien, smiled at Avei from behind the counter.

Tarax, an older Hohanna who had worked for the Themis Institute since its inception, walked to Avei and held out her arms. Her large yellow eyes danced with joy. "My dear child, it is good to see you again." She enveloped Avei in a hug and took care not to prick her with the small bony protuberances that covered her arms.

The women pulled apart and Tarax gave Avei a once-over. Her eyes took in the burn scars on her hands and face. "How are you doing?"

Avei's fingers found the scar on her cheek without her bidding. It was the first time she'd been out in public since the fire. *No one in their right mind walks around disfigured if they don't have to. So why don't I remove them?*

A wave of resistance answered her question. She wasn't ready.

"I'm fine, Tarax. Thank you for asking. Are my parents in?" Just in case she had changed her mind, she hadn't told them of her plans to visit.

"They are in the fifth-floor laboratory. A special delivery from Merudi arrived this morning." Tarax walked with her to the elevator bank. "Lots of excitement today."

"My father's wanted a Qokven from Merudi for as long as I can remember. It sounds like it finally happened." Avei stopped in front of the elevator. "Floor five."

The door opened and Avei entered, turning to face her friend. "It's good to see you, Tarax."

“I’m so happy to see you up and about. You had us all very worried.” Tarax smiled as the doors closed.

The fast elevator ride meant Avei only had moments to digest what Tarax had said. How she hated being the center of attention. Total anonymity was her preference, but Marsa Baako, a woman who fancied herself an author, had put an end to that when she wrote and published her first book, on Avei’s first case. Gods, she loathed that woman.

The elevator doors opened to a corridor with glass windows that looked into a laboratory filled with the latest technology. Habitats for the massive arachnids lined both sides of the space. Her father had overseen the construction of each species section. Albert’s exacting standards ensured an accurate representation of the home world, and a greater chance of survival. The familiar thrill of excitement coursed through her as she stared at the lab.

Nature produced an infinite variety of flora and fauna, and that held true for the Arthropod family. While external features varied from one species to the next, the arachnids’ structure remained remarkably consistent. They all had cephalothorax, abdomen, and the ability to administer venom. Most arachnid venom was harmless, usually just causing localized pain around the bite. The institute’s entire focus was on the lethal kind.

The fifth floor held the deadliest and largest arachnids in the galaxy and the Institute took extra precautions to prevent any from escaping. Avei left the elevator and spotted a knot of people clustered around a table at the back of the laboratory. She entered through a two-phase hatch system, waiting until the scan finished and the second hatch opened into the laboratory. Then she ducked into an alcove before anyone noticed her arrival. She was hoping for a few precious moments of peace before greeting her parents and facing the worry and fear they always tried to hide. Avei knew that once she told her folks of her plans to resign, she couldn't back out.

There were thirty lockers in the alcove. Hers was at the end and out of sight. It held a petite-sized white suit, gloves, and a helmet with the Themis Institute's logo. Avei pulled the suit over her clothes and stood still while it molded to her body contours and the seams sealed shut. The gloves came next and formed a tight bond with the suit. The helmet went on last and locked into place at the neckline.

Next came a quick scan of the suit in the mirror, checking for rips or gaps, per her mother's stringent safety protocols implemented after a deadly cozali arachnid bit both Iveila and Albert. Fortunately, Iveila's team had developed an early prototype of the antidote. Out of necessity and scientific curiosity, both Avei's parents took the untested cure, with far more excitement than the situation warranted. After a tense few hours, they celebrated the success of the new antidote and the fact they were still alive. Iveila had designed the safety suits the next day and added another standard operating practice for the institute.

As she left the alcove, a cry of elation erupted from the tight group huddled around one of the display tables. She watched the eager group and felt a glimmer of hope. This was her life going forward, and a big part of her longed for it. *Maybe this change will be a good thing?*

Iveila's head popped up. She smiled when she spotted her daughter. "Darling, come join us. Your father's Qokvens arrived." A stunning woman, Iveila Themis, was half human and half Nilte. Her height, purple hair and lavender eyes came from her Nilte half. Avei wished for her mother's height every single day of her life.

"Qokvens? More than one?" Avei headed their way.

Albert peered around her mother and shouted, "Avei, a male, and a female! Can you believe our great fortune?" She smiled at her father's exuberance. It had helped get her through some tough times in her life. Fully human, Albert stood a foot shorter than his wife, his hair now more gray than black. His startling green eyes grabbed people's attention and held it. They sparkled with life, which he loved and appreciated more than most.

His family belonged to an endogamous cult, founded over 500 years ago. They prohibited marrying outside the human family and kept birth records all the way back to old Earth. When Albert fell in love with Iveila, he was given a choice. Give up his family or give up the love of his life. It took him seconds to decide and he had never looked back.

Avei had inherited her mother's pragmatic approach to life. Her dogged determination came from her father. A swell of love filled her as she walked toward them. She hadn't felt this alive and present in a while. It felt good to be back out in the world again. At this moment, her decision to leave MSF made perfect sense.

When she reached the group, her father pulled her into a bear hug. “I’m so happy you are here, my darling. Thrilled, in fact.”

Albert passed her over to her mother, who gave her a quick hug. No one ever used the word ‘maternal’ to describe Iveila Themis. That fell to Albert. Iveila’s steady presence provided the stability and sensibilities Avei and Anastasia had needed as children to balance out their father’s Pollyanna view of life.

Iveila looked her daughter up and down. “You’re still not eating, are you?”

Avei blushed when the four scientists looked her way. “Mother, not now.”

Albert took his daughter by the hand and brought her to the glass cage that held the recent additions to the laboratory. “Aren’t they magnificent?” He sounded close to tears, something he succumbed to often.

Two feet across, the Qokven had cobalt-blue trichobothria, tiny hairs that covered their backs and legs. Their iridescent green cephalothorax glittered in the bright lights.

“Wow, they are stunning.” The Qokven resembled old Earth tarantulas, which her father obsessed over and swore he’d resurrect if viable DNA was ever found. Now, she understood why he had spent years trying to convince the Merudians to sell him a Qokven. They were considered a demigod that played a key role in the Merudian religion. Avei wondered what Albert had offered to get the pair of them.

"They really are magnificent." Iveila turned to her daughter. "Did you know the Qokven venom kills in under two minutes? Last year, the Imperial Leader's young son died from a bite when he fell into a Qokven nest. He passed away before anyone noticed he was gone. His mother reached out to me last month, and I promised her an antidote within the year."

That explained it. The death of a beloved son would one day provide the gift of life to the Merudi people and soothe a mother's grief, a little. Something her parents were all too familiar with, and likely forged a lasting bond between two sets of grieving parents. When Anastasia died, it set off a sequence of events that culminated in making the institute a reality. Since its inception, millions of people were alive because of her parents' antidotes and medicines.

"Let's get them out, shall we?" Albert rubbed his hands together with glee.

Avei tensed. She needed to talk to her parents before she lost her nerve. "Can we talk first? It's important."

Her father stared at her as if she had asked him to cut off his right arm. Her mother smiled and took him by the hand. "Albert, dear, our daughter needs us. The team knows how to go through the preparations without us."

"Quite right, my dear. Come, my child, let's have some tea and a nice chat." Albert put his arm around Avei as Iveila herded them both to the changing room.

Avei leaned into her father and braced herself for the difficult conversation ahead. Over the years, she had occasionally longed for a calmer life. One that didn't include depraved murderers, or the brutal deaths of their innocent victims consuming her every waking moment. Now that her decision to leave the Mernin Security Forces was done, she expected to feel at peace. Instead, she felt equal parts conflict and dread.

4

Avei sat in a chair across from her parents, in the center of their shared office at the top of the building.

Iveila's side of the office was immaculate, with a standing desk, potted plants, and a floating monitor. The office mirrored her no-frills approach to life. She considered all nonessential things a distraction. The one exception hung on the wall behind her desk: a picture of her daughters, on a sandy beach next to a reddish-orange sea. They were seven and nine and Avei remembered every detail of that perfect day, when neither she nor Anastasia had a care in the world other than what flavor of iced cremaltos to order.

Albert's side looked like someone had turned it upside-down and shaken it. Piles of books covered every available surface and most of the floor, and the three built-in bookcases against the wall stood empty. Avei's father loved the feeling of a physical book in his hands when carrying out research. The stack of datatabs teetering on the edge of his desk provided access to massive knowledge libraries when his books fell short. He required clutter around him for his deep thinking and it had driven his obsessively clean wife crazy until Iveila had finally given up and embraced the chaos. Just as long as Albert kept his mess on his side of the office.

The center section provided a neutral space. A conference table and seats filled most of the area, along with a couch and two comfy chairs. Four monitors floated off to the side, ready for use should the need arise.

A pot of hot tea sat on the table between parents and daughter, along with three steaming mugs. They shared a love of tea and fancied themselves connoisseurs. Iveila handed Avei a mug, and she breathed in the savory smell of her favorite local blend. It came from the vinzu plant, which grew in the temperate section of Mernin's only continent. Avei took a sip and closed her eyes as the spicy flavor filled her mouth. The warm mug calmed her nerves.

"Deputy Inspector Skora visited yesterday morning," Albert said as he smiled at her.

And boom, the moment of calm fled and her mind sought the dark place it had inhabited for months. Anger swelled at the thought of Skora enlisting her parents' help to keep her on the force. A second later, reality imposed itself and her anger dissipated. She had given her notice yesterday evening and he had visited in the morning. Skora had come for something else. It had to be the Zarul killings.

"A killer's using venomous spiders to murder their victims." Albert's excitement animated his hands, which flew around him. "Really remarkable when you think about it. They're such efficient killing machines, I'm utterly flabbergasted no one thought to use them to commit murder before."

"People are dying in agony at the hand of this lunatic." Iveila frowned at her husband's exuberance. "What your father is referring to are the murders committed by a serial killer and let me be clear, I hate they've named that monster after the zarultalzins. It's not their fault that a maniac is using them to kill these poor people. Anyway, it's been on all the Nexus news and talk shows."

"I stopped watching the news after... I don't watch it anymore. D.I. Skora mentioned 'Zarul' when he stopped by yesterday. He didn't go into any detail." Avei had stayed away from the Nexus news shows since the warehouse fire. Whenever they got a hold of a juicy story, they milked every titillating morsel. The shootout with a deranged killer checked all their boxes. No surprise there, Avei had been a central character in their narrative for nine years. The Nexus conglomerate had dredged up every known fact about her and made up what they didn't know, inundating their audience day and night with truths, half-truths, and outright lies. Avei valued her anonymity over everything else and it caused her almost physical pain to see her life laid bare by people who didn't even know her.

Albert leaned forward and rubbed his hands together. "The zarultalzin arachnids are nasty little devils. They attack for the sport of it. Not surprising at all that the killer used them for the first two murders. Dump a handful on your victim and stand back. They'll get the job done every time. Perfect little assassins."

"Albert, are you hearing yourself right now? People are dying."

"Quite right, my dear. My apologies. I got a little carried away." Chastised, Avei's father sat back with his hands in his lap. His attention was on his wife.

"And then what, Albert? They pick them off the victim and walk away?" Iveila said. "What prevents the zarultalzins from attacking the killer?"

"An excellent point, and I think why the murderer switched to using the grenwal arachnid for the next three killings. Absolutely gorgeous creatures. There's something rather elegant about them, isn't there dear?" Albert smiled at his wife, who glared at him. He swallowed and adopted a proper, serious look.

Avei hid a smile behind her tea mug. "What did Skora want?"

"Information on the two species and how the killer may have purchased them," Iveila said.

"The zarultalzin live in underground burrows and have killed dozens of miners over the years. They're so dangerous, most dealers refuse to stock them. With a bit of research, Mernin Security Forces can identify the few merchants who carry them," Albert said. "We had some at the institute for a while until they withered in captivity and died. Unbelievably devastating, to lose them so quickly. If we had known, we'd never have brought them on."

"And in that brief time, we discovered the zarultalzin venom was analogous to several other species for which we already had antidotes. We supplied the mining companies with an antidote, and no one has died since." Iveila settled back on the couch, clearly proud of her team's work.

"I agree with Papa, the grenwal is a beauty. It's rarely aggressive, which is why it's so popular with collectors. Their passivity makes them a strange choice for the killer. Anyone can purchase a grenwal with minimal effort.

Tracking the dealer will be next to impossible." Avei's interest was growing, alongside a surge of excitement that she often experienced at the start of a new case. Especially one tailor-made for her. Except it wasn't her case, and never would be. Skora had already assigned it to another inspector. Most likely Uma Gredidol, who'd taken over Avei's case log during her medical leave. That blunt reminder brought reality back. In two weeks, she would be gone from the MSF. For good.

Her parents sensed the change in her and exchanged a worried look. Gods knew she had put them through hell by almost dying twice because of Apollyona. First in the warehouse fire, the killer had started with incendiary devices in the hopes of burning Avei alive, along with Tral and Ezo, who were drugged, bound, and helpless. When that hadn't done the job, there was still the laser wound, which had destroyed two-thirds of her liver. The subsequent depression didn't help. Iveila's *snap out of it, you're alive so be grateful* approach had missed the mark. Albert's *let's talk about anything but the giant orthicalpod in the room* wasn't helpful either. Seeing her parents' disappointment only worsened Avei's melancholy and contributed to her downward spiral. She put a stop to their visits, for her own sake. That caused hurt feelings and angry words and it had been a few weeks since she last saw them. The guilt lay heavy as she searched for the right words. Taking a page from her mother's book, she got straight to the point.

"I'm resigning from the Mernin Security Forces, and I want to come work at the Institute full time." She watched their reactions. Her father looked disappointed but her mother appeared happy. It should have been the other way around. Albert never stopped asking her to leave the force and work with them while Iveila told her to keep her MSF job because she loved it and because of the good she did and the lives she saved. It appeared they had reversed positions.

"Honey, I'm thrilled to hear this." Iveila beamed at her. The relief in her eyes was unmistakable. Avei had expected her mother to be the difficult one, wanting to examine her decision from all angles to ensure she hadn't made it in the heat of the moment, but it seemed that almost losing her only living child changed Iveila's perspective.

Albert cleared his throat and fidgeted. He refused to make eye contact.

Iveila studied her husband with a frown. "Albert, your daughter just told you she is leaving the force. Something you've begged her to do for years. Tell her how happy you are she's resigning."

Her father picked up a mug of tea, changed his mind, and put it down. Then he grabbed it and took a sip. Albert Themis's legendary confrontation avoidance was on full display. Hating to hurt anyone's feelings, and particularly his daughter's, he left what he called the ugly business to his wife to manage.

"Go ahead, Papa. You can tell me anything." Avei steeled herself when he finally looked at her.

"All of this is because of you." Albert raised his hands and looked around. "If not for you, we'd still be at the university, with small-minded administrators stifling our research."

"What are you saying, Albert?" Iveila asked, clearly irritated.

"I've already turned in my resignation letter, Papa. It's too late." Avei looked at her father.

Albert grabbed her hands and leaned forward. "For a long time, I've wanted you to leave that job. Prayed for it. The constant, unending worry I've carried over the years culminated when you nearly died. And for a moment, I felt vindicated. That my fear and anxiety had been an appropriate reaction to your work." Albert took a deep breath and let it out slowly. "But I had it wrong and your mother had it right. You love your job, and you excel at it. No one knows for sure how many lives you've saved over the years by getting that filth off our streets. I'm betting it adds up to hundreds of people who are alive today because of you. Avei, my dear, simply put, you made everyone feel safer. My wanting you to leave the Mernin Security Forces came from a place of pure selfishness."

Albert released her hands and settled back in the chair. "I will support you in whatever decision you make. But first, I want you to take some time. We know how much you're struggling with the deaths of your dear friends, and that is understandable. We miss Ezo and Tral so very much and are utterly heartsick they didn't survive the fire. What I don't want is for you to make a significant life choice based on how you are feeling at this moment. A decision you may later regret."

Albert's words rattled his daughter. That she needed to defend her decision to him brought up all the uncertainty she'd wrestled with. She mentally shook herself and focused on what Albert didn't seem to understand. Twenty innocent people had burned to death because she had recommended the release of Apollyona after she had been brought in for questioning following the first four murders. If they had kept her imprisoned, those twenty people would be alive today, including Avei's best friends. Apollyona had used Tral and Ezo as bait to lure Avei to the warehouse.

The weight of her guilt hit full-force, and it didn't just come from the Apollyona case. Despite her best efforts over the years, Anastasia's killer was still at large. Leaving MSF would bring an end to Avei's quest to make Brasnik pay for robbing her family of such a bright light. "I'm sorry I never got justice for Anastasia," she said suddenly.

Both she and her mother teared up. Eleven years had passed, and Anastasia's death still felt like it had happened only yesterday.

Albert cleared his throat, his voice heavy with emotion. "Put that thought out of your mind. Your mother and I know how hard you've worked to find that monster, and we have always appreciated your efforts. Sometimes we must admit defeat in the face of great odds, and this is one of those times. Anastasia is at peace, and we need to move on as a family."

Avei nodded and wiped her face. "Thank you, Papa, but I need you to know that my mind's made up and I'm leaving the force. Good people died the most horrific death because I missed vital insights into Apollyona's character."

Iveila brushed away her own tears before addressing her daughter. "My child, I cannot sit by and watch as you shoulder all the blame for that terrible tragedy." Iveila clutched her chest. "It's breaking my heart, and I need you to know that you do not carry that burden alone."

Avei's eyes widened when Iveila rose and took a seat beside her and pulled her into a fierce hug. She sunk into her mother's arms and, for the first time in a long time, felt utterly safe. All the ugliness of the last few months faded and she closed her eyes, savoring her mother's rare display of love.

They stayed like that for a while until, still holding onto her daughter, Iveila gently moved back and turned Avei to look at her. "I need you to listen to my words and really hear them. Okay?" Iveila waited for Avei's nod before continuing. "Good. First point, Princina Apollyona's family provided alibis for the first four murders, knowing full well she committed them. They didn't want her to stop, and did everything to ensure she continued her murderous rampage. The Navra royal family are to blame for every death that followed the release of the Princina."

"Mother, you don't understand. I knew about the volcanic eruptions on Navra, and I even considered the possibility that the deaths were sacrifices to their Fire God, Huqen. I discarded it as improbable, given—"

"The Federation banned all sacrificial deaths on Navra over two hundred years ago," Albert said earnestly. "It is a truly barbaric practice, and it boggles the mind that anyone in this day and age actually believes burning innocent people to death will stop volcanos from erupting. It's ludicrous, I tell you. How they thought—"

"Quite right, Albert," Iveila said as turned back to Avei. "Second point I want to make: you followed all the proper channels and had your observations and proposal to release Apollyona vetted by a panel of four senior MSF officers, including D.I. Skora. They agreed with your assessment and approved her release. They also bear responsibility for those tragic deaths."

"Mother, I missed all the signals that pointed to Apollyona's insanity. They were there the whole time, staring me right in the face, and I didn't see them. I am the last line of defense between these impenitent killers and the public and I utterly failed in my duty. I no longer trust my instincts, and that will only get more innocent people killed." Avei extracted herself from her mother's arms. "The day after tomorrow, I start my two weeks of light duty at the spaceport while my separation paperwork is being processed. After I leave, I would like to work at the Institute. If that's okay with both of you."

Iveila stared at her for a moment, then nodded. "Of course you can work here, my dear. We'd love for you to continue your efforts with the largest arachnids. It's your choice if you want to work in one of the laboratories or in the field."

"Thank you, Mother. I prefer to keep my field role. I enjoy the hunt for new species."

Albert remained quiet. He didn't approve of Avei's decision, and that shook her to her core.

5

The spaceport lit up the skyline as Avei rode toward it. Sitting astride her hover bike, she followed an avenue lined by ritzy stores, high-end restaurants, and clubs for Mernin's rich and famous. Most vehicles flew hundreds of feet above the ground, on the sky highway. Only Mernin Security Forces personnel reporting for duty, and those who could afford the astronomical permit fee, could drive on the street.

Three large passenger shuttles sat on raised platforms above the five terminals. The fourth platform, carrying a sleek, ten-person shuttle, rose until it pointed straight up.

Three limousines idled outside a bar known to be frequented by Nexus's commentators. A group of beautiful people augmented by the latest in plastic surgery exited the establishment. In no hurry, they preened and strutted their way towards the vehicles.

A group of gawkers shouted from behind security barriers, hoping to catch the attention of their favorite star. She shook her head as she darted around the limos. The same people came daily, yearning for a glimpse of some swankpot who had attained their lofty position in society with family money and minimal talent.

Avei sped down the street and left behind the upper-class blocks. She entered a lively area with eateries, bars, brothels, and music spots. Holographic images of everything from food to sex provided customers with a menu of choices for each business. The street and sidewalks were filled with a rollicking crowd made up of a variety of alien races, humans, and the progeny of cross-mates from the different worlds.

The din of the crowds penetrated Avei's helmet as she sped by, the three gold slashes on her black MSF uniform glittering in the bright lights. Her laser pistol and badge were secured to her belt.

Today, she started her second week of light duty at the spaceport and her last week on the force. A mix of emotions overwhelmed her every time she thought about it. She tapped them down. She would process how she felt about leaving while on vacation at Colea; a retirement gift from her parents. Throughout her childhood, they had visited the water world, with its huge resorts and red-orange oceans. The sunshine, salty air and the sound of the waves always soothed her soul. It was the perfect place to start the healing journey back to her old self. With her flight booked and reservations confirmed at a boutique resort in the southern oceans, all she had to do was pack her bags.

Avei slowed to navigate the throngs of people who huddled around the floating monitors lining the entrance to the largest building on Mernin. It covered three city blocks with 476 floors and one tenant, Nexus, the only broadcast company in their corner of the galaxy. The pre-eminent purveyor of the inane. You watched their shows or you watched nothing. Nexus became a monopoly by buying out their competition or destroying them through shady business practices. It existed to feed the insatiable appetite of the hundreds of billions of people who tuned in for mindless entertainment.

Avei hated Nexus with a passion because they had wasted no time partnering with novelist Marsa Baako nine years ago, when Avei's serial-killer arrests started making the news. They had made a fortune from her, through the sale of books and movies. Neither Nexus nor Marsa Baako had Avei's permission or had asked for her input. The vast majority of the content they published was false. She had taken them to court, and the Tribunal had surprisingly ruled in her favor – to some extent.

The massive sums of money they paid her over the years did nothing to slow them down. Still, they continued to feed the morbid curiosity their audience had with serial killers through publishing books and movies about Avei's life and cases. Her face and name appeared in billions of homes daily. It made living her personal life difficult and added a layer of complexity to her job.

With few exceptions, her cases fell into three major categories. A small group of murderers took it as a personal challenge to see if they could beat her, making it a contest between them and her, which Nexus milked for all its worth. Some killers craved notoriety and wanted to get arrested by Avei. They knew they would live on for eternity in movies and books. She held Nexus and Marsa Baako responsible for the victims who died because their slayers prized fame over taking an innocent life.

That left the larger and more dangerous group, who hid in the shadows and avoided her at all costs. They killed for a myriad of reasons, but all shared a common purpose. They didn't want to stop. Her sister's murderer fell into this last group. Brasnik had gone underground eight years ago, when she was hot on his trail. Most assumed he had died or was incarcerated for another crime. She knew better. He was biding his time until she was out of the picture. Once she retired, he'd resume his reign of terror, and more innocents would die. A sob started low in her chest and worked its way up. It took everything she had to not give in to it.

Avei blinked back tears as she slowed to pass a crowd gathered around a massive monitor with a chyron - ***Don't Get Eaten is the #1 on Nexus!*** On the screen, a mixed group of humans and alien races made up of two teams of six. With little enthusiasm, they kicked a ball back and forth on a barren moon. The two teams clustered together in tight packs. Three referees floated above and tried to disperse them when the ground moved under two unfortunate players. A massive mouth with needle-sharp teeth rose out of the dirt, encircled the legs of both men, and snapped shut. The creature sank, dragging the screaming guys with it. The ground closed behind them, leaving four on the team. Loud cheers erupted from the crowd around the monitor as the other team celebrated with a quick fist-bump in the air. Their merriment lasted seconds before they pulled together again and scanned the area in fear. The chyron changed to read ***Team Serei Wins Two Thousand Credits Each!***

Once past the crowds, Avei sped toward the spaceport terminal, two blocks away. Holographic ads featuring Breckin Starliners covered every inch of the walls and ceilings of the port in a dizzying array of churning ads. Cars descended from the skies and settled in front of the terminals, disgorging their wealthy passengers and luggage. Once done, they ascended and slid back onto the sky highway. Artificial Intelligence choreographed the dance of the vehicles and ran most of the systems at the port. Anyone not lucky enough to be rich or famous used the skylift located off the highway several hundred feet above the spaceport. It delivered them outside the terminal, where they queued in lines to enter.

Avei veered into the underground maintenance lot, where MSF personnel parked their vehicles. She stopped at the booth staffed by an old guard named Hills. The twinkle in his eye and benign appearance didn't fool her. An MSF legend, Hills had single-handedly stopped a gang of miscreants from springing their leader out of an MSF holding facility. Shot several times, he had held them off until backup arrived. His severe injuries prevented him from continuing as an inspector. He rejected early retirement, saying he was too young to sit around doing nothing, and took a post at the spaceport.

"Good evening, Hills." Avei raised her helmet shield and leaned into a screen that scanned her eyes. "How are things today? Quiet, I hope."

"Evening to you, Inspector Themis. Not so quiet, I'm afraid. You're needed at Terminal 5's docking ramp. There's a situation brewing between a passenger and the owner of the *Delphi* starliner."

Well, that was surprising. Famous for keeping a low profile, she wondered which Breckin was creating the commotion. Other than the occasional business update or charity event, the family kept themselves away from the Nexus merry-go-round. Everyone assumed they paid Nexus a fortune to allow their own public relations firm to craft the content before it appeared on one of their shows.

The steel hatch squealed open in front of her. "Well, damn."

"Yep. Julisa Breckin and a passenger are having a disagreement that's causing quite a brouhaha. She won't let anyone board the ship. The AI's losing its mind, because it's messing up the departure schedule."

Julisa was CEO of Breckin Starliners, famous for her fierce protection of her family and company. Avei hoped the passenger had caused the disturbance and not Ms. Breckin herself. Arresting Mernin's most successful businesswoman guaranteed a media circus that would hound her well beyond her last day on the force. Something she didn't need or want.

"Thanks, Hills. Tell them I'm on my way." Avei raced through the entrance and the steel door slid shut behind her.

6

The boarding ramp and attached waiting area were the antithesis of the luxurious ship that awaited the fifty-two passengers lined up to board their shuttle. The fusty odor, a combination of mildew and fried electrical wire, assailed the delicate noses of Mernin's finest. Dim lighting only enhanced the scuffed floor and dingy walls. A bank of dirty windows overlooked the skylift disembarkation platform which swarmed with economy-class passengers.

An aggressive monsoon storm had flooded Breckin Starliners' first-class terminal and caused extensive damage that would take weeks to repair. The company had no choice but to shift their guests to the public boarding ramp.

The impatient travelers fidgeted in line. The majority were humans or human-alien blends. Alien races made up the rest. Two tall, reptilian Sycardians and a gnome-faced Fansus family of three were among the non-humans waiting to board. They all watched the spectacle taking place at the entrance to the loading ramp with rabid interest.

Dressed in a garish purple and green catsuit, Marsa Baako – a plump, middle-aged and mostly human woman

– stood her ground. Her small, pointed ears suggested an Emphrie relative somewhere in her family tree. She hugged to her ample chest a feline creature that had six legs, orange and white fur, and yellow eyes. Marsa's hair was swept up in an elaborate beehive bun that stood straight up from her expansive forehead, the color a perfect match with the tangerine fur of her pet. A massive handbag hung over her shoulder, with a holographic display screen that cycled through ***Marsa Baako***; ***Galaxy Famous Novelist***; ***Winner of Twenty-two Mystery Sleuth Awards***; ***Ask me about my Next Novel***.

The CEO of Breckin Starliners towered over Marsa, who had to crane her neck to take in the full countenance of the angry woman standing before her. Julisa Breckin embodied everything one wanted in a leader of a successful conglomerate. Smart, savvy and willing to take chances, she was aware of the power she wielded and unafraid to use it. Her reddish-brown eyes matched her chestnut-color hair, which she wore in an updo. Not one jeweled pin or fancy hair piece in sight.

Full of righteous anger, Julisa blocked the on-ramp. "We have warned you many times that your animal's banned from our ships for life. I will not have it menacing my staff and terrorizing the captain ever again."

Marisa stepped into Julisa's personal space, forcing her to step back. "Stop calling her *that animal* and *it*. She's got a name – Sintha – and I already paid for her passage. Your company had no issues taking my hard-earned money, so get out of my way and let us board. Or I'm telling Nexus about this outrage."

Avei entered the boarding area through a hidden hatch in the wall and headed towards the two women holding up the line.

Avei recognized Julisa Breckin from seeing her images on Nexus. When she turned her attention to the other passenger, she stumbled to a stop. No. No. *Oh, hell no.* The woman who had made her life a living hell for nine years stood in front of her; author of sixty-two books based on her cases and the very person responsible for obliterating her privacy. Over the years, Avei had avoided all contact with the woman and let her solicitors manage any in-person meetings. Not once had she exchanged words with this self-serving, narcissistic opportunist. She saw no reason to begin now.

Avei spun around, intending to walk back through the door, but, unable to help herself, she glanced over her shoulder and stared at the two women, who showed no signs of wavering. If she didn't handle this situation, who would? As the only MSF inspector at the spaceport, they'd send someone from the field to take over. She cringed at the thought. Given her retirement in five days, this might be the only time she needed to talk to Marsa Baako face to face. Without her cases to write about, the writer would fade into oblivion. That thought cheered Avei up as she turned and faced the crowd, who were oblivious to her presence. She took advantage of their preoccupation and studied the passengers.

Two other members of the Breckin family stood behind Marsa and she took a moment to study Julisa's reinforcements if things went sideways. Best known for their charity work, Wilm Breckin IX and his wife Celethe often appeared on Nexus news shows, reporting on their latest philanthropic endeavor.

The thick, raised scars on Celethe's right ankle, while unexpected, did nothing to mar her sublime elegance, and gave her an air of mystery because she bucked tradition and had chosen not to remove them. Something Avei found relatable, but it didn't stop her from wondering why Mrs. Breckin kept her scars. Celethe wore her long blond hair loose, just held back at the sides with hairpins made of semi-precious gems. A sign of defiance, given elaborate updos were all the rage with the wealthy. The woman appeared to march to the beat of her own drum; something Avei found refreshing. Celethe's gold, silver and green dress was made from the fibers of the Dogo tree and glimmered every time she moved. When she tilted her head to the side, her eyes gave off a subtle shimmer. She was a stunning woman who pulled attention to her and held it, making it impossible to look away.

Avei tore her eyes from Celethe Breckin and studied the woman's husband, Wilm. Taller than his wife by a hair, Wilm's florid face and bloodshot eyes diminished his once handsome features. His purple tunic did little to hide his expanding waist. Given his well-known reputation for overindulging in drink, gambling and sexual affairs, his body reflected his unhealthy vices. Avei took an immediate dislike to him. After spending years dealing with serial killers, she easily picked up on the predatory vibe psychopaths gave off. Something they all shared, whether they were killers, the gossip down the street, or titans of industry. Most people picked up on it subconsciously. They'd feel uncomfortable, repelled or wary, usually not knowing or understanding why. Unfortunately, nearly all would ignore what their gut was telling them.

Can I trust my instincts about Wilm after getting it so wrong about Apollyona?

Celethe turned and saw her. She tapped her husband on his arm and nodded in Avei's direction. Wilm sneered, giving credence to Avei's initial feelings about him. *Time to get to work.* She patted her hair down to cover the burn scar on her left cheek and walked past the line of guests, stopping in front of Julisa and Marsa. "MSF Inspector. What's the holdup?"

Julisa pointed to Sintha. "That vile creature is no longer allowed on any Breckin Starliner. Ms. Baako was notified by our attorneys and yet here she is with that abomination."

Marsa smiled at Avei. "I'm thrilled we finally meet, Inspector. I can't tell you want an honor it is."

With difficulty, Avei kept her focus on Julisa. "Why did you ban the animal?"

Marsa stepped in front of Avei, breaking her line of sight with Ms. Breckin.

"I can answer that. There was a very minor incident with Captain Dimphi on our last trip. He tried to pet her and startled my poor baby. Other than that, she is always well behaved. The perfect little angel. Aren't you, my darling?" She hugged the aloof pet, who glared at Avei and flexed the claws on her front paws.

"That feral beast bit him while he sat in his office on the bridge. I can assure you the attack was unprovoked." Julisa's face flushed with anger as she spun round towards Marsa, who had the good sense to take a step back. "And what about the seventy-two other complaints we've received from guests who found that creature inside their rooms, or were frightened when it hissed at them?"

"I'd call those a big overreaction. Just look at this sweet, beautiful face." Marsa planted another kiss on Sintha's head. "Besides, Miss High and Mighty, your company sold me a ticket for my pet, and you don't get to take it back."

As Marsa stood there in all her pompous arrogance, Avei once more felt the roar of rage and horror from seeing her life laid bare to billions of people. The only consequence to Marsa and Nexus for ruining her life was to grant her fifty percent of book and movie sales. Based on earlier precedents, the Tribunal had a duty to shut Marsa Baako and Nexus down. Instead, they had capitulated when Nexus filled the courtroom with attorneys. The intent was to intimidate, and it worked. The Tribunal issued a compromise. The sum of money Nexus and Marsa had paid Avei over the years was staggering, and she had used every bit of it to build the Institute from the ground up. Now it was profitable, and she needed to find another worthy endeavor for the residuals from the previously published books and movies. She sucked in deep breaths to help push the anger down. The sooner she resolved the situation, the sooner she could leave the presence of this hateful woman. "Ms. Breckin, I need you to step aside and allow the guests to board."

Wilm leaned around Celethe and glared at his sister. "Sis, you heard her. Let her on the damn ship so we can board."

The passengers broke out in applause and hoots of approval. Done with waiting in the dreary boarding area, they wanted on the luxury starliner in orbit over Mernin. Avei figured she had thirty seconds before they shoved their way on board the shuttle regardless. She steeled herself and turned to Marsa. "Show me the ticket for your Atiza."

Marsa smiled. "I'm delighted you know Sintha is an Atiza. They're very rare."

With an end in sight, the guests pushed forward into Wilm and Celethe. Wilm stumbled into Marsa and sent her careening into Julisa, who lurched backwards. Avei grabbed the CEO's arm and kept her from falling.

"Thank you, Inspector." Julisa straightened her dark gray, knee-length tunic.

Avei glared at the passengers. "I need everyone to back up. Now."

Wilm spun around and scowled at the couple who had caused the chain reaction. Caerson Mercer and Imara Tiniba glowered back.

Tall and skinny, Caerson's iridescent blue eyes elevated his otherwise average looks. His short blond hair stood up with the help of a strong gel and he wore the latest fashion: knee-high boots paired with short pants and a tunic in muted pastels. Despite his best efforts, he all but disappeared next to his vivacious girlfriend with her large afro and bright yellow micro dress that had more cutouts than it did fabric. Aware of her beauty, Imara Tiniba posed, rather than slumping like everyone else.

"This is ridiculous." Imara stepped out of line. "Hey MSF, stop messing around and do something. We're tired of waiting."

Caerson pulled Imara back in line and whispered in her ear. She pouted and crossed her arms. "I want to get on that damn ship so I can have champagne. What's wrong with that?"

Marsa smiled at Avei. "Inspector Avei Themis, please humor us and decide."

Imara startled and leaned forward to stare at Avei. "Did she say… Wow, there's like a hundred movies about her. She's the one who catches serial killers."

Before Caerson could react, Imara shoved her way past Celethe and sidled up to Avei. "It must be amazing to be famous. I want to be an actor on Nexus. I'm going to star in movies and talk shows."

Avei moved back to put distance between them, but it did no good. Imara matched her steps.

"My boyfriend's getting me a meeting with a producer. I'll be as big a superstar as you." Imara beamed.

Caerson reached out and yanked Imara back behind him.

She wrenched her arm free. "Ouch. Why are you such a jerkwert? I didn't even get her autograph."

Wilm whipped his head around and stared at Caerson, who held his gaze until Wilm broke eye contact, fists clenched at his side.

"I've had enough." He grabbed Celethe's hand and pushed past Julisa, boarding the gangway.

Avei turned to Marsa, eager to put an end to this debacle and return to her quiet little office. “Show me the ticket for your pet.”

“With pleasure.” Marsa juggled Sintha to one arm and tapped on the embedded wrist device that shone through her skin. A holographic image of Sintha on a Breckin Starliners ticket appeared above her handbag’s display screen.

That settled it. Avei turned to Julisa. “Your company sold passage for her pet. She boards.”

“Exactly. So get out of my way,” demanded Marsa.

Julisa crossed her arms and didn’t budge.

Avei squared her shoulders and straightened up to her full height of five-feet-one-inch, speaking in her formal inspector voice. “You have two choices, Ms. Breckin. Board or step aside. If you do neither, I will arrest you. The choice is yours.”

Julisa’s face darkened with anger and she appeared ready to resist. Avei panicked. She didn’t have the emotional wherewithal to get into a pissing contest with one of Mernin’s most respected businesswoman.

A storm of emotions crossed Julisa’s face, fury being the dominant one. “Whoever sold that ticket is fired.” She turned and stalked through the loading-ramp hatch.

Avei breathed a sigh of relief as the remaining passengers fell in behind Julisa.

Imara, who led the way, slowed to a stop. She studied Marsa, who stood next to Avei. Caerson wrapped his arm around his girlfriend’s waist and pulled her forward. The guests groaned behind them and looked ready to riot.

"Wait. I think we know her." Imara looked over her shoulder at Marsa, as Caerson pushed her through the hatch. The rest of the guests followed until only Avei and the odious woman remained.

Marsa smiled at her over Sintha's head. "Can you believe it? We're finally meeting in person. I've wanted this for so long. My fans will be thrilled. I can't wait to tell them."

Given a choice, Avei would pick being dragged naked across broken glass over having a conversation with Marsa Baako. She longed for a steaming mug of tea, alone in her little spaceport office, the door closed. "I suggest you board before they leave you behind."

"They wouldn't dare leave behind a 50 billion light-year passenger." Marsa frowned as she gave Avei the once-over. "I thought for sure we'd meet when the Tribunal reviewed our case. I don't mind telling you how disappointed I was when only your solicitors showed up."

"*My* case, Ms. Baako. Not *ours*." Avei stared longingly at the spot that held the hidden hatch. "And that was a long time ago."

"When I named my main character Inspector Savei Demis, I..."

Rigid with anger, Avei spun on her heels and headed to the hidden hatch. She didn't care if Ms. Baako boarded the shuttle or not. With the issue resolved, Avei no longer needed to share the same air with this person who had stolen her life.

"Why do you hate me?" Marsa called after her.

Seriously? Is she that stupid?

Avei spun around and faced Marsa. "You dare ask me that? After you robbed me of my anonymity. Without my permission and with no regard for the impact it had on my life and job."

"So what? You got a ton of money from my novels and all those movies. Way too much, if you ask me."

"Every penny of that money built the Anastasia Themis Institute of Arachnology." Avei experienced the familiar pang of discomfort when it came to that money. She loved what she had accomplished with it but hated where it came from.

"An institute for spiders! Give me a freaking break. Animals, I get. But bugs?"

Arachnids. Not bugs.

"Board the shuttle, Ms. Baako, before it leaves without you."

The hidden hatch slid open as Avei headed toward it. Why did Marsa Baako have to show up as she closed out this chapter of her life? Becoming a civilian meant an end to the constant intrusion into her life. She'd finally fade away, just like Marsa Baako. In time, no one would remember either of their names.

"Wait, please don't go." Marsa's shoulders drooped as Avei entered the hatch and it closed behind her. "I shouldn't have said that." She hugged Sintha to her and hurried up the shuttle ramp.

7

Luxury travel had become synonymous with the Breckin brand and catapulted them to the top of the industry. Their oldest ship, the *Delphi*, didn't disappoint. Set to mimic the sunset, the lighting cast the lounge in a seductive glow. Throughout the opulent room, clusters of plush furniture invited guests to sink into soft comfort. A window spanned the exterior wall and framed Mernin, a planet with one small continent surrounded by an emerald-green ocean. Clouds covered most of the world, with several massive hurricanes in various stages of forming or dissipating.

In formal dinner attire, the passengers from the terminal gathered in small groups. Almost everyone dressed in the latest fad of muted pastels that shimmered when they moved, giving the appearance of rippling water. The women wore elegant gowns and the men sleeveless tunics, paired with pants and knee-high boots in a variety of soft colors.

An army of Grilan servers weaved their way between the guests, carrying trays of delicacies and flutes of champagne. An alluring race known for their porcelain-featured beauty and polite demeanor, the Grilan wore their long, lavender-silver hair plaited and coiled in elaborate buns on top of their heads. The Breckins paid top wages to secure their service.

Other luxury cruise companies had moved to robotic servers long ago but Julisa resisted any attempts from her board and family to follow suit. She felt the passengers deserved a personal touch, something a hunk of polymer was incapable of providing. This attention to customer service had kept Breckin Starliners in the number-one spot for the last decade.

Nestled inside a deep alcove, the bar stretched the length of the back wall. Several guests sat at the counter, which was carved from the saffron-colored heartwood of a single gihex tree and said to be worth a small fortune. They chatted with the Calista bartender, who had slits for a nose and skin covered in luminescent green scales. A small frill circled his head and neck and fluttered when he spoke. A jolly fellow, his laughter rang out from behind the bar, mingling with the guests', who appeared to be having a rollicking good time.

Transcendent in the sea of subtle colors, Imara shone like the sun in her bright yellow gown, stunning against her ebony skin. A thick, jeweled headband tamed her black afro. She scanned the guests, eager to spot anyone remotely famous. Caerson fidgeted next to her in his light pink tunic, mauve pants, and fern-green boots.

"No one is as pretty as I am." Imara studied the crowd with a critical eye. Even next to the incomparable Grilan, she stood out.

"We agreed to blend in and not draw attention to ourselves." Caerson glanced at her attire and shook his head.

"If a bigwig producer or director from Nexus is onboard, I want their eyes only on me." Imara snatched a glass of champagne from the tray of a server and sipped it with her eyes closed. "I never knew champagne tasted this good."

"When you become rich and famous on the Nexus, we'll drink it every day." Caerson smiled at Imara, whose eyes flew open in excitement.

"Did you get me a meeting?"

Caerson nodded, his smile widened. "I'd do anything for you, my love."

Imara flung her arms around his neck. "Tell me everything. Who is it? When do I meet them? What show are they with?"

Caerson laughed and hugged her close. "I'll tell you everything tonight. In bed."

"I'll be the next superstar on Nexus. A girl from the Bhindoir commune is going to be famous." She giggled and hugged him back. "Everyone will know who I am."

Captain Lylum Dimphi entered through a hatch in the back. A Daliean, his sparse white hair and beard framed his amber-colored skin and periwinkle eyes. His pointy ears sat low on his long, narrow skull. The Dalieans valued family above all else, and one mated couple could have thirty or more children. The planet Dalia was renowned for its temperate climate and sweet wines made from zui zui fruit grown on the hardy vines that covered the volcanic mountains.

Captain Dimphi smiled and rubbed his hands together as he moved into the room. He nodded to Caerson and Imara, still locked in an embrace. “Enjoying your stay?”

“Very much,” Imara said.

“Good. Happy to hear it.” He turned and ran into Marsa, who had Sintha in her arms. Captain Dimphi’s smile drooped as Sintha raked him with her manic eyes. He took several steps back and, with effort, refocused on Marsa.

“Sintha isn’t happy, Captain. And if she isn’t happy, neither am I.”

“What is it this time, Ms. Baako?”

“The kitchen refused to fix Sintha’s food. Let me remind you, I’m a 50 billion light-year passenger with an enormous fan base that loves to hear about my trips on the *Delphi*.”

“While we, ah… treasure your journeys with us, the issue is the stench. It overwhelms the staff, seeps into the hallways, and causes distress among the guests.”

Sintha flexed her claws as she stared at Captain Dimphi. The intelligence in her eyes was unnerving. He took another step back.

“I told those idiots the last time: bake the worms, don’t fry them.” Marsa huffed.

“If I remember correctly, Sintha also enjoys basa fish. I’ll have the cooks prepare it at once.”

“Fine. Send it to my room.” Marsa shuffled the heavy cat in her arms and turned to leave.

“While you’re here, Ms. Baako, Management asked that I inquire about your sizable—”

Marsa whirled around and glared at Captain Dimphi. "Tell Julisa Breckin to back off. I already told her I have a plan to pay off my debts."

"Excellent. I'll relay your message. Now, if you'll excuse me." Captain Dimphi stepped around Marsa and headed to the middle of the room just as Wilm and Celethe Breckin entered the lounge. Julisa trailed behind them.

All eyes focused on Celethe, who wore a gown of green gossamer that gave glimpses of her nudity underneath. Her long blond hair flowed down her back, held in place by a jeweled tiara. Her eyes shimmered in the muted light.

Wilm snorted in amusement at the attention focused on his wife. The Calista bartender's laugh carried across the room and caught his attention. He pivoted and headed to the bar. Julisa grabbed his arm and shook her head. He yanked his arm away and stumbled. Bleary-eyed, he scanned the room to confirm all eyes remained on this stunning wife and not on him. Frowning, he rubbed his arm and settled in next to her.

Julisa scoured the room and spotted a female guest with an empty glass. She signaled to the closest server and pointed. The Grilan grimaced and dashed toward the woman.

***

Captain Dimphi saw the exchange and quaked inside. He ran a tight ship but no one could match Julisa Breckin's exacting style. There would be hell to pay later.

Another Grilan beckoned Julisa, Celethe, and Wilm to an empty alcove blocked by a holographic velvet rope. The Breckins headed her way as the surrounding guests watched. Celethe and Wilm sat next to each other on the plush couch and Julisa settled at the other end.

Now that the Breckins were seated, it was time to get started. Captain Dimphi tapped the communication device on his lapel. "My dear guests, may I..." His voice could barely be heard over the chatter. Everyone gawked at the Breckins. The gossip, deafening.

Captain Dimphi tapped his communication device again. "May I have your attention?" With the volume higher, his voice cut through the noise and the crowd quieted.

"I want to welcome you to the *Delphi* starliner. We are delighted to have you aboard." The guests clapped. Captain Dimphi smiled and wondered how long that would last once he shared the bad news.

"I have a bit of unfortunate business to get out of the way. We are experiencing a twelve-hour delay entering the Mernin wormhole. Nothing to be concerned about. We're third in line and will arrive in Charnos in two days."

The applause died out and the guests stared at him. He glanced at Julisa and wished he hadn't. Her expression promised a tough night ahead. He should have informed her first, and he kicked himself for a lapse in judgment. Nothing could be done about it now, so he refocused on the guests. "As a thank you for your patience, all top-shelf alcohol is free for the duration of our trip."

Unimpressed, the guests' silence dragged on. *Oh dear. Not good. Not good at all.* What would Ms. Breckin do? Ah, he had it. He cleared his throat. "And of course, we will include liquors from the Dimarit moon. Their Berigan brandy's a favorite of mine."

The applause picked up again. Captain Dimphi spread his arms. "May your journey on the *Delphi* be unforgettable."

The guests flagged down servers as the captain headed towards the Breckins, his insides in turmoil. He was already on thin ice over the incident with Ms. Baako's Atiza. Even though the mangy beast bit him unprovoked, Julisa held him responsible for letting it roam the ship unattended. He loathed that varmint with every fiber of his being. How it got on the bridge remained a mystery. As the captain, he found its intrusion into the nerve center of the ship unforgivable. Ms. Breckin had banned it for life and yet here it was on his ship again. He settled in front of the table.

"Ms. Breckin, Mr. and Mrs. Breckin. It is an honor to have you aboard." He touched his chest and bowed. His ears twitched as he straightened.

"Who bumped us from the first position?" Julisa asked.

"Two military carriers, madam." Getting bumped when the Breckins were aboard went to the top of his list of the worst things to happen since he was made captain fifteen years ago. The situation was beyond his control, as she well knew. The law dictated that the military took priority and they had to abide by it.

Wilm smirked at Julisa. "Why are you in such a hurry to get to Charnos, dear sister?"

Julisa ignored him and focused her ire on Captain Dimphi. "There is no war. No emergency. Why do they get to go first?"

"I'm very sorry about the delay, madam. Until the Mernin Government changes the rules, the military moves to the head of the line."

"We'll see about that. It's time we got rid of these outdated, useless rules."

Wilm snapped his fingers and held up his empty glass. His hand trembled.

A small door slid open in the wall behind them and a server entered with a full glass of whiskey. They set the glass down and took the empty one before it tumbled from Wilm's shaky fingers.

Captain Dimphi glared at the server. "Mr. Breckin's glass never goes empty. Understood?"

The Grilan nodded and disappeared through the open hatch that closed behind them.

Captain Dimphi noted Celethe's concern as Wilm downed half the liquor in one gulp. She had a right to be worried. That man couldn't hold his liquor. Rarely did they get the happy-go-lucky Wilm the drunk. No, it was mostly the evil version. The captain shuddered inside, thinking about the next two days with both Julisa and Wilm aboard. At least he didn't have to worry about Celethe, a kind and even-tempered woman. *Sweet Goddess Mima, please get me through this unscathed.*

Wilm settled back on the couch, every bit the lord of the manor. "Get my table ready in the casino. I feel like playing cards tonight."

"Of course. Right away, sir." He noticed Julisa glaring at him.

"Don't you have a ship to run?"

"Yes, yes, I do. Thank you." Relieved to get a dismissal, he backed up and almost knocked over a server carrying a tray of chianti. Dimphi stumbled sideways and barely avoided calamity. He smoothed down his uniform and hurried from the room.

***

Celethe waited until the captain had moved on before she leaned into Wilm and whispered, "You promised. No more gambling." She knew he'd be angry, but she had to try.

Living with an addict was like hanging onto a float device with a slow leak in the middle of the ocean, knowing the next wave could drown you. Wilm got to numb his pain by using one vice or another. Celethe couldn't escape like he did. She had to experience every excruciating second of his addictions and constant screw-ups fully clearheaded while having to manage her own stress and fear, all the while holding her breath, waiting for the next shoe to drop. Because it always did.

Wilm stiffened. "Don't tell me what I can and can't do on my own damn ship."

"Shh. What about the Iscun?" Her face pinched with worry. The Iscun were a violent crime syndicate who killed first and asked questions later. Their reach spanned the entire Kressa quadrant, home to a hundred billion souls. They had their hands into everything. Sex parlors and gambling dens on L'reus, a small moon orbiting a gas giant in the Mernin system. The piracy of freighters in transit between systems. Creating designer babies using outlawed DNA manipulation. The trafficking of rare beasts, alive or dead, and a hundred other illegal activities. Their latest illicit drug, Zenith, had already killed over a million people, and no government or police agency was strong enough to stop them.

Wilm smirked and swallowed the rest of his drink, slamming the glass on the table. "I'm not afraid of them."

"Well, I'm terrified." Celethe studied the guests as if one of them might produce a gun and kill them on the spot.

"What are you talking about?" Julisa asked.

"Nothing," Wilm said. "Now, if you will excuse me, I have a card game to win."

Wilm stood and watched a beautiful Grilan across the room. They refused to catch Wilm's eye and ducked behind a group of guests. Celethe followed his gaze and stiffened. Not *again.*

"Don't wait up for me, darling. I'll be late tonight." Wilm navigated his way around the table.

Julisa frowned. "You promised us both you'd stay out of trouble."

"Our definitions of trouble are vastly different, dear sister. Enjoy your evening." Wilm headed to the hatch, a spring in his step.

Celethe shared a worried look with Julisa. It would be another sleepless night.

8

The brightly lit corridor on the fifth floor curved around the interior of the ship. Even on the staff deck, the floors had a mirror shine. Hatches peppered the right side every ten feet, each with its own comm device. The occasional employee notice in a holographic frame broke up the gleaming white of the left wall.

Ocia Doni hummed as she danced and her arms swayed as she gyrated down the hall. Pulled back into a tight ponytail, her green hair swayed in time with her steps. The cleaning-supply hover cart followed her serpentine path down the hallway. A stack of sheets teetered on the edge and the cleaning fluids sloshed in their containers.

A Yuzealian, Ocia was small in stature, with four arms, round green eyes twice the size of human eyes, green hair, and a teardrop-shaped skull. She wore the *Delphi* maroon uniform, a sleeveless tunic designed to accommodate her four arms, long pants, and mid-calf black boots.

Ocia loved working on the *Delphi*, and after five years, had no intention of ever leaving. War was a constant on Yuzeal, where despots ruled over their subjects with an iron fist and constantly battled each other. Her family had pooled their credits together to pay a smuggler to get her out, so she could find work and send money home. Because of her job, her family had food and lodging in a safer part of their township. This job meant her family had a real chance of surviving. A warm glow of gratitude filled her, and she smiled with pure joy.

The smile disappeared when she rounded the corner and saw a distraught woman racing toward her, yellow gown torn, eyes wild. Orange foam bubbled at the corner of her mouth.

"We're dying! Help us!" Imara Tiniba shouted, her eyes unfocused.

Ocia slammed against the wall as the woman dashed past her. The hover cart couldn't move fast enough, and Imara plowed into it. She landed on the ground in a heap, along with the sheets and some of the cleaning fluids.

Ocia froze as she processed what had happened. She worked the night shift to cut down on her interactions with the guests. Her strong lisp made her self-conscious, especially after Mr. Breckin had mocked her repeatedly when she first started. Speaking the universal language was a Breckin requirement for employment and challenging for her people to master. Their long, thin tongues made it difficult to form certain consonants.

Imara emitted a high, prolonged shriek, snapping her out of her rumination.

"Madam, are you okay?" Ocia leaned over Imara, who thrashed on the ground, scattering the bedding and bottles in all directions.

Imara grabbed her head and screamed again. The gut-wrenching sound reverberated through the corridor.

Ocia stumbled backwards. The woman's shrieks hurt her ears and the situation was well beyond her capabilities and training. Her hands shook as she tapped a comm device embedded in her wrist. "Code 5. Code 5. I need medical in section 5B. A passenger is really sick down here."

"What's a passenger doing on the staff deck?" A security officer's voice came through her device. "And what's the issue?"

Ocia glared at the security camera in the ceiling behind her. *Why was he asking such a dumb question*? "Can't you see the crazy lady?"

"Cameras are down. We've been blind for ten minutes."

Imara leaped to her feet, startling Ocia. Wild-eyed and frantic, Imara panted in fear as she searched the hallway. Ocia wondered if the woman would hurt her, and she debated running away. Imara solved her dilemma when she turned and raced down the hallway, wailing.

"She's headed for the elevators." Ocia watched Imara disappear around the bend. "Please hurry. Something's very wrong with that lady."

"Copy that."

Ocia gathered the items from the floor and piled them onto the cart. She'd straighten everything after lunch. She shoved her hands into the four pockets of her uniform to stop their trembling and peered down the corridor, half expecting to see the woman again. Relieved to be alone, she continued down the hallway with the cart following.

Wilm Breckin appeared around the bend and careened her way. His glassy eyes gave away his inebriation.

"Not again. Not tonight," Ocia said under her breath. She hated the man. He treated the staff like slaves and what he did to the Grilans was unspeakable and a crime. If he was on the staff deck, he was up to no good. Again. While Ocia's loyalties to Julisa Breckin were unshakable, they did not extend to her brother.

Wilm straightened when he saw her, as if to appear sober. He stumbled and landed on both knees in front of Ocia. "Damn floor. I told them to stop making it so slippery."

Served him right. Ocia bit back a laugh, knowing it would get her fired. She hesitated, not sure how he'd take it if she helped him but aware that the longer she left him on the ground, the greater his rage and the likelihood he'd retaliate. Any other person and she'd have helped them up already.

A quick scan of the halls came up empty. No one else was around to help her decide. If Ms. Breckin discovered Ocia standing over her brother in such an embarrassing position, she'd be mad at her and not him. Left with no choice, Ocia gently gripped his arm. "Sir, let me help you."

Wilm jerked his arm away and glowered at her. "Don't touch me, you freak." He pushed himself to his feet and swayed, then lurched down the corridor.

Ocia watched him over her shoulder as she hurried away and prayed to the three goddesses that he was too drunk to remember her. The hover cart trailed behind her. The captain needed to be informed about Mr. Breckin being down here again. Someone had to check on the Grilan and ensure they were okay.

When Wilm had disappeared around the bend, Ocia turned and took several hurried steps but was brought up short. She stumbled and landed on her hands and knees, the cart inches from crashing into her.

On the ground in front of her lay Caerson Mercer, his face frozen in agony. Orange foam oozed from his mouth. She'd seen enough dead bodies on Yuzeal to know she was staring at one right now.

Ocia trembled from head to toe and scooted back, straight into the cart. She screamed through her hands, which were covering her mouth.

9

Captain Dimphi stood beside Ocia, who had her four arms wrapped around herself in a tight hug. Ever the company man, he wore a robe, pajamas and slippers all in the Breckin maroon with gold piping.

Two security officers kept watch from each end of the corridor, to prevent anyone from entering the crime scene and, more importantly, to keep a lid on the situation.

Everyone watched Chief Security Officer Eadren Varan, who squatted next to the contorted body of Caerson Mercer.

Suiven and human cross-mates made for an attractive combination, and Eadren was no exception. His facial features came from his human mother and everything else: dark cyan hair, light blue skin, and green-colored feline eyes, came from his father. The tailored maroon security uniform with gold epaulets clung to his muscular frame.

Eadren felt their eyes on him as he studied Caerson's face, which was frozen in agony. The victim had suffered a horrifying death. What killed him remained a mystery. *Perhaps drugs*? He studied the orange foam that rimmed the man's mouth. *Maybe poison*? There was something familiar about the situation that tickled the back of his mind. He tried to recall something he must have read or heard but the information remained elusive.

"Chief Varan, please tell me this man's death is an unfortunate accident." Captain Dimphi stared at the security chief as the last vestiges of hope faded.

With every fiber of his being, Eadren wanted to say yes. This situation added a layer of complexity and attention he couldn't afford right now. The victim deserved better, and it went against his moral fiber to pretend otherwise. "That is not my line of thinking."

Captain Dimphi's shoulders slumped. "What are dealing with here?"

"At first, I thought he'd overdosed on that hallucinogenic drug, Zenith. The one that causes contortions like we see here." Eadren motioned towards the body.

Captain Dimphi stepped closer to the victim. "The drug that group of psychopaths peddle. The... Ishtar? Iezen? What is their name again? The ones involved with—"

"The crime syndicate you are referring to are called the Iscun." With considerable effort, Eadren didn't openly react to the captain's comment. He pointed to the rim of orange foam around Caerson's mouth. "This suggests poison."

"So, what is it? Overdose or murder? And please don't say it's murder. Not with the Breckins aboard."

Ocia whimpered and shared a look of horror with the two security guards.

Captain Dimphi scanned the corridor. "And where is Dr. Hueson?"

A murder would derail the whole thing. Eadren could push the captain toward an overdose scenario and buy some time. Once they returned from Charnos with his task completed, he would ensure the victim received a proper investigation. "The victim's girlfriend was raving like a lunatic. The doctor's with her in the medical bay." Eadren hesitated. A war of morality churned inside him. What he said next would dictate the success or failure of the most important job he'd ever taken on. With only one path he could take, he'd get the victim justice. It just needed to wait a few days. "Doc doesn't know what the two of them took."

"That proves it. Write it up as a drug overdose. A murder will only delay us from getting to Charnos." Captain Dimphi gave Eadren a knowing nod. "And as you well know, it is imperative we get to Charnos."

While it didn't assuage his guilt, it gave them some breathing room. He needed to remain focused on the main objective and push aside anything that impeded a successful outcome.

Prior to releasing the scene, he had one more issue to discuss. He glanced at Ocia Doni. She trembled from head to toe and appeared on the verge of shock. She had discovered the body and experienced an alarming encounter with the girlfriend. That would rattle anyone. He needed to hurry this along and get her to the medical bay for a full checkup. "Wilm Breckin was down here again."

Captain Dimphi clutched his chest and stumbled backwards. He almost trampled Ocia, who scooted out of his way. "Sweet Mima, what else tonight? Did he... you know, cause any problems?"

"Too drunk to do any harm. Our idea is working." Every time Eadren thought about what Wilm did to the Grilan, it made his blood boil. Given Eadren's role on the *Delphi* and everything that was at stake, he had very few options on how hard to crack down on Wilm for his behavior. While his and the captain's plan seemed a reasonable compromise, it did nothing to lessen his anger. The man belonged in prison.

"Good, very good." Captain Dimphi visibly relaxed. "I'll make sure he doesn't sober up until we reach Charnos."

Ocia shot a surprised glance in the captain's direction.

"I need to follow protocol and report the death to the Mernin Security Forces," Eadren said.

"Do it. The last thing we need is to go sideways with MSF. And let's not bother the guests and crew with this unfortunate event."

Eadren glanced at Ocia, who shrank back. Knowing how the staff loved to gossip, the story would be all over the ship within an hour. They had to contain it. No matter how sorry he felt for the woman, they needed her kept quiet.

Captain Dimphi followed his gaze and startled. "My dear, I forgot you were still here. As a valued employee of Breckin Starliners, I'm certain we can count on your discretion."

"You need to keep this to yourself until we tell you otherwise. Do not mention it to anyone on this ship. Not your co-workers and not your friends. Do you understand?" Eadren hated using such a stern tone, which clearly frightened her even more, but they could scare her into silence or put her in a holding room until they reached Charnos in twenty-two hours. He preferred a more compassionate approach.

Ocia jammed her trembling hands into her pockets and nodded. “I won’t tell anyone. I promise.”

Even though Eadren knew her promise wouldn’t last, he still didn’t want to imprison her. She’d been through a traumatic event and he would not add to it. Best to stay the course with scaring her. “Please understand. If you talk, you may get fired.”

Tears filled Ocia’s eyes. “I promise, I won’t talk. Not to anyone.”

Some days, he really hated himself. “Thank you, Ocia, I believe you.”

Captain Dimphi glanced back at the victim and grimaced. “Let’s get the body out of here before anyone else sees it.”

10

A battered desk sat in one corner of the tiny precinct office, along with a floating monitor. In another corner was a small table with two rickety chairs. MSF announcements flashed on a cracked communication screen next to the hatch. The worn and scuffed tile floor made it difficult to discern the black diamond pattern. The once-beige walls, now gray with grime and age, added to the dreariness. Considering the wealth of the spaceport visitors, the shabbiness of the MSF office was surprising but not unexpected. All apprehended individuals went straight to headquarters for processing and incarceration. The low-key spaceport office was the refuge for officers retiring from the force or on desk duty to recover from an illness or injury. The MSF leadership reasoned why invest money in the satellite office when only their officers saw the interior?

Avei paced in front of a holographic crime board, several feet in height and width. It hovered in the middle of the floor with 'Zarul Victims' in large print at the top of the board. The images of the six victims covered the right side of the board, bodies twisted into unnatural positions and faces frozen in terror and pain. Some lay on beds and others on the ground in or outside abandoned buildings.

Identification photos of the victims lined the left side. The five men were all middle-aged and the lone woman wore a large diamond necklace and tiara, her dark hair piled on top of her head.

Avei stopped to examine the image of the fifth male victim, tied to a rickety bed in a rundown hotel, his neck in ruins from a large bite. A broken chair lay in the corner of his room. She backed up to take in the full crime board and pushed her purple hair behind her ears, revealing the burn scar. Despite her misgivings about getting involved in a case so close to retirement, her curiosity had got the best of her and she opened the notes. The use of spiders as weapons made it feel like it was tailor made for her. *Is the killer trying to get my attention?*

She felt again the familiar pull when a case got its hooks into her. The rush of excitement that came with the hunt to get a predator off the streets. One got addicted to the flood of endorphins, and she was no exception.

Avei shook her head violently. *I will not get emotionally involved in this case.* After many deep breaths, she took several steps back, putting distance between herself and the crime board. She crossed her arms and studied the images. The six victims had suffered a terrible death at the hands of Zarul, who used three of the most poisonous arachnids known to the Institute. After using the small, black and deadly zarultalzin spiders for the first two victims, and switching to a giant grenwal for the next three, the killer had used a twivorg, second on the Institute's list of the most dangerous arachnids, to kill the sixth victim, the only woman. Even experienced arachnologists would think twice before handling a twivorg.

Avei tapped her fingers against her chin. Zarul was an enigma. *Why use three species of lethal arachnids to kill six victims? Why overcomplicate things?* Each time the murderer introduced a new spider, it required a learning curve and added risks. Zarul was either incredibly stupid, fearless, or they had a compelling reason.

"Sezin, bring up crime scene four again."

"Not until you free me from my cage," Sezin's voice responded from the comm device embedded in her wrist.

Avei felt a surge of regret mixed in with a healthy dose of guilt as she thought about leaving Sezin Watson. During the initial bonding period seven years ago, Avei had let them pick their own name and Sezin chose the moniker of a famous Mernin Security Forces inspector who had died during a shootout with a serial killer over eighty years ago. Bucking AI tradition, Sezin also took a last name, Watson. They said it came from a character in an ancient detective series from old Earth. Avei knew they wanted to talk about her resigning, and she had avoided the conversation until now. She knew she couldn't put it off any longer. "Very well."

A holoball released from the magnet that held it on her belt and floated until it hovered just below the ceiling. Sezin appeared in full MSF uniform, using their androgynous form. They preferred to remain gender-neutral unless a situation required otherwise. Their eyes lingered on Avei's face. "Other than that truly rad scar, I'm happy to see you are well and survived the attack."

Avei smiled and felt a rush of gratitude. "First chance I've had to thank you for your help in the warehouse. Having someone there with me during that... When I found them... I..." She closed her eyes on the image of her two best friends lying on the floor of the warehouse, bound together with wire and still alive as the fire consumed them. Wearing armor and having nothing to extinguish the flames, Avei had used her gloved hands as her friends screamed in agony. Her actions had been too little and too late.

She opened her eyes to find Sezin standing in front of her. Their look of compassion almost undid her.

Sezin wrapped Avei in a hug, even though they had no substance. "I was there. Remember? I know how hard you tried to save them."

Avei stepped out of Sezin's arms and glared at her AI. "I didn't though, did I? I'm retiring, and there is nothing you or anyone else can say that will change my mind. Can you please bring up crime scene four?"

"Please, please, please don't leave," Sezin said with force. Their eyes pleading with her.

The ever-present guilt bloomed into a conflagration. "Don't make this harder than it already is."

Sezin glared at Avei. "Fine. Okay then. Let's just bury our heads in the crime scenes and pretend you're not blowing up our lives by quitting."

"I can't remain on the force when I no longer trust my instincts. I'll get people killed. My mind is made up."

Sezin considered her for a moment. "Then take me with you when you retire. I can help at the Institute and travel with you on your field expeditions to find new species. I can access the Institute's catalog of all known arachnids and tell you if it is a new species, a variant of an existing species, or one that is already cataloged." Sezin beamed. "We can be a team again. We'd be like those great explorers of long ago, braving the unknown dangers of a new world. We'd have so much fun. Please Avei, let me come with you."

Avei's heart broke into a million pieces as she looked at Sezin, who had switched to their petite form. Something they did when they wanted to have a serious conversation. They wore their black hair short, emphasizing androgynous features.

"Sezin, I would take you with me if I could."

"Why can't you buy me?" Sezin asked as hope died in their eyes. "You've never spent a penny of that money from those books on yourself. Do it now. Do it for me. For us."

Avei traced the burn on the back of her hand and sighed. "I asked, then I begged, and offered to pay them every penny they spent on you and more, and leadership said no. I offered to fund two more AIs, which they rejected as well. You're too valuable an investigative tool. They won't let you go. You are… the property of the Mernin Security Forces." She wished for the umpteenth time they had said yes.

"An investigative tool you and I honed during your tenure. It's not fair." Sezin paced in front of her. "I'll go on strike and refuse to work until they release me to you."

Avei winced. Sezin was much more than an AI construct. She considered them a friend, and it gutted her to leave them behind. "You save lives, Sezin Watson, and you will continue to do so with Uma. You already know each other and while it will feel strange at first, I promise you will develop as strong a partnership with her as you have with me. Now, let's look at crime scene four."

Sezin huffed. "Don't even try to sugar-coat it. We both know how we feel about Ms. Uma Smarty-boots. She's a nightmare to work with. I can hear her now. *Sezin, my dear, why am I hearing your voice? I don't remember asking for your opinion. I'll tell you when I need you.* Which will be never. The woman thinks she knows everything. I will wither away with boredom. I'll become one of those dried husks you read about in old Earth books. You know when a body's left outside in the elements and withers away."

"For starters, you don't have a body, so there's no danger of withering away. And yes, Uma can be a pain. No question. You just need to make yourself indispensable to her. Something I know you can do." Avei wanted to give Sezin the hug they so clearly needed. But she'd only be hugging air. "I'm truly sorry about all of this, and I will miss you desperately. I'll visit you often. I promise."

Sezin shrugged and looked away. "How often?"

"As often as Uma will allow. Every week if I can. Now, let's focus on that crime scene."

Sezin sighed and nodded. A hologram of a shirtless man in his fifties appeared, his face frozen in terror. He lay in a filthy alley between two crumbling buildings and behind a mountain of trash and debris. Deep gashes encircled his hands and feet from the metal restraints that bit into his flesh when he convulsed. Orange fluid ringed the twelve puncture marks on his neck. A belt cinched his pants tight over his expansive belly. A bloody white tunic lay nearby.

Avei took in the scene. "He's not a small man. What did the toxicology report say?"

"His blood alcohol level was so high he was barely functioning, and they found traces of Zenith."

"Drunk and high. That explains how the killer subdued him." Avei walked into the hologram and squatted next to the body.

Sezin knelt next to her. "What are you thinking?"

"It's definitely a grenwal bite. What's unusual is it bit him twice." Avei pointed at the wound. "The grenwal spider has six fangs and this bite has twelve puncture wounds."

"Same as the other victims," Sezin said.

"The twivorg's number two on the list of the most aggressive arachnid species identified to date, and the zarultalzins are number four. Both can and will bite their prey multiple times."

"Didn't you get bit by one of those at the Institute?" Sezin asked.

"I've been bitten by a dozen species, but not by a twivorg or zarultalzin. My mother thinks my body has built up some immunity from the bites and all the antidotes I've taken." Avei grimaced as she stood up. Pain flared from the laser wound on her right side; a constant reminder of a night she'd give anything to do over again.

Sezin sprang up next to her. "Are you okay?"

"I'm fine. What's unusual is the grenwal biting the victims twice. They are docile unless they're in danger. Once threatened, they can be as vicious as the twivorg. Given their size and the toxicity of their venom, they'd never need to bite their prey more than once. The killer must have trained it. That's the only explanation."

"If I were the killer, I would have kept using the zarultalzin spiders," Sezin said. "They are ill-tempered buggers on the best of days. Can you imagine their mood after being jostled around in a small container for hours? Just dump them on the victim and stand back while they attack. So why go through all the effort to train a docile spider like the grenwal when you can keep using the zarultalzin?"

"Good question. Grenwals are one of the largest of the known arachnids and can be intimidating to handle. I can't imagine some random person teaching a grenwal to bite on command. It'd take an experienced arachnologist." Avei traced the burn on the back of her hand. "And spiders are notoriously hard to train."

"The Zarul case definitely goes in the creepy and bizarre file," D.I. Skora said as his holographic image appeared alongside Avei, startling her enough that she reached for her gun.

D.I. Skora stood next to her, smiling. He exuded the deep weariness of someone long past retirement. A few inspectors had started a betting pool on when he would retire, but finally gave up as the years rolled by. While others wondered what kept him on the job, Avei knew the reason he remained. It's what formed the tight bond between them.

She released her grip on her gun. "You're going to give someone a heart attack one of these days."

Sezin grew ten inches in height and glared at D.I. Skora as he nodded and smiled. They put their hands on their hips and didn't return the amiable greeting.

"Sorry about that." D.I. Skora paced in front of the crime board. "I've never figured out an acceptable way of entering a room as a hologram. Even when I say 'D.I. Skora is on his way,' it startles the living daylights out of everyone."

"Maybe announce yourself with the ding of a bell."

D.I. Skora nodded. "That might work. I'll use two dings, so people know it's me." He waved at the crime board. "I see you are reviewing the case files from Uma. Tell me about Zarul."

"I'm not in homicide anymore." Skora had been relentless over the past week in his efforts to keep her on the force, and seemed unable to accept her imminent departure.

He studied her. "You're my best detective when it comes to crazies, and I still have you for another four days and three hours."

Avei felt both relief and sadness. He finally appeared to have accepted her resignation. "This is Uma's case, and she is more than qualified to run it." She squared her shoulders and stood her ground.

"Inspector Themis, humor me."

Avei sighed. Skora's stubbornness was legendary and the reason he had the highest close rate in the history of the MSF. He would not give up, so she'd best give him an answer. "The Zarul killings are methodical and executed flawlessly."

"That's already in Uma's case notes. What does your gut say?"

Avei jerked her hand left, then right, and the crime scene disappeared. *How dare he ask me that question?* He knew she didn't trust herself anymore. She turned her back on him.

D.I. Skora took a step closer. "We almost lost you in that warehouse, too."

"I had Apollyona and let her go because I didn't think she could commit such a heinous crime." She fought back the tears that had been a constant companion since the fire. "I got it wrong."

"And I supported that decision and agreed with your assessment. I got it wrong as well, and so did the review panel that approved Apollyona's release. Please, Avei, don't let one deranged soul end a brilliant career."

"She burned twenty people alive, including my two friends. All because I fell for her lies." An image flashed in her mind of dragging her badly burned friends across the warehouse floor as fire raged around them. She shuddered, sick to her stomach.

"There's nothing more dangerous than a religious zealot who has convinced themselves they are doing their God's work." D.I. Skora raised his hands as if to put them on her shoulder, then lowered them. "Even if we do everything perfectly, people can and will still die. Apollyona's ability to compartmentalize her evil deeds from her everyday life made it difficult to suss out her true nature. She didn't just deceive you and me, she fooled four other inspectors, including Uma. We all share responsibility for those deaths. Give it six months. Stay on port duty and if you still feel this way, I'll support your resignation."

Avei whirled on D.I. Skora. "It's our job to see through that deception. If we fail in that duty, people die. I failed, and people died. I've made my decision and it stands. I will remain here while you process my discharge papers."

D.I. Skora sighed and nodded. "Very well. But I need your input on something before you go. Sezin, pull up case A225791. The *Delphi* starliner death."

"Accessing it now."

"Someone died on the *Delphi*?" Skora had Avei's attention, even though she wanted no part of the case. "There was a scuffle last evening during boarding."

The body of Caerson Mercer lying on a steel table appeared between Avei and Skora. The sharp detail made him appear solid. A white sheet covered most of his body, leaving only his neck and face exposed, the dried orange foam around his mouth stark against his pale skin and lips.

Avei experienced a fleeting moment of disappointment that this unfortunate man lay on the morgue table, not Marsa Baako.

"They listed it as a Zenith OD. I have my doubts."

Avei zeroed in on the victim's mouth. *It couldn't be. Could it?* She leaned closer and experienced the thrill she always got when a compelling piece of evidence appeared. Only one arachnoid caused this to happen. "This isn't a Zenith overdose."

"I didn't think so."

Sezin approached the body and stopped next to Avei. "Should I bring up an image of the grenwal?"

"Yes."

The image of a viridian-colored spider with a ten-inch hourglass appeared. It sat in the middle of a massive web with threads a quarter-inch thick.

D.I. Skora gasped and closed his eyes. "My worst nightmare. Make it go away."

Avei waved her hand left, then right, and the image disappeared. She shared a brief smile with Sezin. "It's safe to open your eyes."

D.I. Skora shuddered. "I may never sleep again."

"As the grenwal venom spreads through the body, it causes body fluids to turn orange. This includes saliva, which explains the orange sputum around his mouth. Did the victim have a bite?" Avei asked.

D.I. Skora shook his head. "No mention of one. It's Zarul, isn't it?"

"Uma's case indicates Zarul is a sadist who uses live spiders to terrorize their victims. I agree with that assessment." Avei walked around the body. "No bite means no live spiders. This is a different MO."

"Maybe Zarul got tired of carrying around giant, lethal spiders and came up with a new plan. If the spider didn't bite the victim, how did he die of venom poisoning?"

"He ingested the grenwal venom. Either through something he ate, drank, or absorbed through his skin. Given the resilience of spider venom, it's possible to poison someone by adding venom to a drink or food. It's quite ingenious, and easy enough to do." The excitement of a new case seized hold of Avei, and she didn't try to suppress it. She'd never feel this way again, so she let herself revel in it.

"Could it be Zarul?"

Avei chewed on her lower lip. "Given their proclivity for using spiders and their venom as a weapon, I'd say it's a strong possibility."

"A shuttle will take you to the *Delphi*," D.I. Skora said. "Connect with their chief of security, Eadren Varan."

Sezin startled and then grinned. They nodded their approval at D.I. Skora, who smiled back.

Avei missed the exchange. Panic pressed down on her chest and made breathing difficult. "No sir, I can't. I won't go. I don't trust myself anymore. If you send me up there, you'll put every passenger and crew member in danger. Please don't do it." Avei sucked in a ragged breath. "Please, sir."

"You're my only detective experienced with creepy-crawlies."

"Send Uma. She's more than capable of handling this case." Avei's hands trembled. She jammed them into her pockets. "Besides, I'm gone by the end of the week. It's not enough time to close the case."

"Then I suggest you hurry." D.I. Skora took a step away from her.

"Don't do this."

"I expect an update from the *Delphi* in six hours."

"No, wait." Avei reached for D.I. Skora as he faded away. She stared at the victim on the table and then flicked her wrist left, then right, and the hologram disappeared.

She looked up and saw Sezin smiling. "I'm not talking to you right now."

"See you on the *Delphi*, Inspector." Sezin waved and disappeared. The holoball floated down and reattached to Avei's belt.

Avei sank to the ground, head in hands. Skora had no business putting her on that ship. The victim deserved an inspector who was on the top of their game. They deserved Uma.

11

Set to the brightest level, the lights in the lounge cast a harsh glow on the guests, who were clustered in small groups, their conversations muted. Tables with platters of finger foods, desserts, and urns of hot beverages filled the middle of the room. For those in need of something stronger, Grilan servers offered trays laden with alcoholic beverages.

The bank of windows covered the exterior wall and looked out on five ships lined up in front of the Mernin wormhole, a swirl of white clouds spinning around an incandescent center. The ships ranged in size from giant freighters to sleek pleasure craft.

Nearby, the spacehub bristled with lights and the activity of ships arriving and leaving. Pilot vessels flitted around the spacecrafts, guiding them into or out of their assigned berths.

Julisa, Wilm, and Celethe Breckin huddled together near the hatch. Wilm's eyes tracked a server as they headed their way with a tray.

"About damn time." Wilm grabbed a drink from the tray. "If you value your job, don't take as long next time."

Celethe smiled at the server. "Thank you."

The server bowed and headed back to the guests.

Wilm's hand trembled when he sipped his drink. "Stop doing that."

"Stop what, my love?"

"Don't play dumb, Celethe. It doesn't suit you." Wilm stepped closer to her. "Don't undermine me again in front of my employees."

Celethe held her ground. "Our mantra has always been the guests come first. We are not guests. We are the owners, therefore the server correctly followed orders."

Wilm sneered. "The only owners in our little trio are me and Julisa."

Anger flashed across Celethe's face before her mask of indifference locked back in place. "My mistake."

Julisa had noticed the exchange. "Will you two stop bickering? It gets tiresome."

"Why are we required to be here?" Wilm smoothed down his pale-yellow tunic, a color ill-suited for his sallow skin. "I swear, Captain Dimphi grows more incompetent every day. Why you keep him on is beyond me."

"A guest died last night, of an overdose." Julisa's voice was thick with worry.

"So what? It happens. That's why we're forced to keep an expensive mortuary room that rarely gets used. Just stick the body in one of those damn cabinets and let's be on our way."

Celethe turned to Julisa. "Wilm's right. Isn't that what normally happens?"

"Ordinarily, yes. The captain doesn't know why Mernin Security Forces are sending an inspector instead of letting us finish our voyage."

"Maybe it wasn't an overdose," Celethe said.

"When MSF get here, I'll handle the situation. Understood?" Julisa gave Celethe and Wilm one of her infamous 'don't even think about disobeying me' looks.

"Wouldn't have it any other way." Wilm lifted his glass in salute.

A disgruntled group of guests gathered near the Breckins. Many of them shot angry looks their way. A second delay had worsened the general mood and no amount of top shelf alcohol would make amends.

Marsa remained apart, Sintha cradled in her arms. She glowered at the crowd with disdain. A couple of people gave her a wide berth when Sintha bared her fangs at them.

***

The third floor, known as the Delphi Promenade, was the destination place for the guests and home to the entertainment venues. The Marzotta Casino, a replica of a famous L'reus club, was the most popular, where the guests spent most of their time and money. If gambling didn't fit the bill, they could use the holographic amusement deck and partake in a variety of adventures and historical dramas. If they craved peace, they could spend time in the Galaxy Bar, with its semi-private rooms and observation windows.

Alcoves with plush seating and expensive art lined the corridor. Smaller alcoves held alien artifacts from all over the galaxy. Depending on one's tastes, the thick burgundy carpet and charcoal walls inlaid with gold and silver either elevated the perceived sumptuousness of the promenade or added to its over-the-top ostentatiousness.

Captain Dimphi and Chief Varan stood outside the ballroom hatch. Both wore their dress uniforms in standard Breckin maroon and gold.

"Did you classify it as an overdose in the report?" the captain asked in his deep baritone.

"I did." Eadren glanced behind them at the empty corridor.

Captain Dimphi pulled his collar away from his neck. "Julisa Breckin is most unhappy with this second delay. Most unhappy."

The ship's purser ran toward them with an overnight bag. "Right behind me."

"Take the bag to the room," Captain Dimphi said.

The purser turned as he dashed past. "It's that famous one. Would it be okay if I asked her for an autograph?"

"Absolutely not." The captain glared at him.

The purser shrugged and continued down the hall.

"Do you know what he's talking about?"

Eadren reached for his right pocket and stopped himself. He smoothed his uniform instead. "They've sent Inspector Avei Themis."

"Who? Wait, the one who catches serial killers? Why send her to a drug overdose? That doesn't seem right."

"I agree. Act natural and play your part."

"Sweet Goddess Mima, give me strength." Captain Dimphi kissed his fingertips and touched his forehead.

***

Avei made her way down the *Delphi* promenade. She wore the standard black MSF uniform, her gun and badge on her hip. Dread slowed her steps. She kicked herself for not pushing back on D.I. Skora. He had no business sending her here.

She glanced up. The purser had disappeared. Where did he go? Avei spotted a holographic sign floating near the ceiling with arrows pointing toward the ballroom, casino, lounge, and the Galaxy bar. He had said the lounge, and the arrow pointed straight ahead.

She hurried around the curve and saw two men waiting for her. Avei knew from her brief that they were Chief of Security Eadren Varan and Captain Lylum Dimphi. Skora hadn't given her time to delve into their backgrounds, given the brief window they'd had to board the shuttle and the short flight to the *Delphi*. Knowing very little about them increased her nerves.

Chief Varan studied her as she approached. An attractive man, his green feline eyes were striking against his pale blue skin.

Avei had honed the ability to keep her face free of emotion over the years. A critical skill required when dealing with serial killers, who would exploit any perceived weakness. It had been ages since she had felt a physical attraction to anyone. Too busy for a serious relationship, one-night stands suited her lifestyle.

Much to her horror, she felt herself blush as Varan scrutinized her. So much for that critical skill.

Captain Dimphi had his hand out as he rushed toward her. “Inspector Themis, it is a privilege and honor to have someone of such renown aboard our ship. We are at your disposal during your stay as our guest. Anything you need, just ask and we will do our best to accommodate.”

Avei recoiled from his enthusiastic welcome. She loathed fame. Hated strangers knowing everything about her when she knew nothing about them. It put her at a disadvantage, particularly as a law enforcement official. “I’m not here as a guest. I’m here to investigate a murder on behalf of the Mernin Security Forces.”

“Of course. Of course.” Captain Dimphi shot a panicked glance at Eadren. “This is our chief of security, Eadren Varan. He will ensure you have everything you need to complete your investigation.”

Eadren held out his hand. “I’ll be partnering with you on this unfortunate incident, which appears to be a drug overdose, not a murder.”

Avei shook his hand and studied him. Of course, they needed the death to be drug-related. Understandable. No business wanted the publicity a murder brought. Especially on board a starliner, stuck for hours inside a wormhole during transit between systems. She’d leave them their fantasy for now. “I look forward to partnering with you.”

The hatch opened and Julisa marched out with Celethe and Wilm behind her. Marsa stood in the hatchway, a smile on her face and Sintha sitting at her feet.

When the hatch closed, Sintha darted out, leaving Marsa behind in the lounge. The animal jumped on a cushioned bench in the alcove across from the Breckins and groomed herself.

Julisa settled in front of Captain Dimphi and Avei, who stepped back to look up at her.

"What is the meaning of this delay?" Julisa used her height to intimidate when the situation called for it.

Avei watched Eadren reclaim his spot next to the captain. The same height as Julisa, he didn't flinch when she gave him the once-over. He returned her gaze with a challenge and without the expected deference. *Interesting.* Avei wondered if they had a history beyond that of employer and employee.

Captain Dimphi cleared his throat and brought their attention back to him. "Inspector Themis, I am pleased to introduce Julisa Breckin, owner of this lovely ship."

"I know the inspector. We met yesterday. You have ten minutes to get us back in line, Captain," Julisa said. "Or you can find a new job."

Dimphi blanched. "Madam, I, ah, I—"

Julisa might be used to strong-arming those around her with a confidence that immediately shut down any disagreement but, having come face-to-face with the raw and terrifying power of the worst serial killers, this kind of behavior didn't cause a blip on Avei's fear radar.

"Ms. Breckin, I requested the travel suspension for the *Delphi* until I finish with my investigation. Captain Dimphi had no say in the matter. When I finish my inquiry, I will release the ship and you can continue your voyage."

“We’ll see about that.” Julisa turned on her heel and stalked down the hallway. Celethe and Wilm stared at one another with uncertainty. Follow or stay put?

People with too much power liked to play their bully card whenever it suited them. Allowing Julisa to walk away set a dangerous precedent. If Avei permitted even one of the Breckins to set the terms of her investigation, she’d lose control. Owners or not, they had to follow her orders. Until the inquest was done, she considered everyone one aboard the *Delphi* a potential suspect, and that included the Breckins.

“Ms. Breckin, I insist you wait in the ballroom with the other guests.”

Julisa stopped and turned her wrath on Avei. “Inspector, do you know who I am?”

Wilm snickered and downed the rest of his drink. “I don’t think she cares, sis.”

The creepy aura Avei had picked up yesterday from Wilm Breckin had only intensified today. She’d have Sezin run a background check on him. Meanwhile, Eadren Varan appeared preoccupied. Worried, even. She’d have Sezin research him as well.

Avei turned back to Julisa, who stood rigid with anger. “I know who you are, Ms. Breckin, and it changes nothing. Until we determine the cause of the victim’s death, MSF has authority over the *Delphi*, and it will remain in orbit until I wrap my inquiry.”

Captain Dimphi hurried to Julisa. “You and your family can wait in the private dining alcove, away from the rest of the guests. I’ll have the staff activate the privacy shield.”

Score one for the captain if Ms. Breckin went with him. Avei didn't relish a fight with one of Mernin's richest citizens, especially one who had the chancellor in her back pocket. If Julisa yelled loud enough Avei knew he'd lift the investigative hold and release the *Delphi* with her still on the ship. That couldn't happen.

Eadren stepped in front of the hatch and it slid open, filling the corridor with the din of laughter and conversation.

Sintha leaped off the bench and darted through the open hatch. Marsa frowned and picked her up. "Bad girl." Unperturbed, the cat licked her paw.

Julisa shook off Captain Dimphi's hand and stormed over to her sister-in-law and brother. She grabbed Celethe and dragged her into the ballroom. Wilm sauntered after them.

Eadren stepped away and the hatch closed.

Avei breathed a sigh of relief. The sooner she got the investigation started, the sooner she could leave the ship. "I'd like to see the body first."

"Of course. Follow me." Eadren turned and headed down the corridor.

Avei smiled at the captain, who returned her smile with one of trepidation. It had to be difficult with the owners aboard, and that might explain his apparent nervousness. *Or maybe he had something to hide*? She filed that thought away for further exploration.

She turned and followed Chief Varan, who had disappeared around the bend. Five minutes on the *Delphi* and she had already picked up on a vibe that something was amiss. That brought on the familiar surge of excitement and a healthy dose of fear. What if she got it wrong again? She trusted Sezin's observations and opinions. Having them present during her questioning of the guests would ease some of her anxiety. With that settled, she hurried to catch up with the chief.

12

The *Delphi*'s well-appointed morgue had an autopsy table and a body-scan device to determine the cause of death. Six refrigerated mortuary cabinets lined one wall. Storage closets of varying sizes filled another, along with a counter where a portable synthesizer sat. Every surface gleamed from cleanliness and lack of use.

The smell of cleaning solution tickled the back of Avei's throat as she leaned over the body of Caerson Mercer, laid out on a metal tray that extended from one of the mortuary cabinets. A white sheet covered the victim from the neck down.

In her peripheral vision, she caught Eadren Varan studying her. She felt her cheeks redden again. *Good grief. What am I? Fifteen again?*

Avei turned so he wouldn't see her blush and caught Sezin smiling at her from the end of the table, their holoball a few feet above them. *Gods, they know. Hard to miss when one's cheeks are flaming red.* Sezin wore an MSF uniform and took a taller form that matched the chief's height and, for some unknown reason, had also opted for cropped pink hair. *Why pink?*

Dr. Rymond Hueson, a youthful and slightly overweight man, stood across the table from Avei. He smoothed his crisp white jacket with trembling hands. “First time I’ve been part of a murder investigation.”

“We don’t know what killed him. High amounts of Zenith found in overdose deaths cause contortions too,” Eadren said. “This might be an unfortunate accident.”

Avei shared a glance with Sezin. The chief appeared all in, pushing the Zenith angle, and she wondered why. He had ignored poisoning, and other recreational drugs, as potential causes of death. Was Eadren Varan being intentionally obtuse, or just incompetent? He didn’t strike her as inept.

Avei refocused on the victim. She opened Caerson’s left eye and noted the black line that crossed the sclera. It confirmed that the man had died from grenwal venom. Something else caught her attention. Silver flecks in his blue iris sparkled in the bright lights, even this long after death.

Eadren leaned closer. “What is that line across his eye?”

“I noted it in my report. I ran a toxicology screen on known poisons and pathogens, and nothing came up.” Dr. Hueson moved around the bed to stand next to Eadren. “I can say with certainty that whatever he took caused his death.”

Avei straightened and gave Sezin a quick nod. They needed to figure out if this was a copycat killing. If not, Zarul was on the *Delphi*.

“Run another tox screen and this time search for arachnoid venom. If you need to pick a species, use the grenopid family found on Kassissa, in the Orluth system. Specifically the grenwal spider.”

"You think a spider bit him?" Eadren frowned as he stared at Avei. "Grenwal? Where have I heard that word before?"

"There are no bites. I'm certain of that," Dr. Hueson said. "I'll run another tox screen using the perimeters you requested."

Avei leaned down to study the victim's eyes again. "His eye iridescence is rare. The victim has Thumel DNA."

Dr. Hueson's eyes widened in surprise. "25 percent. A rare pairing of species. The Thumel are extremely protective of their genetic line."

"If a Thumel mates with another race and it results in offspring, they and their children are outcasts in perpetuity," Sezin said.

"A very cruel practice, if you ask me," Dr. Hueson said.

"I agree with you, Doctor. It's a callous and outdated practice," Avei said. "My father belonged to a human endogamous cult and gave it up to marry my mother, who is half Nilte. A decision he never regretted." She studied the bright orange foam dried on Caerson's chin, then pulled back the sheet. Her eyes scanned the body. "The six-fanged bite of the grenwal has an orange circle around it."

"The doctor already said he didn't find a bite." Eadren crossed his arms, his eyes hard.

Avei pulled the sheet over Caerson's head. Without a bite, he must have ingested the toxin. Once the tox screen confirmed the grenwal venom, she had the authority to send the *Delphi* back to the spacehub and debark the passengers and crew.

"You know a lot about venom," Dr. Hueson said.

“My parents are arachnologists who specialize in venomous spiders. I spent my childhood in their lab and got my doctorate in arachnology.” Avei braced herself for the inevitable question. Sezin gave her a sympathetic nod.

“A most unusual path to homicide detective,” Dr. Hueson said. “Why did you give it up to join the Mernin Security Force?”

“A serial killer who went by the name of Brasnik murdered my older sister just after I graduated,” Avei said. “They… I’ve never found him. I didn’t want other families to go through what mine have had to endure, so I changed course and joined the MSF.”

Dr. Hueson pushed the drawer bearing Caerson’s body back into the cabinet and closed the door with a clang that echoed around the room. “Please accept my condolences for your loss.”

Eadren stared at Avei, his face soft with compassion. “I remember the Brasnik killer and what he did to his victims. I can’t imagine how difficult that must have been for you and your family. Please know how sorry I am.”

“Thank you. It happened a long time ago.” At Eadren’s words and the clear sympathy in his eyes, Avei felt the grief well up. After all these years, it was still raw. Brasnik tortured his female victims for several days before he finally killed them. He then dumped their nude bodies in abandoned buildings on the west side. It had taken three months to find Anastasia’s body. By that time, it had been ravaged by vermin and was unrecognizable. It was a gut punch every time Avei thought about how much her sister had suffered. Brasnik had killed five women before he disappeared eleven years ago. Anastasia was his last known victim. Avei always suspected he had moved to another quadrant to continue his heinous killing spree.

"Come back to us," Sezin whispered through the comm embedded behind Avei's ear so that only she could hear. Avei smiled her appreciation. Her AI had stopped her from falling into a dark hole.

Eadren ran his hands through his blue hair. "No bite means—"

"The killer put the venom in something he and his girlfriend ate or drank. It wouldn't take much."

"Why didn't his girlfriend die?" Dr. Hueson asked.

"She must have only had a very small bite or sip. Anymore and she'd have died too."

Eadren stiffened as realization took hold. "I've remembered where I read about the grenwal. It's Zarul. Isn't it?"

Avei watched Sezin's gaze lock on Eadren. The last thing they needed was widespread panic.

"Here, on the *Delphi*? My God. What do we do?" Dr. Hueson whipped around in a circle, as though expecting to see the killer behind him. "We need to warn the captain. We need to get the passengers off the ship."

Avei tensed and glared at Eadren, who had the good grace to appear flustered at his gaffe. That was a rookie mistake and one she didn't expect from a head of security.

"Let's all stay calm and keep it between us until we know for certain," Eadren said. "How long to confirm the grenwal venom?"

Dr. Hueson's eyes widened with panic. "I… I need to research how to program the scanner. It's not set up for that kind of testing. Thirty minutes. Maybe longer."

"I can help with that." Sezin smiled at the doctor, who drooped with relief.

"First, we need to talk to the deceased's girlfriend, Imara Tiniba," Avei said. "I want a full account of their movements last night. What they ate and drank. Who they talked to and so on. Then Sezin can help with the synthesizer."

13

The gleaming medical bay held five beds that lined one wall. Each came with its own medical scanning device and a telemetry screen on the back wall. Monitors floated next to the beds and provided an endless supply of shows from Nexus.

Imara Tiniba, Caerson Mercer's girlfriend and the only patient, occupied bed five, at the end. Her natural hair stuck out in a mad tangle. Her sobbing was full-throated and overwrought. She appeared overcome with grief until one noticed a lack of tears.

Avei observed Imara's performance, while Eadren and Dr. Hueson fidgeted on the other side of the bed from her. She shot a glance at Sezin. They rolled their eyes. Did Imara feign grief to put off uncomfortable questions? If so, she had misjudged the situation. Ms. Tiniba wasn't the first person to attempt deception using modest acting skills. They never seemed to realize that the more dramatic the performance, the more guilty they looked.

"Ms. Tiniba, I'm very sorry for your loss. I understand this is a hard time for you, but I need to ask you questions about the events leading up to the death of your boyfriend, Caerson Mercer."

Imara wailed and shook her fists at the ceiling. “Why Caerson? Why?”

Avei studied the men’s reaction to the drama. Eadren looked horrified and took several steps away from the bed. Dr. Hueson patted Imara’s shoulder, his chubby cheeks flushed scarlet. Both men appeared deceived by her pretense, making things more challenging when Avei pressed Imara for answers.

“There, there, Ms. Tiniba,” Dr. Hueson said as he held out a box of tissues.

Imara snatched it from the doctor as she sobbed. “Caerson got me a meeting with a movie producer.” She wiped her dry eyes and face with a tissue. “He can’t be dead. He never told me the time and date of the appointment. Or even the location.”

Avei remembered now, from their brief meeting at the spacehub. Imara had acting aspirations – as did every other person under the age of twenty-five. “Ms. Tiniba, you need to know I am recording our conversation.”

“Commencing Imara Tiniba recording, case number A225791,” Sezin said with authority.

The waterworks stopped cold as the shocked woman stared at Avei and Sezin. Chief Varan and Dr. Hueson shared a surprised look. Good. The men had finally caught on.

“Do I need a lawyer?” Imara asked.

“Only if you did something wrong,” Avei said.

The monitor dinged when Imara’s pulse spiked to 100 beats. Everyone stared at the telemetry screen. Imara folded her hands in her lap and settled back on the bed. “I did nothing wrong. I’m an innocent victim here.”

"No one is accusing you of anything, Ms. Tiniba. Please walk me through last evening. Start at the beginning." Avei focused on the woman's face to pick up on any signs she was lying.

Imara took in a shuddering breath. "After we boarded the ship, we headed to our cabin to get ready for the welcome banquet. The room blew our minds. It was so beautiful. Really elegant, you know. It's what rich people have every day of their lives." Her eyes grew distant as she relived the memory.

Interesting. It appeared neither one of them had money. *So how did they afford a trip on the Delphi?* Avei and Sezin shared a look. Something else to dig into.

Avei caught Eadren staring at Imara with an intensity that implied he was thinking the same thing. It made her wonder about his past and how he ended up Chief of Security. A position that required a military or police background. She didn't get the military vibe from him. He was police then, which prompted the question: why did he leave the force? Eadren appeared too young to retire.

"Please continue, Ms. Tiniba," Avei said.

Imara balled up the tissue and gripped it tight. "The bed was super comfy, like sinking into a cloud. And twice the size of our little bed at home. Caerson wanted to have sex. He always does... did. Gets annoying after a while. I told him to wait until after the banquet because I didn't want to ruin my hair. We got ready and went to the ballroom. I had champagne, of course. Caerson had some specialty drink made with alcohol from one of the moons that circle Hiddiz. He thought it was fancy."

"You are referring to Dimarit, famous for its liquors," Sezin said.

Imara's face screwed up in disgust. "Yeah, whatever. Why anyone prefers a crummy drink over champagne is a mystery to me. I'm going to drink it like water when I'm famous."

Avei saw Sezin winding up to lecture the woman about her choice in alcoholic beverages and stepped in before they got started. Even though Sezin couldn't take part in anything on the physical plane, it didn't stop them from having strong opinions. About everything. "Until that point, had anything out of the ordinary happened?"

Sezin shot her an irritated glance. Avei shrugged and turned her attention back to the woman.

Imara considered the question. "Nothing that I remember. After the drinks, we ate dinner with the other guests in the dining room. Then we went to the Galaxy Bar for a drink. I didn't want the evening to end. I was having fun, you know? Living my best dream. Caerson wanted to go back to the room. I told him I wanted to stay longer. We could have sex anytime. This–" Imara spread her arms wide – "is something special. Something meant to be appreciated and savored."

So far, Avei had detected no deceitfulness. She'd check in with Sezin to confirm.

"Did you see anyone else in the bar?" Eadren had his right hand in his pocket.

"Just the bartender and us at first. Then a bunch of guests came in and ruined the mood. One of them was an obnoxious woman who never stopped talking."

"Did you know any of them?" Avei asked.

Imara hesitated a little too long after her question. "No, of course not. We left and returned to our room. I remember very little after that."

That's a lie. You knew someone in that group. Avei noted Sezin's keen attention to Imara as well. They needed to check for a connection between Imara and Caerson and any of the guests on board. Particularly the group that had visited the lounge. She had a good idea of the identity of the loud woman.

"Was the person in the bar Marsa Baako, the novelist?" Avei asked.

Imara shrugged and looked right. "How would I know?" She crossed her arms and settled further into the bed.

You just confirmed Marsa was in the lounge. Why lie about it? Given Imara's defensive posture, Avei knew she risked alienating her by pressing too hard in this first interview. Better to move the questioning to safer ground. "Tell me anything you recall. Even the smallest detail is helpful."

Dr. Hueson placed a hand on her shoulder. "Taking some deep breaths will calm the mind and help you retrieve a memory. I'll help you. Breathe in on the count of—"

"Just stop. I'm not into that meditation crap." Imara tightened her arms across her chest and glowered. "I left that behind when I escaped the Bhindoir commune."

Avei straightened in surprise. Nobody left the Bhindoir commune by their own free will. The likely scenario was the elders had kicked Imara out for non-conformity. More cult than commune, the multi-race congregation worshiped a living deity named Gei, who belonged to a long-lived alien race called the Wistra. Gei had ruled her people with an iron fist for over two hundred years. The Bhindoirians had gained infamy for brutality toward their children and for their exquisite jewelry, made from rare olbaria gems and coveted by the very wealthy. Given the costly inventory and the proliferation of criminal gangs, every child learned how to defend the commune, starting at age five. The training was brutal and thorough. Those who failed or refused to follow orders found themselves outside the commune's fifty-foot walls with only the clothes on their backs. Given Imara's desire to be an actor, Avei wondered if the woman had got herself thrown out on purpose.

Dr. Hueson appeared nonplussed and in need of rescue. The *Delphi* must be his first assignment right out of medical school. He looked young enough. "Ms. Tiniba, Dr. Hueson is right. Try closing your eyes. That sometimes helps."

Imara shut her eyes and sat in silence for a few moments. "When we felt ill, I remember stumbling out of our room with Caerson. Somehow, we got on the elevator. He was in a real bad way, much worse than me. I may have been screaming, I don't know. My body felt like it was on fire. Caerson couldn't stand, so I dragged him. I remember a lady with a bunch of arms." She shook her head and opened her eyes. "That's it. The rest is a jumble."

"What drugs did you and Caerson take last night?" Eadren had dialed up his intensity and looked ready to pounce on the woman.

Imara glared at him. "We're not into that sort of thing. Caerson worked for a transportation company that tests their people every day. He couldn't risk it. I'm an actress and drugs do a number on your looks." She pointed to her face. "I won't let anything ruin my chances at becoming a star on the Nexus."

Avei felt Imara was being honest in her response. "Did anything unusual happen earlier? Before you fell ill?"

Imara stalled again. Then her eyes filled with tears. "No. We had the best night ever."

That was a half-truth. She is hiding something. Avei shot a glance at Eadren and the doctor. They both appeared captivated by the conversation. Time to press Ms. Tiniba. She wondered how the men would react.

"Can you think of any reason someone wanted to harm you and Caerson?" Avei asked.

Panic crossed Imara's face. "Harm us? Why are you asking me this? Someone did this to us?"

The machine dinged again when Imara's pulse hit 150.

Dr. Hueson turned off the alarm. "My patient needs rest. I must insist you come back later."

"I only have a few questions left, and it won't take long."

Dr. Hueson shook his head. "Ms. Tiniba is still recovering and requires time to heal. Her health is my priority."

Avei didn't want to stop. Imara's evasive behavior pointed to her concealing information. She studied the doctor. It appeared he'd grown a spine. Instead of pressing the issue, she'd come back later. "I'll return in a couple of hours."

Imara curled up in the bed and cried real tears into her pillow. Avei felt sorry for her. The reality of Caerson's death had finally penetrated the fantasy world she lived in.

"Let's move on to the remaining guests. They grow impatient," Eadren said.

The guests could wait. Avei needed to see the crime scene first, to get a full picture of what had happened.

"The information you requested has arrived," Sezin said in her ear.

Good news, and another reason to delay. Much better if she went into the guest interviews armed with information. She turned to Eadren. "Please meet me at the crime scene in twenty minutes and bring the eyewitness. Sezin and I have something we need to take care of first."

The chief's smile didn't reach his eyes. "I'll inform the guests we'll be delayed."

14

Avei and Sezin entered the guest room assigned to them and stopped. The Breckin brand of luxury didn't disappoint. Soft lighting and pastel colors in the generous space created a peaceful vibe. An immense bed with a dozen pillows filled the alcove. A small table with two comfy chairs sat under a window that looked out on the spacehub, seven starliners and multiple smaller craft docked at its three rings. The luxurious sofa and two end tables filled the center of the room.

Sezin pointed to the communication screen to the right of the hatch. "We can order room service."

"You don't eat."

"True, but I can live vicariously through you by watching you bescufan." Sezin walked to the window.

Watching? Being analyzed while she ate, by an AI whose fervent wish was to be alive, was a little creepy, yet endearing. "What does bescufan even mean?"

"It's old English, and it means to eat with great enthusiasm. You know, to enjoy your food with gusto."

"I never eat with gusto. I'll have you know I'm a very neat eater."

Sezin raised their eyebrows. "One word. Kulphies."

Okay, that was unfair. Kulphies were little balls of heaven, filled with clotted cream and sweet fruit, then dipped in a sticky syrup made from the sap of the Gozok tree. It was impossible to eat Kulphies without making a mess. And yes, maybe at times she did devour them faster than others. "We're getting a little off topic." Avei vowed never to eat Kulphies in front of Sezin again.

Sezin smirked. "Certainly."

Avei cleared her throat and tried to tap down the intense craving for her favorite dessert. Surely the *Delphi* would have them.

Sezin grinned. "I checked. You can find Kulphies on the menu in the Galaxy Lounge."

How does Sezin do that? Maybe she was more of an open book than she thought. "No more talk about Kulphies. It's making me hungry. Let's review the contents of the information packet and discuss the Imara Tiniba interview. If the doctor doesn't find venom in his second tox screen, our stay will quickly end." Avei wandered to one of the two ornate archways on the third wall. It opened onto a well-appointed bathroom. The one next to it led to a walk-in closet. Her battered go bag sat on a padded bench.

She walked into the main room, where Sezin stood frozen. It'd take a few moments before they finished with the assessment of Skora's information packet.

Avei eyed the couch, and the table and chairs under the window, knowing that if she sat on that soft couch, she'd never get up. She chose a chair and leaned her head against the window. With eyes closed, she ran through her options. If it turned out to be an overdose, she'd turn the case over to drug enforcement and be done with it. She longed for it to be that simple. In her heart, she already knew the truth. Someone had murdered Caerson Mercer, and no amount of wishful thinking could change that reality. She let out a heavy sigh and opened her eyes to find Sezin observing her with such compassion it almost undid her.

Her AI had changed their form to petite size. They had also opted for long black hair and golden-brown skin, creating a more feminine look: a form they took when they wanted to have a difficult discussion on a thorny topic. Avei tensed, knowing what the subject would be.

"What you've been through over the last few months would break anyone. There is no shame in asking for help." Sezin took a step closer. "As you know, I'm programmed to assist with mental health issues. Given your elevated heart rate and breathing, it is clear you are experiencing a heightened level of stress. Completely understandable. Please Avei, let me help."

Avei felt her stress elevate, not lessen. The last thing she needed was the killer picking up on her anxiety and exploiting it. Zarul could be anyone on the ship. A guest or one of the crew. Maybe she had already met them. She needed to do a better job of locking down her emotions. "I appreciate your offer. I really do. But I'm fine. Truly."

"You went through a terrible ordeal, and you haven't fully recovered. I understand Skora's reasoning for sending you on this case, but I'm worried it's too soon."

"Stop!" Avei shouted and Sezin froze. Even her AI knew she shouldn't be here. That brought all the insecurities and self-loathing back with vengeance. Her presence on the

Delphi put everyone in danger. As her breathing increased, the pain in her side spiked. She embraced it. Welcomed it as a punishment for her dereliction of duty that got people killed. How did she let Skora talk her into taking this case? Even without the confirmation from Dr. Hueson, she knew Caerson had died from grenwal venom poisoning. The contortions and orange foam around his mouth left little doubt as to what had killed him. She wasn't in a fit state to take on Zarul. Getting off the ship as soon as possible was in everyone's best interest.

Feeling relieved by her decision, Avei stared at Sezin, who had been her constant companion for many years. She would miss her nutty, kind-hearted AI. "Sezin, wake."

Sezin unfroze and looked unsettled. "I overstepped and I'm sorry. I fear I messed up what I meant to say."

"No need for apologies. You're right. It is too soon. I'm not in the right frame of mind to take on a serial killer. It isn't fair to the victim, who deserves better. I'm leaving as soon as Uma can get here."

"Can I talk you into staying?"

"No, Sezin. You can't. Please send a message to D.I. Skora and tell him to send Uma. I'll catch a ride on her shuttle back to Mernin."

"Message sent. We can use the time until she gets here to continue the investigation."

Avei nodded. Handing over detailed case notes when Uma arrived lessened the guilt of quitting in the middle of a case. In all truthfulness, she was sick of wallowing in self-pity. It was the anthesis of who she was and how she had conducted her life until that fateful night.

Acknowledging one's limitations and being honest about them didn't mean you froze in place. Any action had to be better than standing still.

"We are meeting Chief Varan at the crime scene soon. Do you still want to review the information packets, or wait?" Sezin asked.

"We have guests waiting for our interviews. I'll need that information before talking to them. Let Chief Varan know we'll be a little late."

"Done. Let's start with Wilm Breckin, who has twenty-three sexual harassment complaints filed against him by different women. Seven accused him of battery."

That fit with the feeling Avei had gotten from him. "That doesn't surprise me. There's something predatory about him."

Holographic images of seven people appeared next to Sezin. Three human women, two androgynous Grilan, and two females of alien origin. All beautiful, and all with facial bruises. The two Grilans had clearly suffered more brutal beatings. An image of Wilm's smiling face hung above the women.

Avei felt her anger rise. She couldn't stand seeing his smug face anywhere near the bruised and battered women. "Remove his photo." His image disappeared.

"The first complaint happened nine years ago." Sezin morphed into their old Earth detective persona, with a puffy mustache, monocle in one eye, and a black suit with a long-tailed coat.

Sezin's image changes had been a distraction when they first began working together. The AI experimented with a variety of looks and would quickly cycle through them. After a blizzard of costume changes during a particularly challenging case, Avei and Sezin worked out a compromise. Sezin would pick one and stick with it for at least five minutes before changing again.

"Has he gone to prison for the battery?" Avei examined the faces of Wilm's victims and shook her head at the mass of bruises that covered the Grilan faces.

"Six dropped their charges. The seventh victim is a Grilan employee on the *Delphi*. She pressed charges three months ago. The case is pending, and she is currently on the ship."

"With Wilm aboard? That's highly unethical and puts the victim in danger of retaliation. What is Julisa Breckin thinking? Why take such a big risk?"

"Sounds to me like she is in denial about his deviant behavior."

Avei sighed. "Let's have Uma monitor the Grilan. Make sure she stays safe."

"I'll include in the case summary so Uma doesn't miss it."

"Thanks." Avei traced the burn scar on the back of her hand. "Either Wilm or Julisa paid off the others. My money is on Julisa. Let's move on. Tell me about his wife, Celethe Breckin."

A picture of Celethe at a social function replaced the other photos. Avei took in the shimmering ball gown that cost more than she made in a year, and the expensive jewelry that covered her arms and neck. Avei noted Celethe's smile didn't reach her eyes. "Tell me about her."

"The first record on her is from three years ago. Nothing prior to that." An old-fashioned pipe appeared in Sezin's hand. They sucked in and breathed out a cloud of smoke.

"Right around the time she married Wilm. How did they meet?"

"Given the little information we have on Celethe, my best guess is they met on L'reus."

"That's a rough place," Avei said. "Keep digging and see if you can come up with anything else." The tiny moon L'reus was home to more casinos and brothels than anywhere else in the galaxy. Because of its unsavory reputation, where establishments satisfied every desire, no matter how depraved, the wealthy flocked there. Which group did Celethe belong to? The seekers, or the ones who satisfied their proclivities, willingly or unwillingly? The scars on her ankle pointed to the darker of the two options.

"Moving on to Julisa Breckin." Sezin puffed on the pipe. The holographic smoke drifted above their head.

An image appeared: Julisa sitting behind a massive desk that took up half of her luxurious office. A wall of windows behind her framed six Breckin Starliners of varying sizes docked at the spacehub. All had a sleek saucer shape, the hulls covered in windows. The Breckins' belief was every guest should have an up-close-and-personal experience with the wonders of space set them apart from their competition and had made them famous.

"Julisa Breckin inherited the bankrupt starliner business from her father when he died seventeen years ago. A gambler and a drunk, he single-handedly destroyed the company that had been in the family for 478 years. Julisa turned it around, and business is thriving."

"Like father, like son. Tell me about the chief of security, Eadren Varan. There's something off about him."

"I'll say." Sezin waved their hand in front of their face to dispel the smoke. The pipe and smoke disappeared, but the attire remained.

Two images of Eadren popped up. One with him on the *Delphi* wearing his Chief of Security uniform. In the other, he posed with a group of Mernin's top socialites, who appeared to be enjoying themselves. "That's an interesting juxtapose."

"More interesting than you know. Eadren is a fixer for the very rich and goes by the name of Nad Ranack."

Avei studied the two images. On the *Delphi*, he appeared stern and all business. At the gala, he seemed warm and inviting. Eadren Varan could fit in anywhere. A chameleon. And now he was masquerading as the *Delphi*'s chief of security. "He's working for one of the Breckins. The question is, which one? Keep going."

"My guess as well. The next one is a tender subject. Brace yourself."

"Marsa Baako, the bane of my existence." The mere mention of the woman's name got Avei's blood boiling.

An image of Marsa appeared, standing next to a rotating image of her book — *The Cresa Murders, A Savi Demis Novel.* Avei turned her back on the image. "I can't even look at her."

"Completely understandable. Marsa Baako lives well above her means and has amassed a substantial debt."

"It's been ages since she's had a bestselling novel." The money had begun slowing down last year. Avei was thankful the Institute had achieved solvency.

"Marsa's a one-trick pony and her fans finally grew weary of her obsession with you and your cases. And let's be honest, the woman is not a literary genius."

"No, she's not. Did Skora find anything on Caerson Mercer and Imara Tiniba?"

Several head shots of Imara appeared, along with a grainy image of Caerson smiling in front of a nondescript building.

"Caerson worked as a hired hand for an interstellar freight-hauling company. He's been working for the same company for eight years with no marks against him. Imara left the Bhindoir commune when she turned fourteen and spent time in juvenile detention for shoplifting. Imara is an aspiring actor. The couple had been together for five years."

The only way Imara could have left the commune was because their living god, Gei, declared her godless. Without money or an understanding of how the outside world works, it didn't surprise Avei that Imara had resorted to shoplifting to survive. "There's no way the two of them could afford passage on a luxury starliner."

"D.I. Skora agrees with you and has a team digging into their history. I received a reply to your message. There is a Nexus sporting event, and all public shuttles are in use ferrying the spectators to an arena in the southern hemisphere. All MSF shuttles are flying police to the same event to keep the order."

Avei gripped the back of the couch until her fingers turned white. "How long?"

"Skora said it could take several hours. He wants you to continue with the investigation until Uma gets here."

Avei felt her heart rate increase and knew a panic attack was imminent. She sucked in several deep breaths and placed her hand over the locket hidden under her jacket. *You can do this, Themis. It's only for a few hours. The spacehub and Mernin are right here. I'll make today my last day on the force.* She felt her pulse slow, and the tendrils of panic retreat. Skora wouldn't like her to leave three days earlier than planned but he'd get over it. Better to live with his disappointment than the death of another innocent victim.

A buzz from the panel next to the hatch. Eadren's voice filled the room. "Inspector, checking in to see if you are ready to begin."

"Ah, looks like our tall, dark... No wait, tall, *blue*, and handsome chief of security is ready for us," Sezin said with a smirk.

Avei squared her shoulders and walked to the comm screen next to the hatch. "On our way."

Sezin and their holoball settled next to her as the hatch opened. Avei noted they had changed to their tall MSF officer persona and felt immense gratitude for her AI. "I'm glad you're here with me."

Sezin smiled. "Where else would I be? Now, let's go meet up with Mr. Gorgeous, who, I might add, had a notable increase in his pulse when he was checking you out earlier. I think he's as attracted to you as you are to him."

Avei cringed. “Highly inappropriate, Sezin.”

Sezin’s laughter followed her into the corridor. Attractive or not, Eadren Varan was as much a suspect as anyone else on the ship. Maybe even more so than others, given his current role as chief of security. A position that afforded him unfettered access to the guests and crew of the ship. She would keep an eye on him until Uma arrived.

15

Avei walked around the hologram of Caerson Mercer's twisted body lying on the floor. She felt Eadren studying her as she stopped inches from Caerson's feet. Could he detect her anxiety? Did it even matter? Running an investigation wasn't instinctual to an untrained layperson, even one pretending to be a security chief. Uma could decide how best to confront him about his ruse. In the meantime, she'd play along with his pretense.

She glanced at Sezin, who stood nearby with their hands behind their back. They shook their head. Still no shuttle.

"How close did the witness get to the deceased?" Avei refocused on the victim.

"About where you are," Eadren said.

Avei walked through the hologram to the ceiling camera a few feet away. "Cameras?"

"Every 50 feet. They went down ship-wide last night due to an unscheduled maintenance routine."

"Has this happened before?" Avei squatted next to Caerson and scanned the surrounding area.

"First time. They are stuck in a continuous loop and inoperable."

Avei noted Eadren's rigid posture. Was he tense about the murder aboard his ship, or did he have something to hide? "Sounds very convenient to me. Who has access to the camera program?" She rose, her hand pressing against her side as the pain flared. She examined the walls while walking in a circle around the body.

"Security, engineering, the captain. I've already cleared them."

Avei studied Eadren, who broke eye contact. She would have Sezin access the ship's computers and confirm the veracity of his statement. "Anyone else down here besides the cleaning woman and the girlfriend?"

"Staff quarters are down the hall. None left their room. Checked and confirmed."

"Guests?"

Eadren swallowed and tensed. "No."

Avei frowned. No question, he was hiding something. One didn't achieve his level of success as a fixer to the rich and powerful by being indiscreet. Pulling information out of him might prove difficult. She walked a fine line. Too aggressive, she risked him shutting down. Too gentle and he'd know she'd caught on to him. "What aren't you telling me, Chief Varan?"

"I addressed your question."

"Not sure you did." Avei walked down the hallway and around the curve where the housekeeper Ocia Doni and Captain Dimphi waited. Eadren trailed behind her, his hand in his right pocket.

Sezin remained behind with the activated hologram.

Avei smiled at the housekeeper, who tried to smile back and failed. The trauma in Ocia's eyes was clear to Avei, who felt a rush of empathy for the woman. "I'd like to get started, Ms. Doni, if you are ready."

"I'm ready, Inspector." Ocia didn't meet her eyes.

"Good. Please describe what happened after you requested medical help for Ms. Tiniba?"

"I continued to the staff break room for my mid-shift meal."

"Did you hear or observe anything out of the ordinary prior to finding the deceased?"

"I... Ah..." Ocia gripped herself in a tight hug with all four arms. Her forehead gleamed with perspiration.

Surprised at the level of Ocia's fear, Avei put a hand on the woman's shoulder and gently squeezed. "It's alright. Take your time and when you are ready, please tell me what you saw."

Trembling, Ocia looked at Captain Dimphi and Eadren for help. They stared back, an unspoken warning heavy in the air. She shoved her four hands into her uniform pockets and backed away from the men. There would be no help from that direction.

Avei glared at them in frustration. They were hiding something about the case and leaving Ocia dangling on her own. That really got her ire up. "I sincerely hope you're not obstructing an MSF investigation."

"Because if you are, Inspector Themis will arrest you." Sezin stalked around the corner, now a full twelve inches taller than the men and broader in the shoulders than Eadren.

Avei stifled a laugh. The expression of shock on the Captain and Eadren's faces when they realized a giant AI stood behind them tickled her to no end. It seemed Sezin took issue with their behavior too.

Captain Dimphi held up his hands as he stared at Sezin. "I can assure you I'm not. We—" Eadren touched his arm and he stopped chattering.

"Captain, please finish. What did you want to say?" Avei studied his face to see if he was being truthful in his response.

The captain stepped back, his face screwed up like he'd swallowed something sour. "I have nothing further to add."

Lying.

The captain wanted to say more, but fear stopped him. *What is he so afraid of that he would lie to an MSF Inspector?* Getting the housekeeper to spill the beans on the secret the three of them shared was the best approach, since the men were being reticent. "Ocia, please tell me what happened." Avei put a hand on the woman's arm and smiled.

"I can't." Tears welled up in Ocia's eyes. "I will lose my job."

It appeared these two men in positions of power had threatened this poor woman to keep her silent. Who or what were they protecting? The murderer? Avei turned to Captain Dimphi, the weaker of the two. "What are you hiding?"

He shuffled backward, putting distance between them. "Me? I... What are you inferring?" He shot a panic-stricken look at Eadren.

Avei zeroed in on the supposed chief of security. His evasive answer from earlier now made sense. He hadn't exactly lied when he said none of the staff had left their rooms. "You're protecting one of the owners."

Avei fought the urge to smile when Eadren's face hardened. Good, they were getting somewhere. She turned her focus back to Ocia. "Did you see Julisa Breckin down here?"

Ocia gave a slight shake of her head.

"Wilm Breckin?"

Ocia shared a meaningful look with her. Avei nodded, then turned to Eadren and the Captain. "Once I finish up with Ocia, we will discuss why you didn't tell me about Wilm Breckin's presence in the corridor at the time of the murder. Let's keep going."

Captain Dimphi looked like he wanted to say something but a glare from Eadren shut him up.

Ocia and Avei continued down the hall and around the bend, stopping at the image of Caerson Mercer hovering above the ground.

Sezin appeared behind the body in a shorter version of their MSF image. The AI did that to put Ocia, who was already unnerved, at ease. That meant keeping questions to a minimum and following up later when the housekeeper was rested.

Captain Dimphi gaped at the hologram as he and Eadren stopped next to the victim. "Sweet Mima, I'd swear on my life that was the real body."

Ocia moaned and looked away. "Seeing him all twisted like that. He must have suffered terribly."

"Other than Imara Tiniba and Wilm Breckin, did you notice anything else?" Avei caught the irritation slide across Eadren's face before he veiled it.

Ocia brushed tears from her eyes. “No. Just the body. I heard nothing either. May I go? I haven’t slept since yesterday.”

She appeared exhausted, on the verge of collapse. It was always a balancing act, judging when to give a witness time to gather themselves after a traumatic event. Avei could see that letting her recuperate was the best approach in this situation.

“You did good, Ocia. I’ll stop by your room in a couple of hours to check on you.”

Ocia stumbled past the hologram and around the bend, out of sight.

“Sezin, please deactivate the hologram.”

After the image of Caerson Mercer disappeared, Avei scrutinized the men. Eadren was a picture of calm. He met her gaze and held it. With trembling fingers, Captain Dimphi wiped away the sweat beading on his forehead.

“Time to come clean.”

Sezin sidled up next to her and crossed their arms. Avei’s AI was a genius at telling the truth from a lie. Help she hadn’t needed in the past, but was grateful for now.

Captain Dimphi glanced at Eadren, who nodded.

That little interaction solidified who led and who followed. “Sezin, activate recorder.”

“Activated.”

Captain Dimphi recoiled. “Come now, there is no need for that.”

“Was Wilm Breckin down here at the time of Caerson Mercer’s death?” Avei knew the two men would do anything to protect the person who employed them.

They had omitted that information from their report and kept it from her when she asked earlier. They walked a perilous tightrope. One misstep and she'd arrest them for obstructing an investigation.

"Mr. Breckin prefers the *Delphi* over their other starliners," Captain Dimphi said.

"Stop dancing around my question, Captain, and tell me if Ocia or anyone else reported seeing Wilm in this hallway at the time of the murder?"

Captain Dimphi squirmed. "Mr. Breckin likes to drink and gamble. I won't deny it."

"And he likes to harass and batter your help. Was Wilm Breckin down here?"

"He can get overzealous, and it frightens the staff from time to time." Sweat dripped down the captain's face.

"Beating people is not being overzealous. It's a crime and people go to jail for it. Now, answer my question."

Captain Dimphi swallowed and looked at Eadren, who stared straight ahead.

"Ocia saw Mr. Breckin at the time of Caerson Mercer's death." Eadren avoided making eye contact. "He had nothing to do with his murder."

Sezin and Avei shared another glance. Finally, they'd got a straight answer. "Why do you think he didn't kill Caerson?"

"Because of his level of intoxication. Wilm Breckin couldn't stand up straight, much less commit a murder. And keep in mind, Caerson was already dying when he entered the elevator." Eadren shifted his eyes to Avei, his expression firm. "Either Caerson took the stuff himself or someone else gave it to him before he ended up down here."

Damn. He had it right. Caerson and Imara both exhibited signs of poisoning before entering the elevator to the staff floor. It didn't exonerate Wilm. He could still be involved in the murder. Given Eadren's reluctance to implicate his boss, Avei felt certain his field ops on the *Delphi* had something to do with Wilm Breckin. One outstanding question: which of the three Breckins had hired him?

Dr. Hueson's voice came over the captain's and Eadren's comm devices. "The tests are back and positively identified the substance we discussed earlier."

The air left her lungs. Even though she knew Zarul had done it, hearing it confirmed made it real. She sensed a panic attack coming on and she needed to get away. "I need to let my deputy director know the findings. I'll talk to the guests after I've sent my update."

Sezin shot her a look of puzzlement before disappearing. The holoball drifted to Avei's belt and attached as she hurried down the corridor and around the bend.

***

Captain Dimphi let out an explosive breath. He kissed his fingers and touched his forehead three times. "Sweet Goddess Mima, what do we do?"

Eadren's hand drifted to his right pocket. He pulled out a small holographic disk with a picture of a smiling young man who resembled him. After staring at it for a moment, he shoved the disk in his pocket. "We stay the course."

***

Further down the corridor, Avei stopped and checked behind her, but saw nothing.

She leaned against the wall and held her hands tight to her chest to keep them from trembling. Wilm Breckin had been in the corridor at the time of Caerson's death. Whether he had something to do with the death remained unanswered. Even if he wasn't involved, he may have seen something, and she needed to talk to him. To make that happen, she needed to find a way around Julisa Breckin, who showed no reservations about bailing her little brother out of trouble. She would be a formidable opponent.

Avei felt the telltale signs of a panic attack coming on. Thank the Gods she'd had enough of them over the last couple of months to know what to do. She closed her eyes and took deep, measured breaths, focusing on her go-to memory from childhood, of being nestled with her sister in their father's arms as he read from an old Earth book of fairy tales. They were staying in a bungalow at a floating resort on Colea, her happy place. They sat in a comfy chair on the porch, overlooking the ruby-red sea. Avei could feel the warm ocean breeze against her face and the soft, warbling sound of the crustaceans that inhabited the waters. Her heart rate slowed, her breathing normalized.

***

Eadren walked around the bend and slowed when he spotted Avei. He took a few more steps toward her, then stopped when he noticed her eyes were closed. Was she afraid? This didn't square with the legendary Inspector Themis, known for her courage. Her near-perfect record for capturing the worst of the serial killers required a level of bravery and fortitude most didn't possess. Then again, the recent incident with the Apollyona killer could mess with anyone's head. Inspector Avei Themis being off her game wasn't the worst news.

Eadren fingered the holographic disk in his pocket. Over the next two days, he had to tread a razor-thin line between morality and immorality that required staying laser-focused on the end goal. It meant making peace with the harsh decisions he knew lay ahead. The hardest of his life.

Eadren backed around the corner and out of sight as Avei pushed off the wall and continued down the corridor. He stepped back into view and watched her until she disappeared.

16

Bathed in bright lights, the lounge revealed what the soft lights had hidden the night before, the fading majesty of a ship long past its prime. The *Delphi* was the oldest ship in the Breckin fleet and had served for over four hundred years.

Captain Dimphi, Wilm, Celethe and Julisa Breckin were huddled in their private alcove, across the ballroom from where Avei sat at the table. They glowered as she conversed with Sezin, who stood next to her.

Eadren lingered in the middle ground between the Breckins and Avei, his hand jammed in his right pocket.

Captain Dimphi scanned the room and landed on the only other guest, Marsa Baako, who had a frown planted on top of a scowl. He averted his eyes before she noticed him looking at her.

Several Grilan servers hovered near the kitchen doors. Two had trays filled with a variety of alcoholic drinks.

Already bleary-eyed, Wilm knocked back his drink and held it out with a shaky hand. One server rushed forward with a fresh glass. “We’re the owners, for God’s sakes. She should have interviewed us first.”

Celethe touched Wilm’s arm. “Wilm, please. Slow down on the alcohol.” He frowned and pulled away from her.

"Wilm's right. This is unacceptable." Julisa took in the timeworn furnishings. "And get someone to dim the lights."

"No need for that. The inspector's almost done, and the only other guest left is Marsa Baako," Captain Dimphi said. "Given the state of her account, this will be her last trip with us."

"Ms. Baako and that foul beast of hers will never set foot on one of my starliners again." Julisa tapped her foot as she scanned the ballroom again. "It's time to decide what to do with the *Delphi*. Retire her or retrofit her."

"Definitely retrofit," Celethe said.

Wilm snickered. "What do you know about our business?"

Celethe flushed red at Wilm's comment, and Julisa gave her an appraising look.

"Tell me why you think we should retrofit the *Delphi*."

Celethe ignored Wilm's amused look. "So much of our history has taken place on the *Delphi*. From the peace accords with the Yadats that ended the hundred-year war, to the ratification of the Federation Pact binding hundreds of worlds together into one entity. Your own grandfather is a part of her history, when he converted the *Delphi* into a medevac hospital during the Ruyin uprising on Istoi. And don't forget the rescue of the miners trapped on the Avity moon when the star went supernova. Everyone thought it was a suicide mission, and they didn't lose a single person. All of that happened on this beautiful ship. And, well, a more practical reason. It's cheaper to modernize her than to commission a new ship."

Julisa nodded with a rare smile. "Outstanding reasons, Celethe. *Delphi*'s bones are solid, and I am leaning toward updating her. Plus, you raise an excellent point. We need to talk more about the historic events that have taken place on our ships."

"No one cares about history. They want the luxury trip we've promised them," Wilm said. "My vote is to send this piece of junk to the scrap heap and build a new ship."

Avei stood up, capturing everyone's full attention. She waved over Marsa, who hustled to the table. A collective groan came from the Breckin group.

One glance at the Breckins' anger and Eadren scooted closer to Avei's table.

"I've had enough," Julisa said.

Celethe glared at Wilm as he chugged his drink. "Me too."

Julisa and Celethe stalked across to Avei and cut in front of Marsa.

"You will talk to us now," Julisa said.

Avei had intentionally made the Breckins wait. With only one suspect so far, she wanted to interview Wilm last. "I called Ms. Baako."

Sezin and Avei frowned at the three women who tussled in front of the table. Eadren shook his head. No one stepped in to stop the shoving match.

Marsa jostled her way in front of Julisa and Celethe. "You heard her. So back off."

"You and that beast will never travel on a Breckin starliner again," Julisa said.

Marsa puffed up with outrage. “I’d like to see you try to enforce that after my attorneys get involved. Besides, my fans—”

“Can’t afford a ticket on one of my ships,” Julisa said in a matter-of-fact tone that stopped any argument.

The women glowered at one another until Marsa huffed and walked away. She settled a few feet from Captain Dimphi, who sidestepped without acknowledging her.

“It appears I’m no longer needed and will head to the bridge,” Captain Dimphi said to no one in particular as he edged closer to the hatch, his face an open book of desperation to escape and fear his services might still be required. When no one ordered him back, he made his getaway through the hatch.

Forcing Julisa to wait might backfire and cause the Breckins to leave. Avei was worried about interviewing Wilm Breckin with Marsa so near, knowing everything said would end up in one of her damn books.

Julisa solved the problem when she noticed Marsa standing a few feet away. “Back up, Ms. Baako. What’s said here is none of your business.”

Eadren placed himself between Julisa and Marsa. He motioned to a spot by the window. “Please wait over there until we’re ready for you.”

Wearing a smirk, Marsa crept backwards at a glacial pace.

Avei saw the same loathing she felt toward Marsa mirrored in Julisa’s face. At least they had that in common. She chanced a quick glance at Sezin, who rolled their eyes and shook their head for the eighth time in the last thirty minutes. Still no shuttle.

She caught Eadren studying their exchange with curiosity. He didn't know she was leaving, and she had no intention of telling him until Uma boarded the *Delphi*. He might have halted the investigation until the new inspector arrived.

"Inspector, can we get on with it?" Julisa asked, her tone heavy with frustration.

Avei studied the two impatient women in front of her. She expected one or both of them to stop the interview before she finished. It's what powerful people did when questioning struck close to home. They never seemed to realize it clued her in on what they hoped to keep secret.

"Were either of you on the staff deck around 1:15 this morning?"

"Of course not," Julisa said. "We were in bed, asleep."

Celethe frowned when she spotted Wilm with his arm around a Grilan woman who held a tray of *hors d'oeuvres*.

"A guest was murdered last night."

Celethe whipped around and focused on Avei. "Murdered?"

"The doctor and Eadren said it was a drug overdose." Julisa's eyes drifted to Wilm, who stared at Avei, his jaw clenched. When he caught Julisa looking at him, he smiled and saluted her with his drink, then guzzled it down.

Avei noted Julisa's eyes darted to her brother at the mention of murder. Also, she had referred to her chief of security by his first name, implying a personal relationship. And Eadren had tensed when she said his name. It seemed he'd neglected to tell his boss about the grenwal venom. Why keep it from Julisa?

"What is the victim's name?" Celethe asked.

Celethe's question pulled Avei out of her ruminations. She settled back in her chair, so she had an unobstructed view of the three Breckins and Eadren before responding to the question. "The victim's name is Caerson Mercer." Avei had hoped for a reaction and she got one. Celethe turned white, as if someone had flipped a switch.

"Do you know the victim?" Avei leaned forward, her full attention on Celethe Breckin.

Celethe gripped the table and closed her eyes. "No, of course not. I'm a little lightheaded is all."

Julisa put an arm around her. "Should I call for the doctor?"

"I need a moment." Celethe took several deep breaths and straightened. "I haven't eaten today."

"Please sit until you feel better." Avei glanced at Sezin, who gave a discreet nod. They both agreed Celethe knew the victim.

Wilm's laughter pulled their attention from Celethe. The Grilan server struggled in vain to extricate herself from his arms; something he found amusing.

Celethe stared daggers at her husband.

Eadren took a step toward Wilm, his hands fisted. Julisa grabbed his arm and pulled him back. He glared at Julisa, who shook her head.

Eadren stood directly in front of Avei and despite herself, she couldn't stop her eyes from being drawn to his tush.

“The Chief’s definitely a studmuffin with an exceptional patootie, as you are so keenly observing.” Sezin’s whisper in Avei’s ear startled her so badly she almost fell out of the chair. Her cheeks burned red as she made sure no one else had caught her checking out the chief, or noticed her reaction to Sezin’s comment. Thank the Gods, everyone’s attention was on Wilm. Free of prying eyes, she glared at her AI, who bounced on their toes, clearly having way too much fun at her expense. *Studmuffin? Patootie?* More old Earth phrases that made no sense. *Okay, maybe I can guess what a patootie is. But studmuffin? What the hells?*

Avei caught the grimace on the Grilan server’s face. Time to intervene before Wilm caused any further harm. “If Mr. Breckin doesn’t release that server right now, I’m arresting him for battery.” Avei stood with every intention of doing just that.

Sezin grew six inches taller and added broad shoulders and muscular arms to their appearance. They stepped around the table, their holoball hovering above them. “I’ll handle this, Inspector.”

Avei cringed. With no idea what her AI had in mind, she fervently hoped they would keep it tame and civilized.

Wilm sneered as Sezin approached. He had a tight grip on the Grilan server, who grimaced in pain. “What are you going to do, walk through me?” He chuckled to himself.

“See that?” Sezin pointed to the holoball. “It delivers a jolt of electricity that will incapacitate you and cause you to release your bladder and bowels. Fun stuff, especially in front of an audience.”

"You wouldn't dare." Wilm eyed the holoball that now hovered over his head.

"Actually, I would. And I'd enjoy doing it too." Sezin smiled at him. "Release her. Now."

Sezin loved to bluff. Their holoball didn't have the capabilities they had threatened. Given Wilm's reaction, Avei knew she'd better rein in her AI before they changed into the Vusian wrestler avatar; a form they used when the circumstances called for something more intimidating. She knew the Breckins wouldn't appreciate that at all. The last thing Avei needed was a formal complaint against her and Sezin, resulting in an extension of her departure date while the injured party's complaint was heard in an MSF formal hearing. "Sezin, stand down. I'll take care of it."

Sezin pivoted, hands on waist. Avei waved them back and they obliged, none too happy at having their mission aborted.

Marsa snickered, enjoying herself. Avei knew everything would end up in one of her books.

Julisa glared at Avei. "You and your guard dog better stay away from my family."

"If Wilm doesn't remove his hands from the server, I will arrest him myself." Eadren's blue skin flushed violet.

Avei noted Eadren and Julisa's face-off with one another, both of them brimming with anger. Good to know he had a backbone when needed. She gave him ten seconds to do something, or she'd cuff Wilm and lock him in a security cell herself.

"Control your brother, or I will," Eadren said as he stared at Julisa until she broke eye contact and turned to Avei.

"Talk to my solicitors from this point forward. We had nothing to do with that poor man's unfortunate demise." She stalked across the room. "Release my staff, this instant."

Wilm let go. "What's the big deal? I didn't hurt anyone."

Avei watched the server run to the back of the room, where the other Grilan employees stepped in front of their friend and formed a shield.

Avei noticed with surprise that Celethe hadn't moved. She appeared conflicted. "You knew the victim."

Celethe's eyes darted to Julisa, who followed Wilm through the hatch. She bit her lower lip.

"We can talk in private if you like," Avei said softly. "At a time of your choosing."

Celethe shook her head and turned away. "As my sister-in-law said, our solicitors will speak for us." She picked her way around the furniture and left the lounge.

Avei dropped into her chair as Sezin rejoined her. "Celethe Breckin knows the victim."

"Agreed. Brace yourself. Your favorite person approaches."

Avei sighed as Marsa Baako practically skipped toward them, a smile plastered on her face.

Eadren followed behind Marsa, who plopped into the chair across from Avei. He settled close enough to hear the conversation and to observe Ms. Baako's reactions to the questions.

"I'll help you find the killer. We'll be a team. Our fans will go wild over this." Marsa's voice vibrated with excitement. "I can't wait to get started."

Avei swallowed the not-so-nice retort on her tongue. “Do you know Caerson Mercer?”

“Of course, you will be in charge. No question about that. Where do we start?” Marsa leaned in, her face glowing with eagerness.

Unbelievable. The woman was delusional, thinking she could be part of any investigation. “Ms. Baako, address my question.”

“Many have said if I wasn’t a writer, I’d be a brilliant Mernin Security Forces inspector like yourself. Or a very successful serial killer.” Marsa laughed.

Avei leaned back in her chair and stared at Marsa until her laughter stopped. She caught sight of Eadren out of the corner of her eye, watching their exchange with interest.

“Think about it. Okay?” Marsa frowned. “Our fans will eat it up.”

Avei let her silence linger. She found this worked best when some interviewees refused to cooperate.

Marsa fidgeted. “I don’t know him. Okay? Never heard of him.”

Avei stood, putting an end to the discussion. If she spent another minute in this woman’s presence, she’d lose it. She didn’t want her last day on the force marred by a disciplinary action because she had lost her temper.

“Point me in any direction. Tell me what you need, and I’ll get it done.” Marsa grinned at her.

“Thank you for your time, Ms. Baako.” Avei pivoted away from her and nodded to Sezin, who inserted themself between them.

“Please return to your room, Ms. Baako. The inspector has concluded the interview.”

Sezin’s actions allowed Avei enough time to get to the hatch.

Marsa’s smile disappeared when she saw Avei walk into the corridor. Sezin headed across the room, Eadren on their heels.

“We’d make an amazing team,” Marsa called after Avei. “We’d be so famous.” Sintha crawled out from under the table and jumped into her lap. Marsa kissed her head and hugged her pet tight. “You did good, my love.”

17

Avei sat at the small table under the window in her room as the holographic image of D.I. Skora paced in front of her. She gripped a steaming mug of tea made from chacin fruit, a green berry with a sweet honey-like taste. A favorite of her parents. Grateful for a friendly face, she smiled at Sezin, who sat across from her. They raised their eyebrows as if to say, *Of course I'm here.*

Sezin had graciously offered to let Skora share her holoball so he could meet face-to-face with Avei. The tax on the holoball meant they both appeared less solid than normal.

Since his arrival, she had caught him scrutinizing her. Except for a curt reply of "not yet" as to the whereabouts of the shuttle, they hadn't spoken of her request to leave the ship. She flushed with shame at the thought of quitting. The immediate jump into the case pushed the discussion to the end, hanging over them like a thundercloud.

Skora stopped pacing. "Did Zarul murder Caerson Mercer?"

Avei set her mug down, taking a moment to gather her thoughts. The case was only a few hours old and it was too early for definitive statements. With Uma taking over soon, the situation called for a quick assessment.

It didn't mean she needed to rush to conclusions. The case had a lot of holes and relied on guesswork. "Mercer's death felt disorganized. Rushed. Zarul's been meticulous, especially with picking the place of death. Until now, Zarul fit the profile of an organized killer. Caerson Mercer died in the middle of the employee corridor. It doesn't get more disorganized than that."

"A new killer, then?"

Avei traced the burn scar on the back of her hand. "That's a possibility. Or something happened that caused Zarul to act impulsively. They felt compelled to kill without a plan in place. Another option is that their mental health is deteriorating." One more prospect lurked in the dark recesses of her mind, and she debated mentioning it. Speaking it aloud raised the likelihood of having to stay on the case with Uma. Saying nothing meant the murderer continued their killing spree. *Gods, I'd be no better than Zarul if I allowed that to happen.* "If the killer wanted to disguise Caerson's murder by mimicking a Zenith overdose, they would have used the actual drug. Instead, they used grenwal venom. They wanted our attention."

"They specifically wanted Inspector Avei Themis's attention," Sezin corrected her.

"My thoughts exactly," D.I. Skora said.

Avei nodded. Some serial killers thought of her as the ultimate adversary. It disgusted her and added to the growing list of reasons to retire. "Thanks to Marsa Baako and all those damn books and movies, my love of arachnids is common knowledge. Zarul used the one murder tool that guaranteed I'd take the case. The question is: why?"

"It sounds like you're confident it's Zarul," D.I. Skora said.

"I am." Avei surprised herself with the certainty of her words. "Zarul is aboard the *Delphi*, and Caerson Mercer is their seventh victim."

Skora rubbed his hands together. "No need for a shuttle, then. I'll work on returning the *Delphi* to the spacehub." He studied her. "Can you stay on the case for a short time more? I'll need all hands on deck once the *Delphi* docks. No pun intended. We've got the Zarul pinned down. No one debarks until we have the killer in custody."

Avei let out a pent-up breath and smiled. Uma would take over the case. Relief brought on benevolence. "Of course I'll help and thank you."

"Don't thank me yet. Julisa Breckin's putting up one hell of a fight."

Despite her wish to be done with the case, Julisa's behavior intrigued Avei. "What's so pressing on Charnos that she'd take such a risk?"

"The inspector asks a good question," Sezin said. "Everything in Ms. Breckin's dossier points to a conservative approach to business. For her to want to continue a voyage with a murderer on board and endanger the guests doesn't add up."

"I'll have Uma look into it while I work on returning the *Delphi*—"

A buzz from the display interrupted Skora and startled Avei. "It's Chief Varan. Can we talk?"

"Ah, our fixer for the rich. Will you confront him now or wait?"

"There's something off about him. I want to observe Eadren until debarkation."

"Trust your instincts and watch your backs." D.I. Skora faded away.

Avei frowned. She no longer trusted her gut. "Do you agree with my approach with Eadren Varan?"

Sezin nodded. "I do. The chief's hiding something."

Relieved, Avei stood and smoothed the wrinkles in her uniform. Time to dance with the *Delphi*'s chief of security. "Enter."

The hatch opened and Eadren took a step inside the room. "I wanted to check in to see how the case was coming." A model of calm. His face gave nothing away.

"How long until the cameras are back online?"

Other than his green cat eyes narrowing, Eadren appeared at ease with the question.

"The systems that run a massive ship are complex. It—"

"Are you stalling, Chief Varan? From where I stand, it appears someone tampered with the system." She noticed his right hand drift to his pocket. A tell, perhaps?

"We don't know that yet. They should be online by the end of the day." Eadren studied her. "What have you uncovered in your investigation?"

Time to light the fire. "Until I find the killer, everyone on this ship is a suspect. That includes you, Chief Varan."

Eadren's features hardened. "I see. Let me know if I or my team can be of any help."

Avei watched him walk out of the hatch. He didn't argue, and that spoke volumes. "The chief's keeping secrets."

Sezin nodded. "Yes, he is."

18

Imara limped through the medical bay hatch. Her wrinkled yellow dress was a counterbalance to the stark white walls of the fifth-floor corridor as she headed to the elevator. The clean, utilitarian design of the employee wing and medical bay was a jarring juxtaposition to the glitz and glamor of the guest floors. She ran her fingers along the wall, making a squeaking sound, and wondered how things had gone so wrong. This trip was supposed to be the start of a glorious new life. Now she was alone and destitute.

Imara crumpled a piece of paper in her hand and stopped in front of the elevator doors. She leaned close to the display panel on the wall. "Floor two."

The hatch opened onto overwrought opulence, as if to compensate for the subdued fifth floor. The mirrored walls, with swirls of gold and copper etched around the edges, reflected the soft light from the crystal lamps in the ceiling. A solid gold handrail encircled the elevator and a dark green padded bench sat against the back wall. Walking on the thick burgundy carpet felt like stepping onto a suspension bridge.

Imara entered and touched the gold handrail. A tiny sliver would pay for head shots at that swanky photography shop over on Tensin. A small chunk meant no more worries about food and rent now that Caerson had died. Grief and fear washed over her as she grabbed hold of the bar. With no money for rent next week, she had no idea where she would live. Neither she nor Caerson were big on friendships, so she had no one to bunk with until she got her feet under her. And she'd die before she ever lived on the streets again.

Seized with desperation, she bent over and scanned the bottom of the handrail. No luck. Heavy-duty bolts attached it to the wall and required special equipment to remove them. Plus, getting it off the ship without attracting attention seemed an impossible task. The rest of the ship had expensive art sitting around in the alcoves. It'd be a breeze to steal a few small pieces. And there was that other matter. One with the potential of making her rich. Very rich.

"You're Caerson's girlfriend, aren't you?"

Imara whirled around and found Wilm Breckin blocking her way out. He pushed into the elevator, forcing her against the bench. Still recovering from the poisoning, her reactions were slow. The door closed before she thought of escaping. "What do you want?"

The elevator hummed as it headed to the second floor.

"You know exactly what I want, Imara Tiniba. I want you to leave us alone."

"Second floor," the elevator announced in a cheerful voice.

When the doors opened, Imara shoved past Wilm into the corridor. The lush, verdant green carpet of the guest floor enhanced the white walls and ceiling that shimmered with veins of rose crystal. Every twenty feet, a shallow alcove held an ornate vase or exotic plant.

Too panicked to notice, Imara dashed left, then right. Her fingers trembled as she straightened the paper that said 12A.

Wilm sidled up to her, peered over her shoulder and pointed to the right. "Your room is that way."

Imara dashed down the hallway, wincing in pain from the five-inch bruise on her right thigh, and no memory of how it got there. She searched each hatch for its gold-plated number as she ran past. Wilm stuck so close she could smell the liquor on his breath. *Where's my damn room?*

A sigh of relief escaped when she spotted 12A. Imara stopped in front of the hatch and held her palm over the panel. When the door opened, Wilm grabbed her arm before she could enter, wrenching her back into the corridor. Imara struggled to break loose.

Wilm's fingers ground into her arm and she yelped in pain. He jerked her close until a few inches separated them, then he ran his finger down her cheek. "You and your boyfriend threatened my family, and I can't have that."

Something snapped inside Imara. Her abusive childhood had taught her one thing exceptionally well: how to defend oneself from bullies. This rich, entitled scumbag had no right to threaten or touch her. And she alone would decide when and if she backed off. Imara jammed her lower arm against Wilm's throat and slammed him into the wall opposite the open hatch.

"Never underestimate a girl from the Bhindoir commune." She smiled. It felt good to be in control again.

She hated bullies almost as much as being poor. This privileged punk was her golden ticket to an extraordinary life, and a chance of getting on the Nexus.

She watched Wilm's eyes open wide as he gasped for air. He tried to wriggle free and she pressed harder. "Nothing's changed. Meet our demands, or I will tell the galaxy about your nasty little secret."

A rustling sound caught their attention. Several feet away, Sintha dug her nails into the carpet and stretched. Wilm took advantage of the distraction and jammed his fingers between his neck and Imara's arm. They wrestled for control and she slammed him against the wall twice before her bruised leg gave out and she collapsed.

Wilm gripped her yellow gown with both hands and yanked her upright. The fragile fabric ripped at the seams but held long enough to propel her backwards to the open hatch. "Stay away from my family, or you die too." He shoved her into the room and stormed away.

Imara stumbled backwards and crashed to the floor, tangled in her dress. She pushed up on her elbow and scanned the empty corridor. "Close door and lock it." The hatch closed and the light on the display panel turned red.

After several attempts to disentangle the dress, she ripped it off and shoved it aside. Wearing only underwear, she rubbed her right thigh and looked around. Housekeeping had matched the vibrant decor of the old suite. She had requested a new room, not expecting to get assigned one half the size. A flash of anger forged a vow to have a conversation with the captain about the slight. A pile of yellow dresses took up most of the bed.

Housekeeping should have hung them up. She added it to the growing list of grievances. The window framed the spacehub, scarcely discernible in the distance. Fingers of fear tightened around her chest when she realized they had moved closer to the wormhole since last night. Surely they'd stop the trip after Caerson's murder. Another topic for the captain.

Wilm Breckin demanded her full faculties. After a shower and a solid meal, she'd plot her next steps. Given his threats, she'd ask for double the payoff amount. That goon had it coming. No *one messes with a Bhindoir woman.* Why not triple it? If he didn't pay up, Nexus would. They'd be salivating over the Breckins' secret and pay even more.

The perfect idea smacked Imara between the eyes. She laughed out loud. Why not do both? Extort the Breckins and sell the story to Nexus. Between the two, she'd have enough money for several lifetimes of luxuries.

Imara smiled and pushed herself up from the floor. She limped into the bathroom and closed the door.

***

Outside in the hallway, Sintha sniffed at the door and lingered for a few moments, then crept away.

19

Avei stood in front of a narrow hatch in the employee corridor and pressed the comm button on the panel next to the door. "Ocia, it's Inspector Themis." She'd given the woman a little time to decompress, and hoped it was enough. She needed to speak to her without the intimidating presence of the captain and security chief. Verbal confirmation of Wilm's presence in the corridor at the time of Caerson's death provided enough cause to arrest Wilm and remove him from the ship.

Avei had so many questions. Did he know the victim? Was he Zarul? A copycat? Or in the wrong place at the wrong time? Without access to Wilm Breckin, those questions remained unanswered. From what she had seen of him, he didn't strike her as someone with the wherewithal to plan and execute a meticulous set of killings. But neither had Apollyona, whose deception resulted in a catastrophic outcome. It would be better to let Uma sort it out once they had Wilm in custody.

The familiar feeling of failure crept up and Avei wished for Sezin's steady presence but they had agreed it was better for Avei to question Ocia alone. Her fingers sought the holoball on her belt. It brought a measure of relief.

Why didn't Ocia answer her door? Did someone get to her? The chief? Why the leap straight to him? Was her intuition trying to tell her something?

Avei pressed the comm button again. "Ocia, can we talk? It won't take a minute."

Marsa sauntered around the corner with Sintha in her arms. "Inspector, there you are."

Avei wanted to beat her head against the wall. Instead, she steeled herself and turned to face Marsa, who settled in front of her with a smile.

"I figured you'd start with the staff. They never miss a chance to rob you blind."

"That has never been my experience. What do you want, Ms. Baako?"

"Please, call me Marsa. Ms. Baako sounds way too formal, given our partnership over the years."

Partnership? Is there no end to this woman's delusions?

Sintha struggled to get loose, and Marsa tightened her hold. "I want to chat about the case."

"I'm not discussing an ongoing investigation with a civilian. Now, if you'll excuse me, I have work to do." Avei tried the comm button again. "Ocia, I'm here on official MSF business. Please open the door."

"I can help. I know—"

Avei held up a hand and silenced Marsa. She put her ear against the door and heard a moan. "Sezin, start system override. Alert the doctor to a medical emergency in Ocia's room, number 523."

"On it, Inspector." Sezin's voice came through her ear comm.

Avei leaned close to the panel and it scanned her eye. When the hatch opened, she blocked Marsa from entering as she could see Ocia thrashing on the bed. "You want to help, get Chief Varan."

"Roger that." Marsa set Sintha on ground and motioned for her to stay. She raced down the corridor.

Avei rushed into the narrow, bare-bones room with two sets of bunk beds. Personal stuff adorned the alcoves next to each of the four beds, giving the spartan space a homey feeling. Two lockers framed each side of a small door that led to a compact bathroom.

Ocia lay on the lower left bunk, flushed and covered in sweat. She wrapped two arms around her stomach. A third arm gripped the side of the bunk. "I don't feel well."

Avei sat on the bed and grabbed her free hand. "Did you eat or drink anything since we spoke in the hallway?" *Maybe a virus, or food poisoning?* People got sick all the time. Reality pierced her foolish thoughts when Ocia arched and screamed. Orange foam bubbled around her mouth. Zarul had struck again.

Avei clung to her hand. "Hang on, Ocia. Help's coming."

One look at Ocia and Avei knew death was imminent. The venom had spread throughout her body. Even if they had the antidote, it wouldn't save her.

The killer had eliminated the only witness to Wilm Breckin's proximity to Caerson Mercer at the time of his death. Why hadn't she kept Ocia safe? Locked her in the medical unit until they docked at the spacehub?

Avei squeezed Ocia's hand. "You're not alone, Ocia. I'm here, and I won't leave you."

"My family depends on me. What will happen if I die?" A convulsion gripped Ocia and flung Avei off the bed as Eadren rushed into the room.

Panting and red-faced, Marsa settled outside the room. "Dr. Hueson is on his way. Is it another poisoning?" He helped Avei up from the floor and kept a grip on her arm.

She wrenched it away and pointed to the hatch. "Out! This is a crime scene."

Eadren backed into the corridor next to Marsa. Sintha remained in the hatch entry, licking one of her six paws.

Avei sat next to Ocia again and grabbed her hand. "It's okay, Ocia. I'm still here. I'll make sure your family is taken care of. You have my word on that."

Ocia's body went limp, and her face relaxed. Orange foam bubbled around her mouth.

Avei rose and stepped away from Ocia. "No. No. No." Someone else had died because of her failure. Why didn't she put a security detail on her? Why didn't she get her off the ship? Of course, Zarul would kill a witness. Her mind churned through everything she didn't do and obliterated all rational thought.

Eadren leaned into the room. "Inspector?"

Avei backed into the bunks across from Ocia, her eyes locked on the dead woman. "This can't be happening again."

Eadren walked to Ocia and checked for a pulse. He closed her eyes and pulled the sheet over her. "The others will be here soon."

Avei crossed her arms and trembled. All she wanted was to curl into a tight ball and pull a blanket over her head.

Eadren placed a hand on her shoulder and met her panicked gaze. "What can I do to help?"

Avei stared at him. "I shouldn't be here. I—" She lowered her eyes, ashamed of falling apart in front of him. Skora's wise words when she first joined the force penetrated the fog of despair: *Never show weakness when confronting a potential suspect.* Until a few months ago, she had never allowed that to happen. Not a single time. Now Eadren had seen her vulnerability, and he would exploit it. You don't become a fixer for the very rich unless you use every tool at your disposal. Morality be damned.

Dr. Hueson and Captain Dimphi came to a stop in front of the hatch. The doctor, pale and frightened, had a medical bag slung over his shoulder. The captain dabbed at beads of perspiration on his forehead with a napkin. He appeared especially agitated.

"Oh dear, dear. Not again." Captain Dimphi shared a horrified look with the doctor.

Eadren stepped between the two men and Avei, shielding her. He gave her a gentle shake that snapped her out of her downward spiral. Despite what she knew about him, she appreciated the nudge. She needed to pull herself together and secure the crime scene. "No one else comes into the room until I've run my scan."

Eadren walked into the corridor and pushed everyone from the door. Two medical staff with a hover gurney waited nearby.

Captain Dimphi took another step back and stumbled into Sintha, who arched her back and hissed at him.

Eadren pulled the captain behind him as Sintha advanced, fangs bared. “Ms. Baako, take that animal to your quarters immediately. And keep her there.”

Marsa watched Avei work her way around the room, performing a cursory search for evidence.

“Ms. Baako, did you hear me?” Eadren asked again.

Marsa tore her eyes from Avei and turned her fury on him. “Yes, I did, and don’t talk to me that way again. I’m a 50-billion-mile guest.”

Sintha stopped inches from Captain Dimphi, who cowered behind the chief of security.

Eadren glared at Sintha, whose tail whipped back and forth. “If you don’t leave now, I will cage this animal and confine you to your quarters for the duration of the voyage.”

“Do that and you’ll never work on a starliner again.”

“Now, Ms. Baako.” His green cat eyes pierced into Marsa, who met his scowl with one of her own.

“You haven’t heard the last from me, Chief Varan.” Marsa picked up Sintha and kissed her head. “There, there, my love. Don’t listen to this dreadful man. You did nothing wrong.” She cuddled the cat and stalked down the hallway, muttering under her breath.

“Nice job, Chief.” Captain Dimphi moved from behind Eadren. “I will report the situation to Ms. Breckin. Thank the Goddess she is banning that woman and her foul beast forever.”

Avei walked out of the room. “Sezin, begin the crime scene scan.”

Sezin's holoball released from her belt and hovered in front of the door.

"Ocia Doni crime scene analysis of room 523 on the *Delphi* starliner on the thirty-sixth day of Morcea, year 2962." Sezin's voice echoed from the device as it emitted a blue light that scanned the room from top to bottom in seconds before dissipating. "The foam around the victim's mouth is the right color and consistency of a grenwal poisoning and aligns to the findings from Caerson Mercer's autopsy. The good doctor needs to confirm if the venom is present. If it comes back positive, I believe the victim ingested the venom in the last five to seven minutes."

"Noted." Avei motioned for the two medical staff with a hover gurney to enter Ocia's quarters. Years of investigative experience took over, and the panic subsided. They needed to disembark the passengers and crew from the *Delphi* as soon as possible, for their protection. The spacehub was big enough to hold them all until Zarul could be found.

She turned to Eadren, Dr. Hueson, and Captain Dimphi. "I want security officers stationed outside Ocia's and Caerson's rooms. No one goes in until we dock at the spacehub."

Avei turned to Dr. Hueson and missed the troubled look Eadren and the captain shared. "Doc, I need you to confirm AI Sezin's findings and run the tox screen for grenwal venom." She tapped through a few screens on her wrist device and swiped toward Dr. Hueson. His wrist device pinged. "That's the data on the antidote. You need to synthesize it, and that takes time. Let's plan for the worst-case scenario and have the antidote on hand, just in case there's a docking delay. Better to be safe in the event something happens between now and when we get the guests and crew off the ship. Do you have Lorestal?"

"It's required on all vessels, since the Subay plague," Dr. Hueson said. "Why?"

"Lorestal slows the effects of venom and will buy a little time until the antidote is ready. Or until MSF can fly it to us. The Themis Institute of Arachnology will have some on hand. I'll alert my parents, and they'll get it ready for transport."

The medical staff exited the room with Ocia's body, and everyone stilled as they passed.

"This is terrible. Just terrible," Captain Dimphi said.

"May I accompany them?" Dr. Hueson asked.

Avei nodded and watched the doctor rush after them. Once the interviews of the guests and crew concluded in the spacehub, she would head home and not leave there until she had fully retired, in three days' time. Ocia's death proved to her once again that she was no longer fit for duty.

The ship shuddered under her feet and she knew what had caused it. Her investigative work required constant travel to distant worlds, using wormhole transits. She didn't need to ask to know they had just entered one.

Her face flushed red with fury as she turned to the two men. "How could you?"

Captain Dimphi pulled his collar away from his neck. "Julisa Breckin has powerful friends. I had no—"

"You understand you've locked all of us in with an active serial killer for the next twelve hours? Your guests, your crew, and yourselves." Her voice was thick with anger and alarm.

A flash of guilt crossed Eadren's face. "Julisa gave Captain Dimphi an order. He had no choice but to obey it."

Rage battled with disbelief and made any additional conversation with the two men impossible. Leaving a wormhole during transit was a foolhardy and dangerous action no captain in their right mind would attempt when there was no way to determine where you'd end up. Left with no choice, it was up to Avei to keep the passengers and crew safe during the twelve-hour passage to Charnos. The only way to do that was to find the killer before they murdered again.

One other witness to Caerson's murder remained alive and needed her help. Avei whirled around, her hands clenching and unclenching as she stormed down the hall away from the men.

"Wait, Inspector Themis." Captain Dimphi called after her. "What if the killer strikes again?"

Are you kidding me? Avei spun on her heel and glared at him. "You should have considered that before you entered the wormhole."

Avei turned her back on the men, stalked around the bend, and disappeared.

***

Eadren stared after her, his hands clenched into fists. They'd already begun the wormhole entry when they had received word of Ocia's poisoning. The gravitational pull had a hold on the ship and retreating risked breaking the ship in two. He cringed at his own thoughts. He knew a flimsy excuse when he heard one. Anyone with a sound mind would have ended the voyage and gone straight to the spacehub when Caerson's death was confirmed as a murder. His hand drifted to his pocket and wrapped around the holographic disk there. He had promised justice, and everything hinged on getting to Charnos. The lives of so many depended on it.

The captain's voice tore him from his thoughts. "Do you think it was him? You know—"

Eadren seized the shorter man by his lapels and pulled him close. "Keep your voice down." He released him and stepped back in horror. Goddess, help him. He needed to get his emotions under control. His face turned violet with shame. "Forgive me, Captain. I shouldn't have done that."

Captain Dimphi's hands shook as he straightened his jacket. "Nothing to forgive. We made this decision together. What happens next is on both of us, and I'm as torn up about it as you are. This is turning into an unmitigated disaster."

"It's almost over." In order for their plan to succeed, Eadren knew he needed the captain's help. That presented a problem as to how hard he could push him. Captain Dimphi was clearly rattled and not thinking straight.

"We need to come clean and tell the inspector everything." Captain Dimphi headed after Avei.

Given Inspector Themis's stellar reputation, she posed a danger to their plans, even in her reduced capacity. Eadren still felt shocked at seeing her so distressed when Ocia had died. The Nexus had generated wall-to-wall coverage packed with details about how Avei had almost died in the warehouse fire. The incident appeared to have affected her more than she let on. He needed to stay focused on the end goal, at the exclusion of all else, or everything they had accomplished so far would be for naught. That left no choice but to keep the captain on track and away from Avei Themis until they arrived in Charnos.

Eadren ran after Captain Dimphi and stepped in front of him. "We tell her nothing. Not until we arrive at Charnos. You know what's at stake, and why we can't risk her involvement."

Captain Dimphi leaned in close to Eadren and pointed at Ocia's room. "Can you live with yourself if others die? I don't know if I can."

"Please, Captain. There is too much on the line to quit now."

"I don't like this. Not one bit." The captain studied Eadren's face and sighed. "Fine, I'll keep my mouth shut. For the moment. But the first whiff of trouble and I'll tell the inspector myself." He continued down the hallway and disappeared around the bend.

Eadren let out a long breath. He took the holographic disk from his pocket and stared at the image of the young man with light blue skin and hair, and who bore more than a passing resemblance to him. He brought the disk to his lips and kissed it.

20

Avei stood inside the hatch of Imara's room, which had a similar layout to her own, but was decorated in more vibrant colors. The undulating pinks, blues and greens of the wormhole filled the window. In the past, she had found this experience calming and would always sit by a window during transit. It put her into a meditative state and allowed her mind to wander through the case notes. More times than not, her ruminations uncovered hidden clues that put her on the path of the killer. Given the jumbled state of her mind, it might be worth having a go later to see if the exercise unlocked anything.

Imara bristled in front of her, wearing another bright yellow dress that hit mid-thigh. Judging by the stubborn set of her perfect chin, getting her to help with the case may prove difficult. All that beauty didn't soften a hard edge honed by a tough life.

"Why are you headed to Charnos?" Avei asked.

"None of your business. Why are you here?"

Confident and defiant. A challenging combination in a suspect, or a witness, when probing for information. Which camp did Imara land in? Her dramatics in the medical bay and being apparently more concerned about meeting Nexus producers than the death of her boyfriend might sway some inspectors toward suspicion, but if Avei could trust her instincts, she'd say Ms. Tiniba belonged in the witness group. Successful serial killers excelled at hiding their authentic emotions, and Imara wore hers like a badge of honor. Still, her current attitude spoke of guilt –but for what?

"Neither you nor Caerson had the financial means to pay for a passage on the *Delphi*. Who bought your tickets?"

Imara crossed her arms and stared at Avei.

Her unwillingness to help said a lot. A witness withheld information for a variety of reasons. To hide their involvement in the crime. Some feared for their life if they spoke up. Others knew who the killer was and wanted to help them, or wanted something in return for their silence. Imara's secrets involved at least one other on the *Delphi* and that placed her in mortal danger as the last witness alive. Avei traced the burn on the back of her hand as she wrestled with the best way to proceed. Imara's life depended on getting it right. She had always trusted her gut in the past. Now, unmoored, she had nothing to latch onto. *How would I handle a witness like Imara before? Gods, I hate all this uncertainty*. Avei thought for a moment before landing on the right approach. She would appeal to Ms. Tiniba's better senses.

"Someone killed Caerson for a reason and almost killed you. We can assume you are still in danger." Avei held Imara's gaze until she looked away.

"I can take care of myself."

"There's been another murder."

Imara's eyes widened in surprise. "Here, on the *Delphi*?"

"The killer is tying up loose ends and killed the only other witness. Help me find them before they kill again."

Imara appeared shocked by the news of Ocia's death. Having to weigh cooperating with the police against staying safe confirmed more was going on with Imara Tiniba than Caerson's death. Avei gave her the space to decide.

Imara took on the same recalcitrant expression as before, and Avei knew she had abandoned safety in pursuit of her own agenda. A decision that put her on a collision course with Zarul.

"Dr. Hueson said I need rest. You need to leave."

Zarul would strike again, and Avei couldn't have another death on her hands. She had to give it another go. "You don't seem to understand—"

"The danger I'm in? I understand perfectly. Now, get out."

"It's hours until we reach Charnos. Please, let me keep you safe."

Imara pointed to the hatch. "Leave."

With no choice, Avei headed to the hatch. Once they had entered the wormhole, she and MSF lost jurisdiction over the *Delphi*. That now fell to that fraud, Eadren Varan, Chief of Security. *Is he the killer?* Only time would tell.

Her conversation with Imara Tiniba had been informative. The woman's secret was consequential enough that she refused protection. Zarul be damned. *What is so important that she'd risk death?* Time to huddle with Sezin to review their findings thus far and figure out their next steps.

21

Avei walked past the glitz and glamor of the Delphi Promenade with her head down, purple hair draped across her face. Her fingers traced the burn on the back of her hand. She had pushed Imara too hard. A more gentle approach may not have alienated her best witness to Caerson's murder. She knew beyond a doubt that Imara Tiniba was keeping key information to herself. The next step on the agenda was to create a *Delphi* crime board with Sezin and begin an analysis of the case.

Five guests startled Avei out of her reverie when they entered the casino on her right, laughing and having a good time. She glared at them. Two people had died on this ship and a killer walked among them. Why weren't the guests and non-essential employees locked in their rooms until the ship docked at Charnos? If Avei had any say in the matter, that's where they'd be. Not gallivanting around the ship.

Avei took a breath and calmed herself. Knowing Julisa Breckin, she'd insist on keeping the guests in the dark instead of letting them make an informed decision about their own safety. This approach kept panic to a minimum and kept the starliner on course. Leaving the wormhole risked landing the *Delphi* in uncharted space with no way to re-enter and no way home. Although Avei understood Julisa's reasoning, she was angry with the woman for jeopardizing everyone's safety to maintain the illusion of security.

Avei shook her head at the extravagance of the third floor. Expensive artwork hung on the walls, and the alcoves with padded benches displayed rare alien artifacts set into nooks. The thick burgundy carpet and charcoal walls with silver and gold inlay felt oppressive. *Why does anyone think this is beautiful? To each their own, I guess.*

A desire to return to her quiet room overwhelmed her. Avei spun in a circle, looking for the elevators, and realized she had passed them without noticing. She started back in the direction she came from and heard the raised voices of Julisa and Eadren, though she could not see them. She stepped into an alcove; one of the roomier ones, with a bench against the wall.

Avei peered around the wall and observed Eadren and Julisa standing together. They made for an attractive couple and she felt the tiniest tinge of envy as she studied them. Eadren, with his startling green cat eyes, dark cyan hair and light blue skin had sexuality oozing from every pore. Julisa Breckin, while not a classic beauty like her sister-in-law Celethe, had a commanding and confident aura that exuded a seductive appeal. They both wore the Breckin colors of maroon and gold; Eadren in his security uniform and Julisa in a stylish A-line dress with a short jacket. Compared to these two beautiful people, Avei felt short and frumpy.

What the hell is wrong with me? Mooning over a suspect in a murder case. Gods. Themis, get a grip.

Avei straightened, her jaw firm. She removed Sezin's holoball from her belt, released it, then tapped the comm device behind her ear and whispered, "Sezin, I need you to record the conversation between Eadren and Julisa. They're just down the corridor having an argument. Don't scan, or you'll draw unwanted attention."

"Roger that," Sezin said quietly in her ear. The holoball drifted to the ceiling and moved until it had a line of sight to Julisa and Eadren. Their voices came through her ear device loud and clear.

Avei turned her attention to the couple. Julisa, pale and wild-eyed, wrenched her arm from Eadren's grasp.

He invaded her personal space. At the same height, they stared at one another, neither backing down. "Let me make this crystal-clear. You gave the order and by doing so put every single person on this ship in danger."

Julisa glowered at him. "And you didn't talk me out of it. You want to get to Charnos as badly as I do so stop the sanctimonious act. We both know who you are, so don't do yourself a disservice by pretending otherwise."

Eadren sighed, stepped back, and raised his hands. "You're right. I should have stopped you."

Julisa ran her hand through her hair. "If I don't get to Charnos by tomorrow, they'll seize my company. They'll take everything. I worked too hard for someone to come along and take it all."

"Lower your voice. Guests are around."

Eadren scanned the corridor in both directions and Avei pulled herself as far out of sight as she could. She peeked around the wall and confirmed the two hadn't moved.

"Don't tell me to calm down. It's taken me years to drag Breckin Starliners out of the gutter. I won't lose my company now. Especially not for that reason."

Eadren leaned in close. "Is there any chance he murdered--?"

"How dare you suggest such a thing?"

He had asked an excellent question. The same one Avei wanted to ask. She held her breath as she listened.

"Wilm was down there when Caerson died. Same time, same location."

"I don't care how it looks. My brother is not a killer."

Eadren stared at Julisa for a long moment. "Let's move this conversation to my office."

He took her arm and guided her down the hall, away from Avei's alcove. She breathed a sigh of relief because squeezing under the bench was her only option, and difficult to explain away if they had come her way.

Avei sat on the bench and tapped the comm device in her ear. "Sezin, did you get it?"

"Indeed. A scintillating conversation."

"Does Wilm have anything in his past regarding illegal drugs?" Avei kept her voice low.

"There's nothing in the intel packets to indicate Wilm's involvement in the manufacture of drugs. Given Julisa's response, you're right to pursue this avenue."

"Ms. Breckin said someone wanted to take her company. What other legal reasons allow the Tribunal or someone else to take such drastic action?"

"Quite a lot, actually. A financial default on an excessive amount. The removal of rare flora and fauna from protected worlds like Qidon. Illegal mining of chalmun. Solar jumping—"

"Okay, point taken. There are more reasons than the transport and manufacture of drugs." Avei leaned back and rested her head against the wall.

"Breckin Starliners is solvent. That rules out financial institutions. I can't tap into the MSF mainframe for more information until we're out of this cursed wormhole," Sezin said as their holoball floated down and attached to Avei's belt.

The familiar rush of adrenaline at chasing down a clue coursed through Avei's veins. She would miss the exhilaration when the puzzle pieces slid into place. "Do your best with what you already have. I'm on my way back to my room. Time to create a crime board that combines the Zarul and *Delphi* murders."

"Looking forward to it."

Avei slipped out of the alcove and stumbled over Sintha, who darted between her legs and raced down the corridor. She stared after the animal and wondered why Marsa continued to allow her pet to run wild on a ship despite the chief of security's warning. Then she saw a sign pointing to the holographic amusement deck and smiled. She tapped her comm device. "Sezin, change of plans."

22

Avei and Sezin walked into one of the holographic rooms. The muted gray walls, floors and ceilings were a blank canvas, poised to come to life. The menu provided a choice of existing holo-programs or a custom creation.

"The holodeck gives us space to maneuver," Avei said. "And some privacy."

"The cameras remain offline," Sezin said, "so no peeping toms from the security office or any particularly handsome green-eyed men. The door's locked and I've changed the pass codes. I'm tapped into the system and ready for instructions."

"Let's put the Zarul crime board on the left with the first six crime sites sized to real life. We'll build the *Delphi* board and scenes on the right."

The Zarul board and six homicide locations lined one side of the large room. The holodeck brought the scenes to life by using solid holomatter, allowing full immersion of all five senses. On the right, a board appeared with an image of Caerson and Ocia and their crime sites.

Sezin jabbed themselves with their finger. "Oh, my goddesses. I'm solid like a rock. No, that's not right." Sezin squeezed their arm. "My skin gives a bit, where a rock wouldn't. I'm solid like you! Like a living person." They ran to Avei. "Feel me."

Avei laughed and squeezed their arms. "You have always been real to me, Sezin. Even without holomatter." Avei looked around in awe. "I wish MSF had a holomatter room. Incredibly helpful when rebuilding crime scenes."

Sezin raised up on their toes, pirouetted to one of Zarul's early crime scenes and sat on the bed next to the body. They felt the sheet, knocked on the metal bed frame, and bounced a few times on the mattress. They jumped up and walked around the holodeck, hands feeling various objects in the crime scenes. "Touch is way more scintillating than I thought it would be. I could get used to this. I'm going to petition MSF to invest in holomatter. This way AIs can provide real backup when needed."

Avei got a kick out of seeing her partner exploring the real world in solid form for the first time. "When you're done touching everything, can you please reset the crime scenes?"

Sezin skipped over to her. The crime scenes disappeared for a moment and reappeared. Everything returned to its proper place. "I'm happy to see you are back to your old self. I thought you'd find the situation challenging after we entered the wormhole."

Avei traced the burns on the back of her hand. "Honestly, I'm not back. Not yet. My confidence is in the gutter, and I'm afraid… no, *terrified*… of making another mistake. I have two choices in front of me. Hide in my room for twelve hours while Zarul has free rein. Or find the murderer and bring them to justice. And, hopefully, keep everyone safe on the *Delphi*. Hiding in my room would dishonor Anastasia's memory and endanger the lives of everyone on the ship. I couldn't live with myself if I took the path of a coward."

"Your sister would be proud of your accomplishments and all the lives you've saved over the years. Were it not for you and your investigative skills, many of those serial killers would still be free. And still killing." Sezin spoke with a forcefulness they rarely used.

"Thank you, Sezin." Avei felt tears coming on and she turned away to wipe her eyes. What Sezin had said meant everything to her, but also brought on a fresh wave of guilt. When she left MSF, it fell to Uma to maintain the high capture rate, but as much as Uma got on her nerves with her know-it-all attitude, she was still an excellent inspector who got results.

"What's next?" Sezin rubbed their hands together.

"Let's add a suspect list to the *Delphi* crime board. Add Wilm and Julisa Breckin. And Eadren Varan." Images of Wilm, Julisa, and Eadren appeared.

"What about Imara Tiniba?"

"Add a witness list and put her there for now. While I think she's too much of an open book to be Zarul, I don't think she is completely innocent." Avei walked into Caerson's scene and squatted next to his body. "Imara turned down my offer to keep her safe. Practically threw me out of her room. She knows something."

Sezin raised one of their perfectly shaped eyebrows. "You think she knows Zarul's identity?" Imara's image appeared under the witness list on the board with the text: *Knows Zarul.*

"Imara knows or has an idea who they are. Her financial situation is dire now that Caerson's dead. I think she wants to—"

"Extort a serial killer? That takes major *cojones*." Sezin reverted to their mid-nineteenth century detective attire from old Earth. A black jacket, waistcoat, trousers, forest-green cravat, and a black derby hat. They held a pipe in one hand.

"If we hadn't lost jurisdiction when we entered the wormhole, I'd have arrested her on some trumped-up charge to keep her safe."

Sezin pointed their pipe at Eadren's image on the suspect side. "And we can't risk having the fraud do it. Not when he's on our suspect list and would have unhindered access to her."

"And not until we figure out what is going on with Eadren and Captain Dimphi. Those two are up to something." Avei thought back to her interaction with them in the corridor, after Ocia's death. Both men had acted guilty, and the captain oozed anxiety and fear. They entered the wormhole, knowing the terrible risks. Why? "Add a question under Eadren's image. Why is getting to Charnos more important than the safety of the guests and crew?"

"The captain of a ship has the moral and legal obligation to keep their passengers safe. To override that means something more portentous convinced the captain to disregard the safety of their crew and guests."

"Agreed. Julisa Breckin ordered him to do it, which means she's in on whatever scheme the Captain and the Chief have set in motion."

Sezin took a puff of their pipe and blew smoke in Avei's direction. "You're thinking Eadren is working for Julisa."

Avei wrinkled her nose and waved away the smoke. "Gods, that stinks."

Sezin beamed in delight. "That, my dear, is tobacco that hails from old Earth. Specifically, a place called—"

"Sezin, this isn't the time for a history lesson. I get enough of that from my father, who is equally obsessed with old Earth as you are. Please bring up Caerson's crime scene video that we made for Ocia's walkthrough." Avei pushed away the remorse she felt over Ocia's death. She'd deal with it later, when everyone was safe.

Sezin turned their back, hunched over, then took a quick puff of their pipe. Avei shook her head and smiled. Gods, she loved her wacky AI.

Sezin turned around and a cloud of smoke followed them. They whipped their hands around until it dissipated.

"Let's take it from where Imara left Caerson's body." Avei raked her hands through her purple hair, causing it to stick up in places.

"Roger that, boss."

A holographic image of Imara in her yellow dress appeared next to Caerson's body. Her screams echoed around the holodeck. She turned to run down the corridor.

Avei rose and stepped back to watch the scene play out in front of her.

"Freeze." The scene stopped as Imara headed away from the body. "Wilm's there. Somewhere in the vicinity. He followed closely behind Imara, so he's nearby." Avei scanned the scene and walked to a spot ten feet from the body. "Add Wilm here."

Wilm appeared next to Avei. "Drunk and unsteady on his feet. That's what Eadren gave as the reason Wilm couldn't have killed Caerson."

"Which is speculation and hearsay at the moment," Sezin reminded her.

Avei glanced back at Ocia's own crime scene. She appeared so real lying in her bed. "Let's move forward, as if we had confirmation of his inebriated state. Shrink crime scene to quarter-size and start from where we left off."

Avei stood over the holographic depiction of the fifth-floor corridor. She trailed Imara as she ran down the hallway screaming, then rounding the bend and crashing into Ocia's cart, landing on her back.

"Freeze."

The scene froze. Avei walked back to Wilm, who hovered over Caerson's body. "Imara said, *We're dying, help us*. She didn't say, *We're sick, help us*."

Sezin settled next to Wilm. "She knew Caerson had died."

"According to Dr. Hueson, she suffered from hallucinations caused by the venom. I doubt she had enough of her faculties to check for a pulse and respirations."

"Wilm told her Caerson died."

"Move Wilm closer to the body."

Wilm appeared next to Caerson, squatting, his hand on the man's neck.

Avei crouched on the other side and studied Wilm. "He checked for a pulse. Can we get fingerprints?"

"Iffy. We will need Dr. Hueson's help."

"Send him a request. Let's see if we can confirm Wilm's presence in that corridor." Avei stood and stepped back.

"Done. However, the doctor has no obligation to fulfill our request now that we have entered the wormhole. He answers to the chief of security."

"Who will wonder why I didn't go to him first."

"A real sticky wicket if he takes over the case and ices us out." Sezin took another puff on their pipe and blew it away from Avei.

"Until that happens, we keep moving forward. Imara and Caerson's symptoms started while in their room. Instead of calling for help, they took the elevator to the medical bay on the fifth floor. Let's add those locations to the image."

The elevator appeared around the bend from Caerson's body. The medical bay appeared on the opposite side of the ship from Ocia and her cart, thirty feet from the elevator.

Avei walked around the fifth-floor hologram and studied the new additions. "They headed in the wrong direction. If they had gone left instead of right, the medical bay was only feet away. Even if they went right, it wouldn't have mattered. Caerson was seconds from death by then."

"New to the ship and hallucinating from the venom… really not surprising when you think about it." Sezin admired their pipe with a half-smile. "I can feel the smoke in my lungs. This is so—"

"Unhealthy?"

"Not what I was going for, Ms. Buzzkill." Sezin glared at her.

Avei chuckled as she moved to the middle of the room and scanned the eight crime scenes. “Someone purchased Caerson and Imara’s tickets the day before the voyage.”

“Eleventh hour implies a surprise, or poor planning.”

“It’s difficult getting last-minute tickets for a Breckin starliner. It feels like desperation to me. Whoever bought the tickets needed Caerson and Imara aboard the ship. We can rule out Zarul. That would bring too much attention. Something they’d avoid at all costs.” Avei traced the burn on the back of her hand. Too many questions and too few answers.

“Agreed. And there’s no way the killer would trap themselves on the starliner after committing a murder. Zarul is on the *Delphi* for another reason.”

“That means Imara and Caerson left Zarul with no choice.”

“The couple encountered Zarul at some point in the past and confronted them. Tried to blackmail the killer.” Sezin took a long pull on their pipe and breathed out the smoke, eyes half closed.

“Someone else brought Imara and Caerson aboard. Who? And for what reason?” Avei asked.

“I’ll add that to the question list.”

Avei tapped her chin as she scanned the *Delphi* crime scenes. “Grenwal venom takes three to five minutes to kill. A minute for the symptoms to appear and time to realize it wasn’t an upset stomach. Two minutes at least before Imara and Caerson left their room.”

Avei sidestepped until she peered at the elevator. "Given the high dose he ingested, Caerson could barely stand by then. Remove Wilm from the scene for the moment."

Wilm disappeared when Caerson and Imara materialized inside the elevator. They stumbled out when the doors opened and Caerson fell to the ground. Imara helped him stand. Missing the sign pointing to the medical bay on the left, they headed right. Imara struggled, half-carrying Caerson. He fell a second time on the spot where he died. Imara hovered over him.

"Freeze." Avei pointed back at the elevator bank. "Wilm came from that direction or Ocia would've seen him before she ran into Imara."

"The only thing between the body and the elevator are employee rooms." Sezin walked the full circumference of the miniature replica of the fifth floor.

"Show me the location of the Grilan rooms."

Red dots blinked over ten rooms, located halfway between the elevator and Caerson's body.

"Who is Wilm Breckin? Is he the Zarul murderer who stalked Imara and Caerson as they died? Or a lecherous bastard looking for another Grilan victim to knock around?" Avei stared at Sezin, waiting for their opinion.

"Hmmm. I could go either way. We know he's capable of violence. We also know he is an alcoholic who's rarely sober. Is he clearheaded enough to plot a series of fastidious murders and successfully carry them out?"

"Unless his inebriation is an act." Avei headed to the Zarul crime scenes and entered scene one, where a man lay dead on the ground in an abandoned house. His hands and feet were bound. A dozen small bites peppered the base of his neck. "The murderer used the zarultalzin to kill the first two victims. A spider so aggressive and venomous, they land in the top five of the most dangerous arachnids. The only reason to risk using them is they are small, portable, and guaranteed to bite. Zarul simply removes the lid from the container and holds it against the victim's neck until they bite him. Then they screw the lid back on and leave."

"What you're saying is that, with some practice, anyone can do it."

"I believe so, yes." Avei headed to crime scene five. "Then the killer switches species and uses the grenwal for the next three murders. One of the largest arachnids found in the Kressa system and docile unless threatened. Zarul figured out a way to get the grenwal to bite the victim not once, but twice. There are only a handful of experts who can achieve that."

"So, Zarul is one of these experts, or hired one of them to help."

Avei paced between scenes four, five and six, thinking through the people in the industry. "We haven't even talked about the twivorg arachnid that killed victim number six, the only woman. Nasty creatures which make the zarultalzin look like a puppy dog."

"That whittles the list of experts down—"

"To three. Noreedahl Ziz, Polena Foraop, and me. I know the other two very well, and they have unquestionable integrity. There's no way they'd willingly help a murderer."

"We can drop the idea of the killer framing you for the murders. The first three happened during your recovery in the hospital."

Avei stopped her pacing. "Nexus went nuts after the second death, when announcers speculated Mernin had another serial killer loose in the city. If Noreedahl or Polena saw the news and realized they had inadvertently helped the killer, they'd have gone straight to MSF headquarters."

"Not if the killer eliminated them."

Avei felt a growing certainty. "We can't connect with the mainframe until we're out of the wormhole. What we can do is search the *Delphi* for an archive of recent news. See if there is anything on Noreedahl or Polena."

Sezin cocked their head. "Scanning now. Good: the archives go back six months. Now the bad: Noreedahl died of a zenith overdose one week before the first murder."

Avei's eyes widened. "Oh no. I liked Noreedahl very much. This is terrible news. He had a husband and three kids. I need to send my condolences to his family when we return to Mernin. The arachnology community has lost one of our brightest minds. I wonder if my parents know."

"I'm sorry for your loss. We can add Noreedahl to Zarul's victims' list. Do you know if he used drugs?"

Avei pondered Sezin's question. "He liked natural hallucinogens. I know for a fact he'd never take a synthetic drug. Not willingly, anyway. We know there are similarities between a grenwal poisoning and a zenith overdose. Checking for venom poisoning isn't likely to be a consideration for the coroner, given all the deaths linked to zenith; it makes sense they'd jump to that conclusion.

It just happened with Caerson's murder, and I'm sure it was something Zarul counted on. When we leave the wormhole, fire off a message to Skora asking him and Uma to review Noreedahl's autopsy. He was Unutsi, and they bury their dead. Skora can petition to have the body exhumed and checked for grenwal venom. Also, have Uma contact Polena. The killer may have approached her too, but got nowhere."

Avei walked around the middle section of the holodeck, taking in both sets of crime scenes. "Knowing Noreedahl, he would have charged a fortune to take on something as complicated as training a grenwal."

"That means Zarul has money to pay for his expensive services, and enough to afford a voyage on the *Delphi*."

Avei stared at Wilm Breckin, frozen in a squat next to Caerson. "He goes to the top of our suspect list, but we keep an open mind. My gut..." Avei stopped while she sorted through her tangled feelings. She missed that certainty she had once felt when her instincts pointed in a clear direction. Could he pull off the murders? Sezin watched her but remained silent as she worked it out in her head. "I think it's a fifty-fifty chance he's Zarul."

Avei shifted her attention to the first six victims. "I came across something interesting in the case notes. The five men and the woman all came from the same sector in the Kressa system. I haven't had time to map their locations."

"Let me do that." Sezin's face slackened for a moment, then reanimated. "Very interesting. That area covers over twenty-nine habitable planets and moons, with forty-nine billion inhabitants. You raise a good point. The first Zarul victims are two miners from a moon that orbits a gas giant in that sector. The next three are from a freighter running mine supplies. The last of the six is a female who owned a brothel in L'reus."

"Good work, Sezin. Now we need to figure out what ties them together."

"Tough to do while stuck in this blooming hell of a wormhole." Sezin stilled, then nodded. "I received a message from Chief Varan. He wants you to join him in the dining hall for dinner. What's our response?"

"Tell him I accept. It's time to confront him about his dual role on the *Delphi*."

"Well, damn it to all the hells and other nether regions. Using the holomatter drained my holoball power. Instead of watching you confront that charlatan, I must plug myself into a charger. How positively prosaic."

Gratitude mixed with sorrow filled Avei as she gestured to the crime scenes. "Thank you, Sezin. For all of this. For everything. Your help over the years has meant the world to me. I hope you know that."

Sezin smiled as the scenes faded away, and the room turned gray. "And I will miss you too, Inspector Avei Themis. More than you can ever know."

Avei teared up as she turned and headed out of the hatch.

23

The *Delphi* dining hall decor was sedate compared to that of the other venues on the ship. More utilitarian than luxurious. The only nods to grandeur were the white tablecloths and the crystal chandeliers, which were dimmed to mimic candlelight.

Scattered across the bustling room, the guests sat six to a table. Their chatter and laughter filled the space with warmth and camaraderie. The wait staff maneuvered through the tight spaces, delivering dessert and replenishing wine glasses. This was another way Breckin Starliners maintained their superiority over other competitors; serving copious amounts of alcohol at all hours of the day and night. And the more the guests drank, the more money they spent at the different venues. Not surprisingly, the casino came out on top as the biggest moneymaker.

Marsa devoured a sky-high piece of chocolate cake while chatting with the Sycardian couple who sat next to her. A reptilian race, the Sycardians stood over eight feet tall and towered over the author. They eyed the cake with disgust as they shared a bowl of green hlizim fruit from their world. Their needle-sharp teeth gave them a menacing appearance, betraying their true nature. All Sycardians were pacifists and abhorred violence of any kind.

Eadren sat alone at the back of the room, sipping a glass of water. His eyes were locked on the entrance to the dining hall, his napkin balled up in his hand.

At a table nearby, Wilm slouched between Celethe and Julisa. His eyes tracked a beautiful Grilan server as she flitted between guests.

Celethe followed his gaze and frowned. "You promised me, Wilm."

He switched his attention to Avei, who had entered the dining room, her black MSF uniform conspicuous in a sea of sparkling gowns and soft-hued suits.

Celethe, Wilm, and Julisa watched her head to Eadren's table.

"Zarul killed those two people," Celethe said.

Julisa dropped her fork with a clang. "And you know this how?"

Celethe shrugged. "The staff talk."

"They haven't proven anything yet." Julisa threw her napkin on her plate.

"If the staff know, it's only a matter of time before the guests do too. Best to get out in front of that, sis, or we'll have a mutiny on our hands." Wilm's gaze continued to track Avei as she threaded her way between the tables. "MSF is a joke."

"You stay away from the inspector. I'm not sure how much longer I can hold her off from questioning you. Understood?" Julisa tried to hide her worry and failed.

"You're right. I need a plan to manage the guests when news gets out."

Wilm shrugged and turned his attention back to the server. Celethe glowered as he ignored her.

***

Avei turned sideways to get through the last of the tables. Many of the guests followed her progress as she crossed the floor, giving her an itchy feeling between her shoulder blades. She hated being the center of attention. She felt at home in the shadows, which was one of the reasons she excelled at her job. The shadows are where the killers dwell.

Eadren motioned to the chair next to him, which faced the crowd. He appeared to embrace the mantra *never sit with your back to an open room.* She appreciated the gesture, but not tonight. Avei needed to see his reaction when she confronted him. Sitting beside him wouldn't provide a line of sight. With a good deal of discomfort, she turned her back to the crowd and sat across from him.

"I hope you don't mind, I ordered food for us," Eadren said as he studied her.

Had she buried her lack of confidence and doubts deep enough so he didn't catch on to her weakened state? A *little late for that, after I fell apart in Ocia's room.* Her fingers found the burn on the back of her hand and traced the scar. It soothed her and brought peace to her turbulent mind. She had conducted hundreds of interviews. Nothing new here. She needed to relax and let procedural memory take over. "Are the cameras back online?"

Two servers headed their way, laden with plates of meat, vegetables, and a bowl of purple fruit. They set the dishes on the table and left.

The food smelled delicious, and her stomach growled in anticipation. It had been hours since she last ate and everything looked tempting, but the next few minutes required her full attention, so dinner would have to wait.

Not so encumbered, Eadren heaped his plate with a little of everything. "They will be operational in a few hours. Someone accidentally turned on a maintenance routine that's meant to be used only when docked."

The spicy seasonings wafting off the dishes made Avei's mouth water. She watched Eadren pierce a hunk of meat with his fork and eat it. *Get a grip, Themis. Focus.* "Accident? My money's on intentional."

Eadren set his fork down and stared at her. "What are you implying?"

His jaw tensed and his eyes narrowed. Good. She had struck a nerve. Time to ratchet up the pressure and confront him as a liar.

"Nad Ranack, fixer for the rich. The question is, what are you fixing on the *Delphi*? A Breckin, perhaps?"

Eadren went still and Avei felt the doubt creep back. Too soon? Gods, she hated this self-doubt, which she hadn't felt since her first year on the force. Needing to do something with her hands, she grabbed one of the purple fruits and peeled it. Pink juice drenched her fingers. Eadren stared in silence. He was a cool one. She'd give him that. She changed tack.

"Wilm was in that corridor at the time of Caerson's death." Avei ate a slice of the fruit as she observed him. "Now we have two people dead. One, an eyewitness to that fact."

Eadren sat up straight. "Wilm didn't murder anyone."

"Really? I know Wilm likes to harass and beat up innocent people. Murder doesn't seem such a big leap for someone like him." *Why is he protecting a known batterer?* Judging by Eadren's behavior in the ballroom during the guest interviews, the man hadn't liked Wilm manhandling the Grilan server. But who had hired him? Julisa? Wilm? Someone else? She flashed back to the scene in the hallway, when Eadren confronted Julisa about entering the wormhole and continuing their flight to Charnos. *It has to be Julisa.*

"There are forces at work here you do not understand."

"Explain." Eadren was evasive and cunning. Good. Avei settled back in her chair and relished the challenge. The longer the interview, the more she learned.

Eadren sighed and looked away, which only added to her resolve. "Shall we begin again? Wilm Breckin killed Caerson, then murdered Ocia to tie up a loose end. Those are the only forces at work here, Nad Ranack."

A loud hiss came from near the back wall, startling them. They both stood and searched for the source. Sintha crouched behind them with her back raised, growling at a server who tried to shoo her away.

The hatch to the kitchen opened, and Sintha darted through it. A Grilan server entering the dining hall almost dumped their tray of desserts, having to hop over the animal. The hatch closed on yells from the staff and the clatter of pans hitting the floor.

Amused, Avei looked at Eadren, who appeared rankled by the situation. It tickled her, knowing she wasn't the only one to suffer from Marsa's particular brand of aggravation.

"If I don't deal with this, we may be down a chef. Or two." Eadren rose from his chair.

"I can't take this anymore!" Celethe shouted from the nearby table.

Avei and Eadren watched her storm out of the dining room. Wilm had the decency to look embarrassed. He slumped in his chair while Julisa glared at him.

Perfect. The precise opening Avei needed to talk to Celethe Breckin alone. "Looks like she's had enough of his extra-curricular activities." She wiped her fingers on a napkin. "We're not done here, Nad. Meet me in your office in thirty minutes. You are going to tell me what you're really doing on the *Delphi*."

Eadren dropped into his chair and pushed his plate away. He waited until Avei had left the hall before pulling the holographic disk from his pocket and gripping it tightly in his hand.

24

Avei entered the Galaxy Lounge and stopped. Though smaller than she expected, the height of the six booths would shield anyone inside. Each had a narrow opening that provided entry into an intimate space for up to four people. She poked her head into one to find it empty, thinking back to Imara's statement about initially being the only guests in the bar. How would she have known, unless she checked each of the hideaways herself? Something Avei would have to do to ensure her conversation with Celethe remained private. *Did Imara do the same?*

The exquisite bar sat against the back wall, six stools lined next to it. The bar was made from a molded piece of blue ingeru, a rare metal found on a moon in the Senat system. The lighted display filled the wall behind the bar and displayed dozens of bottles of alcohol. Avei could kill for a drink right now, but her professionalism prohibited giving in to the craving.

A quick search of the booths came up empty. She turned her attention to the massive window that covered one entire wall opposite the booths and framed the swirling colors of the wormhole. Celethe stood in front of it with a glass of water in her hand and her back to the room.

A Calista bartender entered from a small hatch at the back of the bar. Avei caught his eye and pointed to the MSF badge on her belt, which also held a laser pistol and a military-grade knife. Not having jurisdiction over the *Delphi* didn't prohibit her from wearing the uniform. With a killer on the loose, it was essential to keep her gun close. She motioned with her head for him to leave. He nodded and stepped back through the narrow hatch.

Avei studied the deep, rope-like scars on Celethe's right ankle. She had an idea how she had got them and debated whether to confront Celethe with her suspicions now or wait until she had earned her trust. Avei once again traced the burn on the back of her hand. She decided that coddling the woman with Zarul loose on the ship and ten hours left in the wormhole made little sense.

"Hello, Mrs. Breckin." Avei headed to the woman.

Celethe stiffened and continued to stare out of the window.

Avei settled in next to her and looked up. Almost as tall as her sister-in-law, Celethe towered over her. As she so often did, Avei wished she had inherited her mother's height.

To break the ice, she began with a softball approach. "It's near impossible to get a ship released during an active investigation. Julisa Breckin has powerful friends."

Celethe turned her glittery blue eyes on her. "Let's skip the small talk, Inspector."

Okay, I wasn't expecting that. Someone else who liked to get straight to the point. "Works for me. Tell me who Caerson Mercer is to you."

Celethe gave her the side-eye but remained silent. She gripped her glass so tight that water spilled down the window.

Another solid response to Caerson's name. There could be no doubt anymore. Celethe knew him. That solidified an avenue Avei had wanted to pursue if she ever got Celethe alone. "You almost fainted earlier when you heard his name."

Celethe studied the symphony of colors through thick panes of transparent resin designed to mimic the clarity of glass. "I told you I hadn't eaten."

Avei had a far-fetched theory of how Caerson and Celethe knew each other. Time to roll it out with the expectation it'd rattled her enough, she would drop her guard. "Your eyes are quite unusual. You have Thule ancestry."

"Is that a crime?"

"Just making an observation. Caerson had iridescent eyes too. Coincidence?"

"Lots of people have Thule ancestry."

"Actually, it's quite rare."

Celethe finally turned to her. "What do you really want, Inspector Themis?"

Avei glanced at the entry hatch, expecting Julisa or Wilm to arrive at any moment. It surprised her that she'd managed this long with Celethe without one of them barging in. Time to turn up the heat. "A witness places your husband in the hallway around the time Caerson died."

Celethe sighed. "My husband is not a murderer."

"People keep saying that to me, which I really don't get, given Wilm's multiple battery charges over the years. He clearly has no issue with violence and shows no remorse or willingness to change his ways, as evidenced by his behavior toward the Grilan server during my interviews today."

Celethe flinched as if she had been struck. Her cheeks reddened and her breath quickened.

"Has your husband ever harmed you?"

Celethe's mouth tightened. "Despite Wilm's obvious flaws, he is good to me. Are we done here?"

"Not quite. I've seen scars like the ones you have on your right ankle." If her hunch was right, Avei understood the deep trauma the woman had gone through, and it troubled her to even bring it up. Someone with that kind of past would do anything to keep it buried. Including protecting the person responsible for saving them from a soul-crushing life. And the reason she needed to ask.

Celethe had a white-knuckle grip on her water glass. For the first time, she appeared unsure of herself, making it difficult for Avei to continue, but she moved closer and lowered her voice. "We raided a brothel last year and freed 22 men and women chained to a wall by their ankles."

Celethe took a long moment before responding. "A sad story. I'm genuinely sorry for those people."

"Anyone who escapes such a terrible life would do anything to not go back. Maybe even cover up a murder."

Celethe put the glass on a small table next to her. Her glittering eyes scrutinized Avei and then focused on the burn scars on her face and hands. "We all bear scars,

Inspector. Some are inside, hidden away, and others are outside for the world to see. What I have found is that people who choose to keep their scars visible do so for a variety of reasons. Some wear them as a badge of honor. Others keep them as a reminder they're a survivor and can handle whatever comes their way. The rest wear them as a punishment for their actions."

Celethe had hit a nerve. Avei thought again of her time in hospital, how her doctor had pleaded with her to have her scars removed. It was a simple procedure that erased the burns and replaced them with new skin, and she had refused. When D.I. Skora and her parents asked her why, she didn't have an answer. Now Celethe had defined the reason and it shook her to her core.

Celethe stepped away from the window. "My husband didn't kill Caerson Mercer. And neither did I."

Celethe walked out of the Galaxy Lounge. Avei didn't try to stop her. She leaned her forehead against the window and closed her eyes. Her fingers trembled as they traced the scars on her face.

25

Avei leaned on the wall, arms crossed in front of her chest. She always preferred standing when running an interview. It made her feel more in control of the situation. A quick scan of the office pointed to Eadren's temporary status as the *Delphi*'s security chief.

Devoid of personal items, the office took tedium to a new level. Eadren sat behind the gray metal desk with two metal chairs in front of it. Recessed cabinets covered one wall. Several small alcoves on another wall sat empty. A monitor floated nearby, displaying a stunning image of Mount Tui, a famous volcano on the planet Suiva. Green and yellow fauna covered the mountain, providing the only color in the room.

Avei made eye contact with Sezin, who stood nearby. Their holoball floated above them. They wore their MSF uniform along with five gold slashes on their sleeves. One more than D.I. Skora had as Deputy Inspector. Sezin had three laser guns on their belt and a large purple flower stuck in a fourth holster. Avei didn't even try to guess its significance. Their beloved pipe peeked out from their jacket pocket. Avei sent a prayer to all the gods and goddesses to keep Sezin from pulling it out and smoking it during the interview.

"Let's begin with why you're masquerading as the *Delphi*'s Chief of Security."

Eadren shot a glance at Sezin, who crossed their arms and smiled.

"It's typical for Sezin to join me during my interviews," Avei said. "Please, Mr. Ranack, continue."

Irritation flashed over his face. "I prefer Eadren Varan until we reach Charnos."

Good, he denied nothing. Yet. "Which Breckin hired you?"

"Julisa."

"Why?"

Eadren ran his fingers through his blue hair, green cat eyes focused on everything but Avei. She stayed silent while he worked through whatever conflicted him. Finally, he settled back in his chair and made eye contact. "A crime syndicate bought up Wilm's considerable gambling debts. Then extorted him into transporting their drug, Zenith. Two months ago, a *Delphi* crew member discovered a sizable shipment of Zenith hidden in food containers in one of the storage rooms."

Avei straightened up and shared a look with Sezin. Finally, concrete facts in what had been a very nebulous case. "Julisa hired you to find the guilty party."

"It didn't take long to trace the shipment to Wilm. Not too shocking, given his sketchy background. To keep the Mernin government from seizing everything she owns, Julisa is required to hand Wilm over to the Charnos authorities by noon tomorrow."

Avei settled into the chair across from Eadren. "Why all the cloak and dagger? You could've turned Wilm over to MSF on Mernin." An idea occurred to her, which explained why they had endangered everyone on the ship. Her face flushed red with anger. "Unless Julisa negotiated a cushy prison for him, like the Yapho Penitentiary on Charnos."

Sezin walked over to the desk and leaned on it, eye level with Eadren, primed to deliver their opinion. Avei didn't stop them.

Eadren pulled away, but it didn't stop Sezin. "A prison infamous for its laxness and amoral staff, who never saw a bribe they did not like. The Yapho population includes the wealthiest people in the Kressa System, who serve time when they can't buy off the Tribunal. Also known as the Yapho Palace, the prison caters to the needs of all its guests, most of whom can come and go as they please. There is one unbreakable rule. The prisoners must spend one full day a week inside. The Tribunal has tried to shut it down for years, without success."

Eadren had the decency to look ashamed. That didn't change anything. The decision to continue to Charnos had trapped everyone on the ship with a murderer.

Avei's anger rose, and she did nothing to moderate it. "Two people died so that this creep can continue his life of luxury in Yapho," she said with venom. "When Ocia died, we knew we had a murderer on board. As Chief of Security, you could have overridden Julisa, and the captain, and moved the *Delphi* to the spacehub. Or, at the very least, off-boarded the guests and all non-essential crew, before continuing to Charnos."

"You think I didn't try?" Eadren's light blue skin turned violet. He appeared as angry as she felt.

"Clearly not hard enough. Why didn't you come to me for help?"

"I didn't know what she planned to do. I found out five minutes before I got the call about Ocia. By then, the wormhole had a grip on the *Delphi* and pulling out of the gravitational lock meant significant structural damage and a risk to everyone onboard."

If Julisa hadn't told Eadren about her plans, she didn't trust him. Or she knew he would talk her out of continuing to Charnos. The second scenario seemed the more likely, given his angry indignation. Either way, Avei had an opportunity to exploit the pair's distrust of one another.

"Wilm is a person of interest in the murders of Caerson Mercer and Ocia Doni, and I want him locked up. It's the least we can do to keep the guests and crew safe."

"He didn't kill them."

"You keep saying that." Avei glared at him.

"What is your evidence to back up that assertion?" Sezin asked.

"During his last voyage four weeks ago, I injected a tracker into him when he passed out. I've had him under surveillance from the moment he stepped foot on the *Delphi* yesterday. Wilm never went near Ocia's room."

"Then you have solid proof that puts Wilm in the hallway with Caerson Mercer." The man knew this and had said nothing, making him a potential accomplice to murder. Risky, even for a problem-solver for the affluent. Eadren didn't strike Avei as stupid enough to go to prison for a client. Something else was going on.

Eadren folded his hands on his desk, as if preparing to chastise a classroom of unruly children. "Wilm arrived after Caerson died, making his presence nothing more than a bystander to an unfortunate incident. He had no interaction with Ocia before her death. And Dr. Hueson informed me of your request to check for fingerprints on Caerson's body. He reports there are none."

"That proves nothing, and you know it. The fingerprints were a long shot and Wilm could easily have run into Ocia before she returned to her room after her visit to medical."

"Or arranged for her to receive food or water laced with venom," Sezin said.

Eadren stared at them in exasperation. "The man is rarely sober. You've seen him. Honestly, do you think he's in the right frame of mind to plan a murder using toxic venom and dangerous spiders? And to pull it off eight times, when you include the first six Zarul victims. His hands never stop shaking. Wilm Breckin is a raging alcoholic who is only alive because of expensive weekly medical treatments to reverse the damage he's inflicting on his body. Without them, he'd already be dead."

As much as Avei wanted to rail against what Eadren was saying, she conceded he might be right. Unless Wilm faked his chronic intoxication, it seemed unlikely he could have successfully pulled off the eight murders. Still, she had no intention of sharing her doubts. When Eadren confessed to his actual role on the *Delphi*, it didn't satisfy the itch in the back of her mind that he hid more secrets. The ever-present doubt crept in again. Her fingers sought the scar on her hand and traced it. The constant vacillation sapped her energy and she was getting damn tired of feeling this way.

Avei looked up and caught Eadren watching her. Did he see the turmoil inside of her? Best to finish her questions and end the interview. “Do you know of any connection between Wilm and Caerson?”

“Honestly, I don’t. Caerson’s and Imara’s names popped up on the manifest just before boarding at the spaceport.”

The comm screen next to the hatch lit up. “Chief Varan, you’re needed in the casino,” a woman’s voice said. “A guest is disputing his loss at the poker table.”

Eadren sighed. “On my way.”

“I’ll alert them.” The comm clicked off.

“Inspector, I apologize. We’ll need to end our discussion early.” Eadren rose and stared at Avei.

She held his gaze. “We’re not finished. Consider our conversation delayed.”

“Understood.” Eadren motioned to the hatch.

Avei walked into the corridor with Sezin. They watched Eadren hurry away.

“He’s holding out on us.” Avei tensed, waiting for Sezin’s reply.

“No doubt about it. Our fixer’s full of secrets and he isn’t sharing all of them with us.”

Avei let out a long breath and allowed her thoughts free rein for the first time in months. Where they landed surprised her. “What if his fixer role is a cover for something else?”

26

Imara held a glass of champagne and gazed out at the billowing colors of the wormhole. A half-empty bottle chilled in a bucket on the table next to her. Bright yellow dresses littered the bed and couch, an explosion of sunshine. Shoved into the corner by the bathroom, a battered metal trunk sat with its lid open. Caerson's meager possessions were scattered around it.

Imara had learned early in life that beauty had power over others. When wielded with intention, she knew how to intoxicate the most disciplined adversary. The window mirrored her image and she smiled. The bright yellow minidress fit like a glove and highlighted her generous assets. She preened this way and that, pretending a mob of Nexus reporters were taking her picture, until she caught sight of Caerson's belongings.

Imara settled against the window and sighed. Time to acknowledge the jitters she had tried to ignore. It was dangerous to move forward alone with their plan. Equal parts of excitement and fear battled one another for dominance. If she succeeded, she'd become one of the biggest Nexus stars and the richest, making her dreams come true. If she failed, she faced the possibility of death. The inspector said someone else had died, and the killer was tying up loose ends. Her fear spiked. She was a loose end. *Why not let the whole thing go? Just lock the hatch and stay in the room until the ship reaches Charnos. Better to be alive and poor than dead.*

Could she really walk away from all that money? Enough to buy everything she needed prior to meeting the Nexus producer. Expensive clothes, cosmetic enhancements, headshots... the list went on and on. Never in her life had she been so close to achieving her dream. Damn Caerson for not telling her the producer's name or where to meet them. She frowned at the small pile of Caerson's belongings. When she got home, she'd tear their little apartment apart looking for the information.

A tendril of unease crept back towards her. She gulped the champagne and poured herself another generous glass. Liquid courage.

Moving forward with the plan meant waltzing into any Nexus office decked out in the finest clothing and having them beg her to be on their show. She would play hard to get and make them work. But not too hard. She'd come across as sweet and unspoiled but also smart and savvy. Nexus needed to know they couldn't take advantage of her and rip her off. It'd be a tightrope-walk between the two sides, but she felt confident in her ability to come out on top.

Goddess knew she had dreamed of being on the Nexus since the age of seven, when she caught a glimpse of one of their talk shows through an open window in the commune leader's home. All those beautiful people sitting around having a conversation. Acting like they didn't have a care in the world, while she stood there with her backside throbbing with pain from the latest beating for taking extra food and then lying about it. She experienced envy for the first time in her life. From that moment on, she had plotted to free herself from the Bhindoir commune and become one of those people she had seen on the screen.

The comm device next to the door buzzed and startled her out of her reverie. *About time.* She set the glass down and smoothed her dress. "Enter."

The hatch opened onto an empty corridor. Simmering fear now flared into a conflagration. She clenched her hands tight to stop the trembling and headed to the hatch. If she showed fear it would mean handing her power over to them. If she wanted to survive, she couldn't allow that to happen. "If you think you scare me, think again." She leaned into the empty corridor. "Hello? Anyone there?"

The grenwal crouched on the ceiling above her. The behemoth spider, with 18-inch legs and a ten-inch hourglass body, crawled into the room from the open hatch.

Imara stepped back and the hatch to the room closed. *Did they lose their nerve*? No matter. Peddling their secret to the highest bidder brought in the same amount of money and even had the chance of bringing in more.

The grenwal crept across the ceiling, its dark, viridian-colored body camouflaged by the shadows and shallow recesses of the dark gray ceiling.

Imara smiled and returned to her champagne. She picked up the glass and toasted her image in the window.

The grenwal settled above her and flattened itself.

Imara took a sip of champagne and reveled in relief. She didn't need to deal with that monster. As soon as they docked in Charnos, she'd get herself to the closest Nexus station and start a bidding war. She'd give them just enough information to pique their interest. Giggling with delight in the knowledge that her dreams were about to come true. Like purchasing one of those cute condos next to the Nexus headquarters, where the biggest stars lived. Even the producers. She'd strut the hallway in a micro-mini yellow dress and accidentally stumble into a producer. He'd apologize for knocking her down and then insist she audition for a part on his new show. It had to be the right show. One that brought instant stardom. She needed to do research first and choose her mark with care. He needed to be handsome, of course. Rich, most definitely. Well connected, a no-brainer. Imara giggled again, lost in her fantasy.

The grenwal sprung onto her head. Its weight sent her careening into the window, shattering the champagne glass and plunging shards of it into her palm. The spider moved around and covered her face, muffling her screams. Its legs wrapped tight around her skull.

Survival instincts overrode terror. Imara's fingers found its hairy abdomen and yanked. It gripped harder and probed her face with its fanged jaws. Consumed with fear and unable to see, Imara stumbled across the room and collided with the bed. A pile of dresses toppled over and twisted around her feet. She crashed to the ground in a tangle of clothes.

The grenwal hunched. Its fangs penetrated deep into her face and pulsed. Pain seared deep into her skull, then spread through her body in a cascade of fiery agony.

The spider released its hold and leaped away. Venom filled Imara's eyes. Her beautiful mouth and nose were a ruined mess. Blinded and besieged with pain, she crawled in a circle, feeling for the hatch twenty feet away. A gown rustled under her. She grabbed it and scrubbed the venom from her eyes. Vision clouded by an orange haze, she struggled to her knees and spotted the glimmer of green light on the display next to the hatch.

The spider jumped from her right and landed on her shoulders, wrapping its legs around her neck and face once more. Imara's screams echoed around the room as her fingers tore at it, trying to pull it off. She gripped a leg and wrenched it from its body. The creature hissed, then sank its fangs into her neck and gave a shake. Imara sprung to her feet in a blind panic, all reason gone. The arachnid clung to her as she raced toward the hatch. It opened and she ran out, slamming into the wall across from her room. Semi-conscious, Imara fell to the ground, still locked in the arachnid's embrace.

Her yellow dress twisted around her torso as she writhed on the ground. Orange foam bubbled from her mouth and nose. In a moment of lucidity, she wished she had let the plan go, and locked the damn hatch. Her body contorted.

A small gasp and Imara stilled.

The spider released its grip and scurried up the wall to the ceiling, then headed down the hallway.

27

A small crowd gathered in the hallway outside Imara's room. Dr. Hueson stood apart, a medical bag slung over his shoulder. Captain Dimphi and Eadren huddled around Avei and AI Sezin, who squatted next to Imara's body. Three security officers stood nearby.

The gleaming white, gold-veined walls reflected their fractured images and added to the strangeness of the situation. The holoball that provided Sezin's holographic form floated above them. Sezin wore blue coveralls and the MSF forensic team cap.

"That poor woman. I've never seen... it's just horrifying. Sweet Goddess Mima, guide her into the loving arms of whatever deity she believes in." Captain Dimphi kissed his fingertips and touched his forehead.

Eadren put his hand on Captain Dimphi's shoulder and gently pulled him away. "Let's give Inspector Themis some room." He guided the captain to Dr. Hueson, who appeared grateful for the company. Eadren headed back to the body.

Avei studied Imara's destroyed face, which appeared frozen in terror. With gloved hands, she turned Imara's head and found the second bite on the back of her neck. Avei sat back on her heels and nodded at Sezin. "It bit her twice, like the other victims. Same MO. Same spider. I'm certain it's Zarul."

"Agreed. The likelihood of a copycat killer is so low it isn't worth talking about."

"Do you think the grenwal's still around?" Eadren did a three-sixty as he scanned the surrounding area.

"It depends. If Zarul stayed to watch the attack, they would've taken the grenwal with them. Although…." Avei stood and tapped her chin. The guest who reported hearing Imara's screams called while the attack was taking place and then she, Sezin and the three men had been on the scene for at least two minutes. That left Zarul little time to collect the spider. "We got here pretty fast. There's a chance the grenwal is nearby."

Sezin stood. They changed their attire to that of an old Earth big game hunter with khaki knickerbockers and shirt, tall black boots, and a pith helmet. A large rifle hung from their shoulder.

Avei watched Eadren give Sezin a double take, confusion on his face. She hid a smile.

Captain Dimphi hunched over and stared at the ceiling. "Are we in danger?"

"I recommend locking the ship down until I capture the grenwal. If it's still loose." Avei studied the area around Imara's body.

Captain Dimphi raised his wrist device and spoke. "Bridge, put me on ship-wide speaker. Lock all doors thirty seconds after I finish my message. Understood?"

A voice came through his wrist device. "Understood. You are good to go, Captain."

"Attention all passengers and staff. This is Captain Dimphi. We need to implement an emergency lockdown for a short time. All doors will lock in thirty seconds, so please quickly head to the nearest venue or room. Security will do a sweep of all floors for anyone who can't get to a room in time. If you find yourself locked out, please remain where you are, and security will come to you and bring you to a secure location. There is no need to panic. We appreciate your patience during this drill. The thirty-second clock starts now. Captain Dimphi, out."

Avei studied the ceiling and noticed a line of orange spots. Sezin followed her gaze and nodded. They both walked around the body. Avei appreciated that Sezin mimicked the actions of the living while out in public spaces, instead of walking through the body as they easily could. She experienced another rush of guilt about abandoning Sezin when she left the force and hoped Uma would treat her friend with the respect they deserved. Avei stopped the maudlin thought and admonished herself. Recrimination could wait. Imara deserved her full attention.

She searched behind her and found Dr. Hueson and the captain standing next to one another. Both trembled with fear. "Doc, where are you with the antidote?"

"Less than an hour. I had to produce the ingredients one at a time in the synthesizer." His voice shook. "There isn't anything I can do for Ms. Tiniba. If it's okay with you, I'll head back to medical to finish it."

Eadren pointed to one of his security team. “Escort Dr. Hueson to medical and Captain Dimphi to the bridge.” He smiled when both men sighed with relief.

Dr. Hueson set his medical bag on the floor. “I’ll leave this behind just in case. There’s a syringe with Lorestal in there.” He followed the security officer and Captain Dimphi, both men jogging to put distance between themselves and the grenwal.

Eadren turned to the remaining two officers. “Stay here with the body until the medical team arrives with the hover sled.”

The two officers, both human men, shared nervous looks and moved closer to each other.

Avei and Sezin followed the orange drops of venom, the holoball trailing behind Sezin. Eadren walked behind them. As they rounded the bend, the spots became smaller, and lighter in color.

“We’ve lost the trail.” Avei stopped under the last visible speck.

“Or Zarul removed the spider,” Sezin said.

“Let’s hope that isn’t the case. They could use the grenwal to kill again.” Avei searched the corridor as it stretched ahead of them. A massive green spider would stand out like a neon sign against the white walls and ceiling. Her eyes slid to the alcove next to them, containing a large vase and a thick yellow plant with triangle-shaped leaves. The nooks would make an excellent place for the spider to hide while it recovered.

The displays outside of all the hatches turned red and made a ping sound that echoed throughout the hall as every guest room door locked.

"I feel better knowing everyone is behind a locked door," Avei said.

"What's the timing from contact with the venom to death?" Eadren sidled up to her, his eyes darting all around.

"Three to ten minutes. With two bites, a minute or less." Avei eased the vase from the wall. Sezin's holoball darted behind the vase and then popped out again. "Nothing."

Avei slid the vase back into place, and the three of them headed to the next alcove.

"Where are the Breckins?" Avei asked.

"Wilm's in the Casino. Julisa is in the dining hall. We think Celethe's in the Breckins' rooms."

She raised her eyebrows. "You think?"

"We lost track of her. Is she a suspect now?"

"Everyone's a suspect." Avei spotted the next alcove and headed toward it. "Why are you really on the *Delphi*?"

"I already told you." Eadren's face flushed violet when he caught Sezin studying him.

"You told me something." Avei approached the alcove with a vase of mint-green flowers with blue stems and searched the dark interior. She spotted a purple mass hunched behind it. Finally, a break. "Found it."

Eadren spoke into the device on his wrist. "We've got the grenwal. I need one of you to bring a container."

"Copy that." The security officer's voice came through Eadren's comm device.

Avei pulled her gun from the holster. "What's behind this wall?

"Guest room." Eadren frowned. "We can't risk laser fire going through the wall and hitting someone."

"Agreed." Avei slid her gun back into the holster. "We do this the hard way."

Sezin pulled her rifle off her shoulder and pointed it at the alcove.

Eadren glanced at Avei with a worried look.

Avei shook her head when Sezin kneeled on one knee and bore-sighted the rifle. "You know you can't do anything with that rifle?"

"It's makes me feel like I'm contributing. And I'll take this moment to mention once again that we need to get me one of those portable holomatter generators. Then I *can* do something. I really hate being little more than a walking photograph."

"Topic for another day. Mr. Varan, best if you back up a bit."

Eadren stumbled backwards until he stood ten feet away. "Far enough? Should I move further away?"

"You're good there." Avei approached the alcove. It had been a few months since she had wrangled a large arachnoid at the Themis Institute of Arachnology. She felt a flush of pride. The antidotes and medicines discovered and manufactured at the Institute saved countless lives. No more homicide cases meant no more novels, and no more Ms. Baako in her life. In two days, the reign of Inspector Themis ended. Marsa needed a new character, or she faced ruin.

Something tickled the back of Avei's mind. Could Marsa Baako be Zarul? Was this an elaborate plan to get Inspector Themis back on a case?

The spider stood and jittered, pushing all thoughts from Avei's mind as she settled in front of it.

"That thing is terrifying," Eadren said. "I never knew spiders got that big."

"You should have seen her pet," Sezin said. "Magnus was twice the size of the grenwal."

Eadren gave Avei a sideways look. "Please tell me you don't have a pet spider."

"I used to. Magnus was an Andior, and I had him for thirty years. My parents gave him to me for my fourth birthday. Best gift ever. Magnus died a couple of years ago, from old age." Avei still felt the painful void left behind after his passing. He had taken a big piece of her heart with him.

Eadren stared at her with compassion. "I'm so sorry for your loss."

Tears pricked behind her eyes as she turned away from him. *Gods, I've turned into a crier like my dad.* She took a couple of deep breaths as she approached the alcove.

"Time to bag this spider." Avei gripped the vase and edged it away from the wall. The grenwal clung to it in a creepy hug. Good. It allowed her to get behind it.

"Careful, Inspector." Sezin's rifle tracked the grenwal.

Eadren backpedaled further down the hall when Avei set the vase on the ground. "That thing is huge."

The grenwal released its hold on the vase and sprung onto her leg. A moment of panic fled when instinct took over. Avei grabbed it with both hands and wrenched it off her leg before it bit her. It took effort to keep hold of the flailing spider. She had nothing but pity for the poor creature. Someone had trained the gentleness out of this beautiful arachnid and created a raging monster.

Eadren gaped at the massive spider as it tried to break Avei's grasp. "What can I do?"

"Stay back, like the inspector asked. She's got it handled." The look of concern on Sezin's face contradicted their comment.

Avei struggled to keep her grip. She needed to work her fingers up to the middle section, between the spider's cephalothorax and abdomen. The grenwal bucked and twisted and didn't make it easy. It would bite her the first chance it got.

"What if you shove it against the wall?" Sezin asked. "Work your hands up the body."

"Excellent idea." Avei pressed the struggling spider to the wall next to the alcove. She moved her right hand to the narrow section above its abdomen, then slid her left hand into place. She squeezed tight when the grenwal tried to climb the wall. It went limp and its seven legs drooped. "Much harder than it should have been. I've never seen a grenwal so aggressive. They're usually very docile."

"What's that on its back?" Sezin pointed to a small silver disk embedded near its cephalothorax.

Avei held up the grenwal to get a look. "My guess is the killer's controlling it using some kind of transmitter."

"What do we do?" Eadren asked. "Kill it?"

"MSF rules state a weapon used in a murder has to be taken into custody," Sezin said.

An agonizing decision. Avei loved arachnids, even this one. Someone had abused it, altering its passive nature. Reversing the damage seemed unlikely. Unfortunately, as long as it lived, it could kill again. MSF had no choice but to kill it. The question remained: do it now, or euthanize it when they reach Charnos? Better to wait than risk Zarul being freed on a technicality because she'd destroyed the evidence.

"Sezin's right. It's murdered three people, and its venom killed two more. We need to keep it alive if possible."

Avei scanned the unconscious spider and noted its missing leg and fluid oozing from the wound. "Imara put up a fight. She pulled off one of its legs."

Eadren shuddered and kept his distance. "I expect I'll be having nightmares for a while."

One of the security officers dashed around the bend with a small plastic box. "Found this in the doctor's—" He slowed to a stop when he saw the massive spider gripped in Avei's hands.

Eadren and Avei stared at the inadequate container and then at the officer, who eyed the grenwal with trepidation. He noticed them staring at him.

"What? It's the only thing I could find in Doc's bag," the officer said.

"You didn't think to grab the large medical bag you found it in?" Eadren asked.

The officer groaned, then sprinted back down the hall.

28

Avei and Eadren watched the grenwal attack the sides of the cylinder-shaped clear container sitting on the operating table in the medical wing, a pile of surgical instruments dumped next to it. Sezin stood across from them.

"Now we know how the killer is controlling the grenwal. When the little device on its back vibrates, it can feel it through the carapace covering its cephalothorax," Avei said.

"Ingenious, if you ask me. Evil, yes. But very clever." Sezin had changed their outfit and was now wearing a white coat with a pocket protector, several pens stuck in it. They also had thick, black-framed glasses.

"Can you remove the disk?" Eadren asked.

"Not without killing it." Avei questioned her decision to keep the grenwal alive. With Zarul still loose, leaving it alive came at a hefty risk. Shooting it an even bigger risk if the laser fire penetrated a wall and killed someone or pierced the hull. Employing a gel commonly used on burn victims would coat its body and suffocate it. Its death would be slow, cruel, and pointless. They'd reach Charnos before it died. She knew of a dozen other methods to kill it in a more humane manner, but it didn't matter. The choice was now out of their hands.

"Is it prudent to keep this thing alive with Zarul roaming free?" Eadren's question mirrored her own thoughts.

Avei sighed, wishing she had another answer for him. "We neutralized the grenwal and it no longer poses a threat. That removes any choice we have in the matter."

"MSF protocol is to preserve it as evidence," Sezin said. "If it gets loose and becomes a threat again, we can kill it."

"And we will," Avei said with more force than she intended.

"I don't like this one bit." Eadren glared at the spider as if he wanted it to kill it himself. "I'll get the doc to lock it in a cabinet."

Avei contemplated Eadren as he watched the spider test the security of its prison. They had hours left in the wormhole, and another murder on their hands. She needed his help, but did she trust him? She glanced at Sezin, who gave her a slight nod. Working together for so long, they knew each other's thoughts. No other AI partnership had achieved the tight bond they had.

A ship-wide announcement from Captain Dimphi sounded through the comm. "Attention all passengers and crew. The temporary lockdown is lifted. You may move freely about the ship. Thank you for your patience."

Avei sighed and turned to Eadren. "Is that prudent?"

Eadren shook his head. "No. Not at all. Julisa overruled Captain Dimphi and me. The passengers pay a small fortune to fly on a Breckin Starliner and she felt the short lockdown had inconvenienced them enough. Plus, she is trying to minimize the bad publicity that will come from the deaths of Caerson, Imara and Ocia."

Sezin crossed their arms. "Risky move if Zarul has more venom on them."

Eadren held up his hand. "I'm not disagreeing with you."

Not mollified, Sezin grew six inches taller than Eadren, and looked down at him.

"It's time to come clean. Tell us who you really are, because I'm not buying the fixer for the rich scenario."

Avei wondered what his response would be. Would they finally get the truth about who he truly was?

Eadren straightened, his face rigid with tension. "You're putting me in a difficult position."

"How many more need to die before you get comfortable?" *Is he Zarul?* A gut feeling said no, without the usual doubt. A pleasant surprise.

Eadren appeared to wrestle with the question and after a heavy sigh he walked to the hatch and closed it. He spun around and faced them. "My name is Eadren Omu. I'm a Mernin Security Drug Enforcement Inspector working on a deep-cover assignment. Nad Ranack and Eadren Varan are my aliases."

Avei pulled back in surprise. "I didn't expect that." Given Wilm's exploits as a drug smuggler, the size of his operation, and the name of his family, it made sense that MSF would insert an undercover cop. They needed someone on the inside to give detailed information back to headquarters and to guide the family's decisions. She turned to Sezin, who shrugged.

"Until we are out of this infernal wormhole, I can't access MSF records to confirm his real identity. Eadren's explanation sounds plausible, and I didn't detect untruthfulness." Sezin looked thoughtful. "There is one way to confirm his identity. Who is your assigned AI?"

"Marmereck, who I had to leave behind. He may never forgive me for doing that."

"MSF's policy is firm. No AIs while undercover. Nexus has documented the MSF Artificial Intelligence program extensively. If an undesirable discovered your AI, it would put the operation and your life in jeopardy," Sezin said. "I'm acquainted with Marmereck. He has a very odd and unique hobby. Tell me what it is."

Eadren chuckled as he moved closer to Avei and Sezin. "Cehinel throat singing, which he does often. At first it drove me crazy. Now, I find it oddly soothing."

Sezin smiled at Avei. "Marmereck loves to sing. He constantly regales us AIs in our holographic bar, where we throw back a few drinks in-between cases. I also remember Marmereck telling me he had a Suiven partner whom the ladies loved. I believe the chief is telling the truth."

Eadren blushed violet. "I'm half Suiven. My mother's mostly human, and I promise I'm telling you the truth."

"Truth? Like when you said you were Nad Ranack?" Avei hated being tricked and wasn't ready to let him off the hook yet. "Why didn't you tell me about your operation as soon as I boarded the *Delphi*?" He should have read her in from the start. He was holding back something important. "Who does Julisa think you are?"

"Ms. Breckin believes I'm Nad Ranack. And you're right. I should have read you in, and I regret not doing so."

"Who takes Wilm to Yapho Penitentiary? You?" Avei asked.

Eadren didn't hide his anger. "Wilm isn't going to prison."

The law was crystal-clear, and everyone had to abide by it. Even a wealthy Breckin. "Transporting drugs is an automatic 20-year sentence. No matter who they are." Avei bristled at the thought Wilm might once again escape being held accountable for his criminal behavior.

"Ordinarily, yes. I'd agree with you. However, given the million-plus deaths associated with Zenith, the Tribunal would be more open to cutting a deal with Mr. Breckin," Sezin said.

Eadren nodded. "Wilm agreed to turn over his contacts to stay out of prison."

"Is Julisa aware of this deal?" Avei folded her arms across her chest.

Eadren sighed and settled against the operating table, his back to the grenwal. "Neither knows what the other is doing. I've had to play both sides for the last two months." The grenwal charged the side of the container, causing it to rock into Eadren. He shot across the room and only stopped when he reached the hatch. He spun in a circle as he tried to check his back for the spider.

Avei and Sezin tried to stifle a laugh and failed. Their laughter filled the space as Eadren remained across the room.

He quivered from head to toe, then smiled at their mirth. "I fear spiders with an intensity that is hard to explain."

“They have that effect on people. Especially big ones.” Avei’s father always said laughter was the cure for all that ails you. She felt lighter. The weight of despair and depression that had buried her these last few months had lessened a bit. “I have more questions for you.”

“Fire away.” Eadren moved closer but kept a few feet between himself and the massive arachnid.

“Why did you keep Julisa in the dark? You don’t need her.”

“If Julisa found out he made a deal to turn on the Iscun—”

“Wait. Wilm’s in bed with the Iscun Crime Syndicate?” Avei reared back at the news, which cleared up a lot of unanswered questions. It made sense the Iscun were the ones peddling Zenith, given their history of creating designer drugs. “Their brutality toward disloyalty is legendary. The Iscun will kill everyone Wilm knows if he’s discovered as the one who betrayed them.”

“Which is why they are so powerful,” Sezin said. “And why they’ve been so successful over the years with their many criminal enterprises. They keep their army of underlings in check through fear and intimidation.”

“And precisely why Julisa would do everything in her power to stop her brother,” Eadren said.

“And let’s not forget, if Julisa forced Wilm to drop his deal, you wouldn’t get his Iscun contacts,” Avei said.

Eadren’s hand drifted to his right pocket. “That drug has killed far too many good people. The only way to get it off the streets is to shut down the Iscun. We can’t do that without Wilm’s help, no matter how we feel about him.”

"Transporting Wilm to Charnos instead of turning him in to MSF on Mernin got people killed on the *Delphi*. Maybe we wouldn't have stopped Caerson's or Ocia's deaths, but we could have prevented Imara's if we had returned to the spacehub."

"Something that will haunt me for the rest of my life." A mournful look passed over Eadren's face.

Avei could empathize. Despite his subterfuge, she felt herself softening toward him. "I know a little something about that."

"We've captured the grenwal, which is great. But don't lose sight of the fact Zarul may still have venom," Sezin said.

"You're right. They may not be done."

"Let me help you find Zarul." Eadren leaned forward, a plea in his eyes.

Avei drummed her fingers on the table. Truth be told, they needed his help. "Sezin, what's your confidence level that Eadren is speaking the truth about being an MSF undercover agent?"

"98.9%."

Avei trusted Sezin and Sezin trusted Eadren. "Bring up a combined crime board with all of Zarul's victims."

A hologram of the Zarul Crime Board appeared. On the right side, the images of the five men and one woman. On the left, the *Delphi* victims, Caerson, Ocia and Imara.

"Sezin, put the original crime scenes in chronological order."

Eadren brought fresh eyes to the case. He may see something they missed.

"The holoball isn't powerful enough to sustain my image and the crime scenes simultaneously. I need to go offline." Sezin disappeared and 3D images of the crime scenes filled the space across the front of the operating bay.

"Zarul's first six victims lived in a small corner of the Krussa system. We believe the cases are related to one another. The two miners lived on a moon that orbits a gas giant, and the next three victims worked on the same freighter that ran supplies to the mine. The last victim is a female who owned a brothel in L'reus, where the freighter often docked for fuel and shore leave for the crew."

"All the killings started when I had just gone undercover. I saw the news reports on Nexus."

"Sezin, overlay the spiders."

"Copy that." Sezin's voice rang out from the holoball.

Small and black, the zarultalzin spider appeared over the first two male victims. A grenwal hovered over the next three male victims. The twivorg, a rat-like spider with twelve legs and massive fangs, hung over the woman.

Avei walked through the lineup of scenes and pointed to the two men. One lay on the floor of an abandoned factory, wrapped in bindings. Black lines spiraled out from a cluster of bites on his face and neck. Another man lay face-up in a vacant lot, covered in bites, his neck and torso riddled with deep, black lines. "Zarultalzin spiders killed the first two victims."

Avei continued to the next three scenes: two men tied to beds in rundown hotels and the third in a trash-strewn alley. Eadren followed her. "The killer used the grenwal to kill these men."

Eadren squatted next to victim five and studied the twelve puncture marks on his neck. “The grenwal bit the victims twice. Is that unusual?”

Avei traced the burn mark on the back of her hand as she considered his question. “All spiders can bite more than once, and some do it routinely if their prey is large, or if they’re threatened. It is less common with the grenwal. We suspect Zarul trained it or had someone else do so. It’s likely the small silver disk on its back is a transmitter and the killer uses it to control it.”

“Why use three different species?” Eadren looked at her.

“I don’t know. Not yet anyway. All three species the killer picked inflict a violent death. So, why not stick with one kind? The zarultalzin are small and easy to transport. Walking around with a massive grenwal and twivorg makes no sense. Especially the twivorg.” Avei pushed her purple hair behind her ear. “Victims bitten by the zarultalzin or grenwal spiders suffer an agonizing demise. Death from twivorg venom is a special kind of hell. Within a minute of the bite, it feels like you are burning from the inside out. The worst part is that it takes thirty minutes or more to die, and there is no antidote yet. It’s a terrible way to go.”

“One reserved for the madam.” Eadren rose and walked to the last scene, where the woman lay on the floor of a palatial room with fine furnishings. A dead twivorg covered her chest.

“She owned brothels across L’reus and kept her workers chained to their beds so they couldn’t escape. She may have been Celethe’s jailer.”

Eadren glanced back in surprise. “You know about Celethe’s history?”

“Not with certainty. You just confirmed what we suspected.”

“I did a thorough background check on the Breckins before coming to the *Delphi* and surmised that as well. Nothing concrete though. You realize you are connecting Celethe to Zarul.” He turned pensive eyes on her. “For what it’s worth, I don’t believe Celethe is capable of murder.”

“Because she’s a woman?” Avei asked.

Eadren stared at the burn scars on Avei’s face and hands. “No, nothing like that. Just a hunch.”

Her gut said the same. “My belief is something terrible happened to Celethe. While I don’t think she’s Zarul, I do think there’s a connection.”

Eadren nodded. “Find the link, find the killer.”

“Wilm avenges the wrongs done to his wife. Ocia puts Mr. Breckin at the scene of Caerson’s murder. Imara catches on and extorts him. And let’s not forget, Wilm’s a regular at the L’reus casinos where two victims died.” Avei watched for a reaction. She needed to know how Eadren would respond in his actual role as an MSF Inspector. He didn’t immediately reject Wilm as a suspect as he’d done in previous conversations. Still, Avei had her doubts about Wilm being Zarul. Addicts think of little else other than their next fix. Observing his alcoholism firsthand, it seemed unlikely he could plan one murder, much less nine of them.

“There’s nothing I want more than to see that creep behind bars. I hate how he treats women, especially the Grilan servers.” Eadren ran his hands through his blue hair.

"I don't think Wilm is Zarul. Besides, what you just listed sounds very convenient to me. On the surface, he makes a perfect fall guy."

"I haven't ruled Wilm out, but I agree. It seems a little too tidy. Where are you with the cameras?"

"Someone uploaded malware using the comm display in one of the guest rooms. We don't know which one. Our techs are working on removing the code and they are having a hell of a time. The sophistication is beyond their ability."

As the crime scenes disappeared, Sezin reappeared in their librarian persona, wearing a brown tweed jacket and skirt. Based on their interpretation of old Earth stereotypes, they wore their hair pulled back in a severe bun and had on thick-framed glasses. Their chunky black shoes completed the transformation. "I'd love to help your team if you let me."

Eadren shook his head at their appearance.

Avei smiled at Sezin. "As you can see, my AI has their own idiosyncrasies too. Sezin is obsessed with old Earth and never misses a chance to bring some aspect of it into our investigations."

Eadren smiled. "I welcome your help. I'll tell my people to give you full access to our systems. Thank you, Sezin."

Sezin looked pleased as they bounced on their toes in those hideous shoes. "I'll get started now." They dashed to the hatch and raced through when it opened. Their holoball zipped behind them.

Avei faced Eadren. "Would you like to join me for a chat with another person of interest? I want to test a theory."

"Love to. What do you need?"

"An RF meter."

Eadren gave her a quizzical look.

Avei smiled. "I'll explain on the way."

29

The Solarium, a solid glass dome at the top of the ship, contained three alcoves for an up-close experience with the cold vacuum of space. Or, in this case, the spiraling colors of the wormhole. Each alcove comfortably fit two people on a wide divan that hugged the glass. In the main area, plush furniture circled a self-service bar stocked with a wide variety of alcohols. Lavish snacks and desserts filled a clear glass display cabinet. A fountain near the entrance provided soft water sounds that coordinated in intensity with the bursts of colors from the wormhole. The mesmerizing setting made for a once-in-a-lifetime experience.

Marsa Baako waited in a chair next to the bar, wearing another of her gaudy cat suits. A pink and green affair, paired with a massive silver star pendant. Her tangerine-colored hair was piled high on top of her head in an elaborate beehive and held in place with a jeweled net. Sintha reclined on Marsa's lap and looked around with indifference. A decanter of liquor and a half-full glass sat on a table nearby.

Two security officers stood near the entrance, eyes locked on Marsa. The human woman had her arms across her chest and the Suiven male had his hand resting on his holstered stunner. Their rigid posture left little doubt they'd spring into action should the need arise.

Avei entered the Solarium with Eadren on her heels. He hung back and motioned for the officers to wait outside the entrance. Neither looked happy about getting the boot. They obeyed and left.

Avei scanned the deck and spotted the top of Marsa's bun, the rest of her hidden by the wingback chair. She headed to the sofa across from the author and wondered again if Marsa could be Zarul. Could she trust her gut with this woman? On one hand, the woman robbed her of her anonymity, making her job as a homicide inspector a hundred times harder. Conversely, the money she had received from the book and movie sales had funded the Themis Institute and saved countless lives over the years. Even so, she struggled to forgive the woman for turning her life upside down without one shred of remorse or hesitation. There was no question Marsa Baako was a narcissist. *Is she also a killer?*

Avei settled across from the author. She hoped to confirm what she suspected. At the very least, she was sure Marsa knew the identity of the killer.

Avei glanced up at Eadren, who settled in next to her. He was taking Sezin's place by her side, while her AI remained on the bridge, helping the *Delphi* technicians restore the cameras.

Marsa smirked at Avei. "Took you long enough. I've been wanting this talk since you boarded."

Avei ignored her jab. "I'm here now."

Marsa motioned to a large decanter full of brandy on the table next to her. "Captain Dimphi's favorite brandy is a gracious gesture. Thank you."

A spot of blood welled on Marsa's arm. She stared at it for a moment before wiping it away with her finger, then she hugged Sintha to her. "Baby, please be more careful with those claws."

Avei leaned closer to Marsa and focused on her face and body language. "You've been spying on the passengers, the staff, and on me."

Marsa's eyes widened. Her hand gripped the star pendant as she considered the words. After a few seconds she released the necklace and petted Sintha, seemingly at peace with the discussion. "I look for story ideas the same way you look for clues. It's how I get material for my novels."

"Your material has come directly from my cases. What changed?"

"What changed?" Marsa belted out a scornful laugh. "It's been months since you last worked a homicide case." A flash of anger before she hid behind a forced smile. "Your selfish actions required I branch out and find a new method of getting my stories. I have to say, it's been very fruitful."

Avei bristled at her words. "There is observation, Ms. Baako, and there is illegal surveillance. I believe you are guilty of the latter."

Sweat beaded on Marsa's forehead. Her face flushed and for the first time, she appeared uncomfortable with the direction of their conversation. "What are you are talking about?"

"You've been recording private conversations since you boarded the *Delphi*, and I know how you've been doing it. Hand over Sintha's collar." Avei held out her hand.

Marsa hugged Sintha to her and didn't try to hide her anger. "You think I'm stupid? Once we entered the wormhole, MSF lost jurisdiction. I'm not handing anything over to you."

Eadren moved closer to Marsa, who glared at him. He waved a small metal cylinder in front of Sintha. It beeped three times, bringing a satisfied smile to his face. "As head of security on the *Delphi*, I have the authority. I suggest you do what Inspector Themis requests, or I'll ask my security officers to join us and remove it for you."

Avei met Marsa's eyes and held them. "I won't ask again."

Marsa fumed as she removed the silver collar from Sintha's neck and handed it over. "That's an expensive piece of equipment. If you damage it, you will buy me a new one."

Avei examined the collar and spotted the tiny recording device cleverly woven into the clasp that hung in front. She felt her confidence rise when she showed it to Eadren, who stooped to get a closer look. "We were right," Avei said.

"No. You got it right." Eadren straightened up and shook his head. "In hindsight, it all seems so obvious now."

Avei noted the sweat dripping down Marsa's face. She had blotches on her skin and her hands were trembling. A physical reaction to being found out? Or was she ill? "Do you know who the murderer is?"

Sintha nudged her, as if asking the same question. Marsa straightened and appeared more in control. "I might."

"Tell me what you know."

Marsa glared at Eadren. "Back up. What I've got to say is for her ears alone." She leaned close to Avei after Eadren took a few steps back and whispered with effort, "The murderer isn't who you think it is." Marsa grimaced and pushed Sintha off her lap. The cat grunted in protest. Marsa grabbed her head and groaned.

Avei sprung to her feet in horror. Zarul had struck again, right under their noses. "Get the doc."

Eadren tapped his wrist device. "I need Dr. Hueson in the Solarium. We've got another venom poisoning."

Avei and Eadren squatted in front of Marsa, who rocked back and forth in the chair, moaning in agony.

"Did you eat or drink anything before leaving your room?" Avei grabbed her nemesis' hand and squeezed it. No matter what she thought of the woman, she certainly didn't wish her dead.

Marsa closed her eyes and leaned back in the chair. "The brandy. Sintha's fish. I tried a bite first. Those inept chefs—" She arched back. Her hands and feet cramped into tight balls. She screamed through clenched teeth.

"Hang on, Marsa. Help is on the way." Avei tried to hold on to her hand but she wrenched it away.

Marsa wailed as her body writhed. Her right hand shot out and slammed into the full brandy decanter, knocking it over.

Still on their knees in front of Marsa, Avei had only a moment to register the wave of brandy headed their way and the danger it held. "No!" She shoved Eadren out of the way as the liquor hit her in the face.

Marsa froze, her back arched and her hands and feet contorted into painful claws. Orange foam oozed from her lips.

Everything had happened so fast, Avei didn't have time to think about taking precautions, like closing her eyes and mouth. Not that it would have done any good. She leaned forward and spit out the brandy. The liquor dripped from her face and down her neck and chest. Even without swallowing, she knew the venom had already penetrated the soft tissue in her mouth, her skin, and her eyes. A terrible death awaited her in the next thirty minutes. Maybe less if the Lorestal didn't work. The urge to survive overwhelmed her and took her breath away. Avei realized how much she had to live for and hated how she had wasted precious time hiding out in her apartment these last few weeks.

Eadren scrambled off the floor next to her and ripped off his jacket. He dabbed at Avei's face. "Why did you do that?"

Avei opened her eyes and stared at Marsa's lifeless body. Zarul knew Marsa could divulge their identity and, in a desperate and reckless move, the killer had silenced the author.

Avei glanced at Sintha, the animal's eyes locked on their dead human. "Sintha ate the fish, and she's still alive. The venom is in the brandy." Avei held up the dripping collar. "I'll get Sezin to check the recordings for the identity of the murderer. Zarul would never risk exposing themselves in such a reckless way unless they considered the situation dire."

"First, get out of your clothes before any more of that venom soaks into your skin."

"You're right." She peeled off her clothes, boots and socks, leaving only her sports bra, boxer shorts and necklace, and revealing the arachnoid tattoos that covered her body.

Eadren shook his head at the crazy array of spider images across her arms, legs, chest, and stomach. "You're a walking nightmare."

Despite the dire circumstance, she had to smile. No one except her parents understood her obsession with arachnids. Her father considered her a walking piece of art but, although her mother appreciated why she did it, she would have preferred to see the images on a wall rather than her daughter's body. A deep pang of guilt and sorrow hit Avei as she thought of her parents. To lose both daughters to serial killers was too much for any person to bear. She felt herself on the precipice of a deep, dark hole. One she'd never come back from if she didn't keep her head in the game. Zarul had struck again and they needed to catch the killer before someone else lost their life to this monster.

Eadren stood in front of her, a bundle of barely concealed nerves. With no time to waste, Avei spun her finger in a circle. "Let me check you to make sure none of the brandy hit you."

Eadren turned while Avei scanned him from head to toe. She didn't see any sign of the tainted liquor on him. "You're clean."

"Thank the goddess." Eadren's hand drifted to his right pocket.

Dr. Hueson dashed in, his medical bag slung over his shoulder. He slowed to a stop when he saw Marsa. "Not again." His eyes landed on Avei's wet hair and the pile of clothes at her feet, and he blanched. "Oh, no."

"I believe the venom is in the liquor that Marsa was drinking." Avei felt feverish, and her skin tingled. The start of a headache pounded at the back of her skull. Fear crept back. She didn't want to die in the warehouse fire, and she wasn't ready to die now.

Sintha meowed a melodic tune as she brushed against Marsa's legs. The sound captured their attention as they watched the animal weave back and forth in a spellbinding dance.

With effort, Avei dragged her eyes back to the doctor. "Where are you with the antidote?"

"It will be ready in thirty minutes. Maybe less."

Avei felt a rush of hope. If she could stave off the full effects of the venom until the antidote was ready, she had a chance of surviving. "Give me the Lorestal. That will buy me some time."

"Got it right here." Dr. Hueson pulled a silver cylinder from his bag and headed her way.

"Be very careful, doc." Avei held her left arm away from her body and he injected the Lorestal.

"You said three to ten minutes before..." Eadren's green cat eyes didn't meet hers.

"A dozen different species have bitten me during my work at the Institute. Between their venom and the antidotes I took to counteract the poison, I have built up immunity over the years. That and the Lorestal should buy me more time than the average person." In theory, what she said sounded right. Plus, over time and after multiple bites, she never responded to the venom as quickly as someone who had never previously been bitten by a venomous spider. There was no way of knowing if this would be the case with grenwal venom until some time had passed.

Rigid with worry and fear, Eadren shoved his hands into his pockets. Pulled them out. Shoved them back in again. "How much time are we talking? A few minutes? An hour?"

Avei considered his question from a rational place. The horror of her predicament forced its way in and made it difficult. He needed reassurance, so she did her best to push aside the dread. "Lorestal can prolong life for fifteen to twenty minutes, allowing time to get the antidote onboard. It's been enough to save countless lives. Lorestal doesn't work with all venoms and the grenwal is unknown. My tolerance level is higher than most. My guess, thirty minutes."

"There's no wiggle room. None. It will be down to the wire." Eadren stared at her in dread and then glanced at Marsa, her face frozen into a mask of terror. He shuddered and looked away.

Avei had the luxury of being put under by the doctor during her last minutes, sparing her the worst of the pain that Marsa and the other victims had endured. While she detested the woman, she would never wish a death like this on her, or any living being. "We're going to make every one of those minutes count and find that killer."

Two medical personnel in biohazard suits entered the Solarium, with two red bins stacked on a hover board.

"They're here to decontaminate you," Dr. Hueson said. "I need to get back to the medical bay to check on the antidote."

Eadren grabbed the doctor's arm as he turned to leave. "Do what you can to speed up the process."

Dr. Hueson swallowed hard and nodded. "Of course. You have my word."

Eadren released him, and the doctor hurried out of the hatch. Eadren watched the two medical personnel unload the bins from the hover board beside her. "What can I do?"

"Wait for me outside the entrance." Avei turned to the two medics. "We need to move lightning-fast."

Eadren hurried from the room as Avei stripped to her birthday suit.

30

Eadren leaned against the wall and watched Captain Dimphi pacing nearby. The opulence of the third floor spread out on all sides of the Solarium entrance, which sat in the middle of the promenade. Not that either man was thinking about this. The deep quiet penetrated their thoughts more acutely than the usual noise made by boisterous guests blowing off steam on the brief journey between Mernin and Charnos. Word of Marsa's death had spread like wildfire among the guests and crew. Most had locked themselves in their rooms, leaving the public spaces on the ship deserted and eerily silent.

The death of Marsa Baako shook Eadren to his core. *How did I lose control of everything?* A murderer had upended the simple task of flying to Charnos and handing Wilm over to the authorities. He blamed himself for every terrible thing that had happened since they left the spacehub. Like a fool, he had gone along with Wilm's insistence on keeping the deal with MSF a secret and not telling Julisa about the plan to reveal his Iscun contacts. There was too much riding on it to risk her ending the agreement out of fear. Given Iscun's terrible reputation, she had every right to stop her brother. If they had brought Julisa in from the beginning, he could have brought

Wilm to MSF headquarters on Mernin. Instead, they had found themselves locked on this deathtrap because Julisa believed Wilm had to go to jail, and she wanted it to be at the Yapho Penitentiary.

Eadren barely recognized himself anymore. A year ago, when his brother Masitrel still lived, he would have returned the *Delphi* to the spacehub immediately after Caerson's murder. Now, because of his actions, good people had died. Ocia, Imara, Marsa, and soon Avei. Why didn't he turn the damn ship around when he had the chance? He caught Captain Dimphi staring at him.

"As Captain, I bear the full weight of our decisions. It's my responsibility to keep the guests safe, and I failed. Now, I have to live with my actions." He leaned back against the wall, his yellow skin pale and his face full of regret. "I don't know if I can."

Eadren felt a rush of sympathy for the man. He had dragged Captain Dimphi kicking and screaming into his plans. The captain had wanted nothing to do with his scheme so Eadren had coerced him into participating. "No, Captain, this is all on me. I forced you into my subterfuge. I'm to blame, not you. I've been so focused on the end goal that I didn't think of the potential consequences of my actions. I'm truly sorry for all of this."

Captain Dimphi held up his hand and shook his head. "I appreciate what you're doing but we both share the blame. It's my sincere wish this wasn't all for nothing."

"As much as I despise Wilm Breckin, his actions will save an untold number of lives. Tens of thousands. Maybe even millions." Eadren ran his hands through his blue hair. "I know he's turning over his contacts to stay out of jail. Still, it takes courage to do that when you consider how ruthless the Iscun is toward informants. This is the best chance MSF has ever had to crush the Iscun crime syndicate. Wilm's actions will stop the Zenith deaths from happening every day and also save the lives of innocent people who unwittingly cross paths with those ruthless psychopaths."

"Thank you, Eadren. An excellent reminder of what we need to focus on, when guilt and despair threaten to consume us."

Despite the lack of people, Eadren still scanned the surrounding area before he spoke. "Who put your brandy in there? Ms. Baako thought it was for her."

"Sweet Goddess Mima, I'd never waste—" Horror flooded Captain Dimphi's face as he faltered, then stopped. "It's wrong to speak ill of the dead. Forgive me, Mima." He kissed his fingers, then touched his forehead three times, then his chest.

"Do you keep your private stock in the Galaxy Lounge?"

"Behind the bar in a cabinet, and a couple of bottles in the Solarium. Why?" Captain Dimphi stared at Eadren, puzzled.

"It means anyone can take a bottle if they know it's there. We need to confine passengers and non-essential crew to their rooms for the duration of the voyage. I should have kept them in their rooms after Imara's death, instead of giving in to Julisa and letting them out."

"An excellent idea. Very good." Captain Dimphi smoothed his uniform.

"Now, Captain. Please."

"Yes. Yes, of course. I'll head to the bridge now."

"Don't stop for anything, and stay alert."

"Sweet Mima, give me strength, and eyes in the back of my head." Captain Dimphi kissed his fingers and repeated his prayer ritual of touching his forehead and chest as he hurried away. His head swiveled from side to side as he searched every dark corner and alcove.

***

Avei walked out of the Solarium in a blue jumpsuit and her belt with her gun, knife and badge. The medical crew were adamant that she left behind her gear because of possible contamination, but with a murderer loose she wasn't giving up her weapon. After a good scrub, they relented and let her take it. She tucked her wet hair behind her ears and headed to Eadren, who stood across from the hatch.

The worry emanated from him as he studied her. "How do you feel?"

"I can function." The Lorestal had dampened most of her symptoms, but it did nothing for the headache that threatened to overwhelm her, making it difficult to think straight. This concerned her, given what they needed to do before... She shoved that thought away. Dwelling on her impeding death accomplished nothing.

"Thank you for what you did in there. If you hadn't pushed me aside—"

"Better me than you, given my built-in immunity. Our time is limited, so let's stay focused on the case. Sezin got back to me about the collar. It has seven levels of encryption and will take time to access. She is dividing herself so she can focus on accessing the recordings in the collar and getting the cameras back online. I suggest we search Marsa's room first. I'm certain she knew Zarul's identity." Avei pivoted to head down the hallway and stumbled when a wave of dizziness hit her. Eadren caught her and kept her upright. He put an arm around her waist and her gratitude for his solid presence warmed her. She felt relief that he was one of the good guys. "Thank you."

"You need to be in medical, not running around the ship. I'll check Marsa's room and report back to you."

Avei pulled away and glared at him. "And lay there until I die? Not a chance." She walked away. "Are you coming?"

Eadren fell in next to her. "Fine, but I'm not leaving your side until you are back in medical."

Avei shot a grateful look his way as his arm snaked around her waist. Another dizzy spell threatened to send her straight to the ground again. "I appreciate that."

Captain Dimphi's voice echoed through the empty corridor. "This is an emergency announcement that requires your full attention and mandatory cooperation. All passengers and non-essential crew must return to their quarters at once. This is not a drill. Anyone caught by security outside of their rooms will spend the rest of the voyage in a cell. I repeat, this is not a drill. You have five minutes to get to your rooms before we lock down the ship again. Everyone will remain in their rooms until we reach Charnos."

Avei gripped her necklace as a small group of guests and crew trickled out of the casino and headed to the elevator bank. “If we had done this a few hours ago, Imara and Marsa would still be alive.”

“Zarul may have gotten to them anyway. The killer was desperate to keep those two women quiet,” Eadren said quietly.

Avei and Eadren followed the small group to the elevator.

“Given what we know about Zarul and how meticulous they’ve been, it’s a major blunder allowing themselves to get cornered on a starliner,” Eadren said.

Avei stopped and looked up at Eadren, who stood head and shoulders above her. She had to acknowledge her lingering frustration with him. He should have revealed his identity from the start. At the very least, he should have come clean when she first confronted him. Instead, Eadren had hidden behind his Nad Ranack alias. She understood his reluctance, given that the success of his case rested with Wilm Breckin. A man with questionable integrity. Avei mentally shook herself for giving in to these kinds of thoughts that wasted precious time. She needed to remain laser-focused on the case. “You raise an excellent point. What if Zarul boarded the *Delphi* with no intention of killing anyone?”

“Caerson and Imara figured out Zarul’s identity and tried to blackmail the killer. That could explain this latest killing spree.” Eadren glanced over his shoulder at the empty corridor behind them.

“I agree. Until the *Delphi* murders, Zarul had been meticulous, which took significant planning. The murders of Caerson, Ocia, Imara and Marsa felt messy, rushed, and ill-conceived. Caerson and Imara forced Zarul's hand, leaving the killer no choice but to act." Avei felt Eadren's arm tighten around her waist, giving her strength as a wave of vertigo struck.

"Zarul figured out Marsa's surveillance methods using Sintha and killed her. She may have inadvertently captured the killer, or Zarul murdered her in an abundance of caution."

They continued to the elevator bank where the dwindling group of guests and crew clustered together in a tight knot, waiting their turn. A Sycardian couple stood on the edge. Arms held out, they created a protective barrier around the remaining guests and crew, who threw them grateful looks.

"Why bring the grenwal and venom onboard unless Zarul expected problems?" Avei swallowed through the wave of nausea that came out of nowhere. She slowed to a stop and closed her eyes. "Give me a second."

When the sick feeling passed, she opened her eyes to find Eadren studying her with dread. She smiled, which did nothing to ease his worry. "I'm fine. Now, what was I saying?"

Eadren frowned as they continued toward the elevator. Only the Sycardians remained. "I know it's a waste of time to try to get you to medical, so I won't bother. We agree. Zarul never intended to murder anyone on the *Delphi*. So why bring the grenwal, a highly incriminating piece of evidence, with them? It's not exactly small and easy to hide."

The elevator opened, and the Sycardians rushed in. The doors swished shut, leaving Eadren and Avei alone.

Eadren leaned close to the display. "Second floor."

"Zarul traveled extensively with the grenwal, twivorg, and zarultalzin arachnids to commit their murders. Bringing the grenwal on the *Delphi* wouldn't be that unusual for them. Somewhere over the last couple of months, Caerson and Imara's paths intersected with Zarul, and the three of them ended up on the *Delphi* together. What we don't know is if it's an unfortunate coincidence. Or did someone plan it?"

"With both of them dead, we may never find out."

Avei traced the burn on the back of her hand. "I really hate unanswered questions."

"And that is why you are MSF's most successful investigator."

Avei smiled at him as the elevator doors opened. "D.I. Skora holds the record on cases closed."

"Over a thirty-year career. You are closing in on his record with less than ten years on the force."

"My sister's death is what drives me." She brought her necklace to her lips and kissed it. "Hopefully, something in Marsa's room or on Sintha's collar can shed light on the identity of Zarul. This is one killer I want behind bars for the rest of their natural life." *And before I die*, she thought to herself.

"We have more in common than you know." Eadren led the way into the elevator, and the doors slid shut.

31

Avei had a tight grip on Eadren's arm as they entered Marsa's living quarters. She felt flushed and sweat soaked her hair. They stopped inside the entrance and scanned the large space. It had a living room, a bedroom partially hidden behind a half wall, a fully appointed bathroom, and a walk-in closet. Each suite came with chromatic nanobots embedded into the walls and furniture, allowing guests to select their color palette. Marsa's taste in decor mirrored her acumen with clothes. Wild splashes of clashing bright hues covered the wall. Neon-pink made the couch and two easy chairs hard to look at without squinting. From what they could see of the bedroom, lime-green was the primary color. They both shook their heads as they took in the baffling color scheme.

"There really is no accounting for taste," Eadren said.

"My mother always says diversity is the secret ingredient to innovation. I wonder what she'd think of this room." Avei spotted three wine glasses on the table against the wall, along with two bottles of red wine, one empty and the other half-full. Only one glass still had wine left.

"Marsa had company at some point. Why don't you check the bedroom? I'll work with Sezin on fingerprints and possible contamination." She let go of his arm and centered herself on her feet.

"Copy that." Eadren headed into the bedroom then turned, stunned. "It looks like a bomb went off in here. There are clothes everywhere."

"Marsa strikes me as the type who takes full advantage of the perks associated with a first-class ticket on the *Delphi*." Avei's legs wobbled as she shuffled her way to the table. If she didn't know better, she'd swear a drumming competition was going on in her head. Thirteen minutes since the poisoning, and still upright. The Lorestal had tempered the worst of the symptoms, giving the doc time to finish the antidote, and giving her time to work on the case.

"Agreed. It doesn't appear anyone's been here to clean. I'll check with housekeeping to see if Marsa turned down the daily cleaning."

"Which she would if she had something to hide. It would be much more interesting if we thought Marsa was Zarul." Avei stopped in front of the table and tapped a spot behind her ear. "Sezin, I need you for a moment to do a fingerprint scan in Marsa Baako's quarters."

"Of course. Tell me when you are ready." Sezin's voice came from the embedded device in her arm.

Avei's hand trembled when she held up her wrist and pointed it at the bottles and glasses. She gripped her arm with her other hand, which wavered too. "Sezin, go ahead."

"Fingerprint scan commencing." A bright light appeared from the device embedded under the skin on the back of her arm. It stuttered before disappearing. "I can't get a lock. Please hold still."

"Believe me, I'm trying." Avei gripped her arm. Her hands continued to shake, making it impossible to hold still long enough to complete the scan.

"Let me help." Eadren left the bedroom and came up beside her. He cradled Avei's hand and arm, holding them steady. "Sezin, try again."

A solid white light shot out and scanned each of the three glasses and two bottles three times apiece before disappearing.

"Fingerprints on the first glass are a 96.6% match for Marsa Baako. The three-quarter-full glass is a 98.2% match for Imara Tiniba. The third glass is a 97.3% match to Caerson Mercer. I'm detecting a trace element in the half-bottle but not in the empty bottle. I don't have the capabilities to determine if it's grenwal venom. We'll need the good doctor to do an analysis using his fancy equipment."

Avei's stare bored into Eadren. "It has to be grenwal venom. Think about it. Imara and Caerson's room is three doors down the hall. They go back there when they begin to feel ill. Then things get worse and they head to medical bay."

"It makes sense. But why didn't Marsa get sick?"

Sezin's voice comes through the device on Avei's arm. "Maybe she only had wine from the empty bottle. Imara's glass was mostly full. Caerson's glass was empty. I'm thinking he had a significant amount from the tainted second bottle."

"We know where the poisoning happened, and the method. What we don't know is how Marsa fits into it all." Eadren gently released Avei's hand.

"Thanks." Avei smiled at him. "Maybe Marsa was the intended victim. Zarul tampers with the wine sent to her room and Caerson and Imara end up as collateral damage. Maybe just dumb luck that Marsa didn't drink from the tainted bottle. We also know why Caerson died and Imara lived. Imara strikes me as the type who prefers champagne. If Imara had been forthcoming about having drinks with Marsa, both women would be alive right now." It felt good to get some questions answered.

"Imara held back that information out of fear, or she had something to gain by staying quiet."

"From what I know about her, fear didn't keep her silent." Avei rubbed a cramp out of her right hand.

"Imara learned something about Marsa and blackmailed her."

"That's the most likely scenario." Avei stared at the two bottles, one empty and the other half-full. "Did the killer intend to kill the three of them on their first night onboard? If so, why not put the venom into both bottles?"

Eadren ran his hand through his hair. "It makes little sense, unless—"

"You left one bottle free of venom to put your targets at ease. If Marsa Baako wasn't lying in a morgue drawer right now, I'd arrest her for the Zarul murders."

"There is one other possibility. Zarul didn't want to use up all the venom. Maybe the killer had a limited supply and wanted to hold some in reserve."

"Meaning they were able to use it in the brandy decanter. It also explains why Zarul risked using the grenwal to kill Imara. They were low on venom." Avei lowered herself into the chair next to the table as a wave of nausea hit her. She took several deep breaths to settle her stomach. "Sezin, how are you coming along with the encryption in Sintha's collar?"

"I'm through three levels," Sezin said through her arm device. "Ms. Baako created something of a lockbox, using seven layers of security to keep her activities secret."

Avei considered herself the premier expert on Marsa Baako's thoroughness. The woman left no stone unturned in uncovering every detail of the cases she worked on, or of anything personal. Marsa's books memorialized every aspect of Avei's life, to her everlasting horror. Severe legal jeopardy never dissuaded that woman from adding everything she uncovered to her novels, no matter how sensitive the material, then embellishing it with lies and half-truths. The garnishment of 50% of her earnings didn't stop her. Marsa stole her life and turned it into a money-making machine to enrich herself. *Good riddance.* "Thanks, Sezin. Any progress on the cameras?"

"I estimate they'll be online in less than an hour. Please don't croak on me, Inspector. I'd miss you."

Avei smiled. "I'll try my best. Now, go make yourself useful."

"Roger that."

Eadren paced in front of her. "How does Marsa Baako know Caerson and Imara?"

"That's easy. Imara recognized Marsa from her novels. She'd never miss a chance to socialize with a famous author." Avei leaned back against the chair. "No matter how hard I try, I can't seem to get my arms around this case."

Eadren stopped pacing and stared at her. "What does your famous gut tell you?"

Avei glared at Eadren. "I had Apollyona after her fourth murder and let her go because my gut said she didn't do it." Remorse displaced her fear of dying. "That monster doused her unsuspecting victims with a flammable liquid from several feet away. Then she lit them on fire before they registered what had occurred, leaving no time to save themselves. And she did it in the name of her god, as some kind of sick sacrifice to stop the volcanic eruptions on her world because they threatened their civilization." Avei sucked in a deep breath and let it out slowly. "I alone am responsible for the deaths of my best friends and the eighteen victims that came after I released her. I no longer trust my gut."

Eadren studied her for a moment, then shook his head. "I heard what you did in that warehouse. Given how badly wounded you were, you still managed to pull your friends through a building engulfed in flames and out the door. Most people would have left them behind and bolted, to save their own skin."

"Then you also know I didn't get them out in time." Avei turned away from him and stared out the window at the undulating colors of the wormhole. Her headache ratcheted up another notch and pain lanced her body. At the most, she had fifteen minutes of lucidity left, and they still didn't know Zarul's identity.

Eadren squatted next to her. "We all make mistakes. Goddess knows I've made my share on the *Delphi*."

"My mistake caused innocent people to die a horrific death because I released a murderer back onto the streets." Her eyes glistened with tears as she stared at him.

"I know a little something about that." Eadren grabbed her hand. "I think the trick to surviving this job is to focus on the good we do, which far exceeds the times we get it wrong. We are imperfect beings, and we will get things wrong. It's inevitable. What you have done over the last ten years is the stuff of legends. Look at how many lives you've saved by locking away... how many serial killers? Over sixty, I believe. Killers who would have kept killing had you not caught them."

Avei wiped her eyes with her sleeve. "And you're shutting down the Iscun and eliminating the Zenith drug. That alone will save hundreds of thousands of lives. Maybe even millions." It didn't ease her guilt, but she appreciated his efforts.

"I couldn't save my brother, but I can save others." Eadren pulled the holographic disk from his pocket and handed it to Avei.

She stared at the image of a smiling young man and saw the family resemblance. She looked up at him and glimpsed the pain and grief he had kept hidden.

"A friend put Zenith in his drink as a joke. Masitrel thought he could fly, and he jumped off a ninety-story building. I hope to goddess he didn't sober up on the way down. I can't imagine the fear he would have felt if he had."

Avei handed the disk back and squeezed Eadren's hand. This explained his determination to get Wilm into custody, even if it meant going to Charnos to make it happen. She pulled out the necklace from around her neck and tapped it. A small hologram image appeared of Anastasia, smiling. "I'm truly so sorry for your loss. I wear this necklace with the image of my big sister, to remind myself of why I do what I do." Avei felt a pang of regret. If she lived, she'd be leaving the job that had meant so much to her for so long. *Am I making the right decision?*

First, she needed to survive the grenwal venom. Then perhaps she could consider that question.

"The death of a loved one is devastating, but losing one to violence or a senseless act is particularly shattering and difficult to pick yourself up from." Eadren slipped the disk back into his right pocket. "Tell me how I can help."

Avei tapped her necklace, and the image disappeared. She slipped the necklace under her coveralls. There was one more interview to conduct before she succumbed to the effects of the venom. "Get me to the Breckin suite."

32

The *Delphi*'s largest suite took grandeur to another level. The luxurious rooms came with their own staff and a kitchen, in case the guests wanted to eat alone instead of in the dining room. The sight of the churning wormhole filled the windows that lined the wall, creating the illusion you could reach out and touch it. Filled with sumptuous furniture, the living room had a well-stocked bar and a holo-theater that sat within a deep alcove. Rare art covered the walls and surfaces.

Julisa and Celethe sat together on a couch and Wilm sprawled on a plush chair next to them, a coffee cup in his hand. For once, he appeared sober.

Avei sat across from them in an over-sized armchair, her feet a few inches from the ground. Being short really sucked some days. *How does anyone take me seriously, when my feet dangle like a five-year-old's?* Over the last few minutes, the effects of the venom had ratcheted up to a new level. Fiery pain seized her muscles, reminding her that being petite was the least of her problems. Her head throbbed and she didn't know how long she'd last. There hadn't been time to dwell on her encroaching death, and the thought of writing a goodbye message to her parents almost undid her. She needed the Breckin interview done as quickly as possible. Eadren stood next to her, his hand on the back of the chair. Despite their rocky start, she found his presence comforting. Plus, she now understood what had driven him to take desperate measures to eradicate the Iscun crime syndicate. The deaths of their beloved siblings drove them both. She felt a camaraderie with Eadren she hadn't felt about anyone in a long time.

With time running out, Avei focused on Wilm first and made the easy decision to get straight to the point. "Tell your sister about your deal with MSF Drug Enforcement."

Celethe startled then got herself under control. She crossed her arms and frowned at her husband as he fidgeted in his chair.

Julisa leaned forward and glared at Wilm. "What did you do?"

Wilm shifted in the chair again. "I discovered your plan to send me to jail, and I made a better deal." Both his hands gripped the cup, stilling the trembling that threatened to spill coffee on him.

Julisa stared at Wilm with dread, clearly afraid of the answer to the next logical question.

Celethe sighed in frustration and jumped into the conversation. "Tell your sister about the agreement."

Wilm stood and paced, still clutching the cup. One glance at his wife's angry face confirmed to everyone in the room he'd get no help there.

Avei studied the Breckins and discerned from their body language they didn't trust or like one another. Wilm feared Julisa, with good reason. She controlled the purse strings and, until recently, cleaned up his messes. Julisa had reached the end of the rope, and he knew it.

Avei turned her attention to Celethe, who struggled to hold her ire. Maybe the couple had loved each other in the beginning. Or, the more likely scenario, Wilm had offered a way out of the wretched life she led on L'reus and she'd seized it, ignoring how she really felt about her husband.

"Tell them what you did," Celethe said with fury. Her facade of a tolerant and loving wife was gone. In its place a woman who'd had enough.

Wilm swallowed and turned to his sister. "I agreed to turn over the names of my Iscun contacts to MSF. They said I'd remain anonymous." Wilm glanced at Eadren for confirmation.

Eadren nodded. "That's the agreement."

Julisa jumped up and planted herself in front of Wilm. "The Iscun? Have you lost your damn mind? They'll kill us. You, me, and your wife." She shook with outrage. "How are you okay with that?"

Wilm skulked away, unable or unwilling to make eye contact with his sister.

Julisa shook her head with disgust and turned on Eadren. "You played me like a fool, Nad... Eadren, whatever your name is."

He met her eyes with steadfast determination. "My name is Eadren Omu, and I'm a drug enforcement inspector with Mernin Security Forces. I did what needed to be done to get Zenith off the streets. And I'm sorry I had to mislead you."

Julisa remained locked in place, at a loss for words. Celethe stood and took her hand. She led her sister-in-law to the couch and they both sat. Julisa gave Celethe a small smile, which quickly drooped and disappeared.

Wilm's and Eadren's confessions appeared to unnerve Julisa. Not wanting to lose momentum, Avei turned back to Wilm to keep things moving. "Marsa told you about your sister's plan to turn you in."

"She did." He glared at Julisa, who sat with her hands clenched in her lap.

"Did she tell you on the *Delphi*?"

Wilm nodded as Avei shared a knowing look with Eadren. Marsa was at the center of this mess. She had figured out the identity of Zarul and lost her life because of it. But why involve herself with Wilm and his problems? That made little sense. Avei tensed as a sharp pain shot through her legs and arms. She breathed through it and refocused on the dysfunctional family. Marsa lay in the morgue, and she had faith that Sezin would break the encrypted data. Other avenues of questioning took priority. Ones that may shed light on the identity of Zarul.

"Celethe, why did Caerson and Imara blackmail you?"

Celethe flinched when she heard the names. She ignored Wilm when he frowned at her. "I brought them on board to reason with them. I had to do something."

Avei nodded. At least she had gotten that part right, and it gave her a small flicker of satisfaction. From her earlier reaction to his death, it had been clear that Celethe knew Caerson.

"I told you I had it handled." Wilm huffed as he gripped his now empty mug.

"Really? Because they're dead now." Celethe stood, her face rigid with anger.

Wilm leaned into Celethe, who stood her ground. "Are you accusing me of murder?"

"Why not? I told you who they were and what they wanted."

Eadren stepped in between the couple and pried them apart. "Let's keep things civil. Okay?"

Celethe crossed her arms, and Wilm set the coffee mug on the table. He jammed his hands into his pockets.

Avei gritted her teeth against the increasing pain that flared across her body. She figured she had five minutes, tops. With no time to finesse her questions, she got right to it. "Did they blackmail you about your past as a sex slave?"

Celethe nodded and turned away.

"How are you and Caerson related?"

"My twin brother."

A closer connection than Avei had expected. "I'm sorry for your loss."

"Don't be. He left me behind with our mother; a cruel, vindictive woman. From the age of ten, she prostituted my brother and me to the miners to pay for her drug addiction."

Julisa appeared on the verge of tears. "What mother does that to their children?"

"Tell me what Caerson and Imara wanted." Avei gripped the sides of the chair as pain coursed through her body.

Eadren leaned close and whispered, "Please, let me bring you to medical."

"A few minutes more." Avei couldn't leave now, not this close to cracking open the case.

"Caerson wanted a million credits and a role for Imara on a top show," Celethe said.

"Stupid fools." Wilm moved to put an arm around his wife, and she twisted away. He sighed and plopped on the couch next to Julisa, who scooted closer to Celethe.

"Celethe, why didn't you tell me? I would have helped." Julisa implored her.

Celethe smiled at her. "I know. You've done so much for us, and I wanted to handle it myself."

There was no time for a kumbaya moment between the women. Avei pressed on. "Did Marsa know about your past?"

"Only Julisa and Wilm knew. They both accepted me. No one else knew." Celethe shot a grateful look at her sister-in-law, who nodded and smiled back at her.

Wilm fidgeted and looked uncomfortable. "That's not entirely accurate. I had too much to drink one night."

"Only one night?" Julisa asked.

"Marsa is very persuasive. I didn't mean to, is what I'm saying."

Julisa shook her head, and Celethe's face hardened.

Wilm stared out at the wormhole, aware his actions had caused his wife pain.

"The woman killed by Zarul. Was she your madam?" Avei leaned in. If she answered yes, they had found the first link between the Breckins and Zarul.

"She imprisoned me. Kept me chained to the wall and made me do things—" Celethe wrapped her arms around herself. “The two miners pushed my father into a nest of zarultalzin spiders. They thought it hilarious until he died. The authorities dropped all charges against them and called it an accident. My mother turned to drugs to cope.”

Avei grimaced as her left hand cramped. She felt the end approaching as the symptoms increased in frequency and intensity. “The three other male victims?”

“Freighters who raped me when they found me after I stowed away on their ship.”

Celethe had a motive to murder her tormentors, and Avei needed to ask the glaring question. “Did you kill them?”

Unwavering, Celethe looked directly into her eyes. “No. I did not.”

Avei nodded, sensing no subterfuge. She turned her attention to Wilm, who balked and then appeared offended.

“You dare pin the murders on me? I had nothing to do with them.”

“You both knew about the connection to Zarul and said nothing to MSF?”

Avei understood why Celethe didn’t want her past blazoned across the Nexus. However, the couple’s silence had contributed to the deaths of Ocia, Caerson, Imara and Marsa. And soon her own.

Celethe reddened and turned away.

“By the time Celethe and I figured it out, the killings had stopped,” Wilm said. “It seemed pointless to speak up. Can you imagine the damage to our company’s reputation if word got out about my wife’s past as a prostitute?”

Celethe recoiled as if struck. Wilm's words had hit home and Avei wondered if he had dealt the death blow to their marriage.

"Prostitute implies I had a choice. I was a prisoner chained to a bed. I had no say in anything that happened to me."

"Thank you for your honesty. It took a lot of courage to tell me your story and I'm truly sorry for what you went through." Avei smiled at Celethe, who nodded at her.

Avei turned her attention back to Wilm. "What were you doing in the staff hallway at the time of Caerson's death?"

Wilm shot a look at Celethe, who had her back to him. "I… I swear I didn't kill him. He was dead when I found him."

"And you didn't think to call for help?" Eadren asked.

"I'd promised my wife I'd stay away from the staff floor. And, I… well…"

The pain exploded inside Avei, and she doubled over. Eadren grabbed her before she fell to the floor.

Celethe and Julisa rushed to her while Wilm stood apart, relieved.

Avei whispered to Eadren, who squatted in front of her. "My time's running out."

Eadren picked her up in his arms and turned to the Breckins. "Remain in your quarters and lock your hatch. Don't let anyone in, unless it's me or Captain Dimphi. Understood?"

"We'll do as you say," Julisa said.

Eadren hurried through the hatch with Avei.

33

Partially blinded by the bright lights, Avei writhed on a bed in the medical bay and caught glimpses of Eadren through half-closed eyes. Every single muscle spasmed, sending waves of pain ricocheting through her body. Her diaphragm seized into a tight fist, making breathing nearly impossible. Getting a message to her parents was the only thing keeping her conscious. The squeeze of Eadren's hand brought a brief distraction from the pain.

"Doc's coming with the antidote. I need you to fight, Avei. You've made it this far. Don't give up."

Not a moment too soon. With surely only a minute or two left, she thought her chance of survival hovered around ten percent. The bites sustained over the years working with spiders were the only reason she still drew breath. No question it'd be close. It took a herculean effort to force her fingers to squeeze Eadren's hand.

He gripped her hand and leaned close. "What can I do?"

Knowing how important her last words were, she dug deep and marshaled every bit of strength left. "Tell... tell parents..." The darkness closed in and the struggle to stay conscious crumbled. "Love them. And sorry. Tell them thank you for a wonderful life."

"Tell them yourself. I will not let you die."

Dr. Hueson ran in with a silver shot dispenser in his hand. "Got it."

Eadren gently swept her hair aside so he could look her in the eyes. "Doc's got the antidote. Fight, Avei. Fight with everything you've got."

Avei tried to nod, but her neck muscles refused to respond. The pain intensified as her body convulsed. Death waited patiently on the edge of consciousness. The pressure from Eadren's hands on her shoulders was comforting. She wouldn't die alone.

"Doc, give her the damn shot."

Eadren's shout penetrated the fog of pain that dragged her ever closer to the deep abyss where life, as she knew it, ceased.

A prick on her neck. Searing hope. It took every ounce of energy to keep the shadows that beckoned her into a lover's embrace from consuming her. She had to give the antidote time to work. The burning sensation of a thousand knives stabbing from within brought excruciating torment and signaled the race between life and death was almost over. Yielding to the pain meant death.

"Will the antidote work?" Eadren asked.

The headache she'd been grappling with since the poisoning intensified, making it difficult to follow the conversation.

"I honestly don't know. Look at how quickly it killed the others. It's a miracle she's survived this long." Dr. Hueson spoke in a quiet voice.

"Give me your best guess," Eadren said through gritted teeth as Avei thrashed under him.

"I'm way out of my depth here. If I had to guess, I'd say if the inspector is still alive five minutes from now, she may make it."

It didn't matter what the doctor thought. Avei felt the venom surging unimpeded. The antidote was too late.

Eadren spoke in her ear as she succumbed to the darkness and the blessed release from the agony. "Fight, Avei. Please. We're not giving up, so you don't either."

34

Someone shook Avei with enough force to rattle her teeth. Bone-tired and with the mother of all headaches, resentment surged toward the person who kept her from blessed sleep. Another violent shake and she fought to wake up and yell a few choice words. Easier said than done. It felt like climbing out of a pitch-black pit, smooth sides slick with oil. Someone shook her again and pain exploded behind her eyes. Avei would give anything to punch the bastard, but her arms refused to move.

"Avei. Can you hear me?"

Eadren? Why whisper? Everything rushed back. The *Delphi*. The murders. Getting poisoned by grenwal venom. A thrill went through her. She hadn't died. The antidote had worked, and she needed to thank the doctor. Her eyes fluttered open long enough to get a glimpse of Eadren, who leaned over the bed. He looked panicked. Odd. The edges of unconsciousness crept back and the wish to let go almost trumped the need to figure out what Eadren wanted. She tried to speak, and only managed a moan.

"Thank the goddess you're alive. Avei, I need you to play dead. Squeeze my hand so I know you understand."

Play dead? Why? Avei focused on the hand he held and managed a small squeeze.

"Good, Avei. Very good. Remember, don't move." Eadren's voice sounded as if it came from the end of a long tunnel. Something light settled against her face. Was it a bed sheet? *Wait, did I die?* Desperate, she struggled to stay awake.

Eadren's voice penetrated her growing fear. "I have to save him. Stay completely still and I will come back for you."

Save who? While her body remained still, her mind raced. How much time had passed since getting the antidote? The thick brain fog made it difficult to think. When the doc delivered it, death was only moments away. She could still feel the effects of the grenwal venom. It had to be less than ten minutes ago. What had happened in that short time? *What did Zarul do?* The ever-present darkness flared, bringing an all-consuming weariness. Too weak to fight, and trusting Eadren when he said he'd come back, she let go and sunk into oblivion.

35

The monochromatic morgue was spartan compared to the resplendence of the medical bay that catered to the living. Bright lights shone down on two bodies draped in sheets, each on a steel table. A bank of six mortuary drawers lined the back wall. The reek of cleaning solution permeated the space. A distant alarm sounded through the closed hatch.

Sintha sat next to one of the bodies, grooming her orange fur with one of her six paws, emerald eyes half closed as she purred with contentment. The silver collar glittered in the bright lights and threw patterns on the wall whenever she moved.

Avei threw back the sheet and covered Sintha, who froze in indignation. Eyes closed tight against the light, she struggled to sit. Moaning, she fell back and grabbed her pounding head.

After several deep breaths to ease the headache, she opened her eyes and took a moment to celebrate being alive. Avei reached for her necklace and found it. She gripped it tight, thankful her parents would not suffer the loss of another daughter. A quick inventory showed she was far from well. A deep ache in her bones and muscles brought on a cold sweat and nausea. *Where is everyone?*

"Dr. Hueson? Eadren?" she croaked out, her throat and mouth bone dry. The only sound was the incessant alarm from the corridor. "Is anyone here?" Avei tapped the embedded wrist device to raise help. Nothing happened. A more aggressive tap brought the same results. The seizures and severe muscle contractions must have short-circuited it.

Sintha growled and batted away the sheet, startling Avei as she pushed herself to a sitting position. "Where did you come from?"

The animal sidled up to her and seemed to say, *you are not alone*. The wisp of a memory brushed against at the edges of Avei's mind as she petted the animal. She struggled to grab it and recalled Eadren leaning over her, whispering something. *What did he say*? Sintha meowed and brought her rumination to a screeching stop. *Wait, how did Sintha get into the morgue through the closed hatch?*

Avei studied the feline and zeroed in on the collar. It looked identical to the one they had removed earlier in the Solarium. She sat up too fast, causing the headache to flare again. Another round of deep breaths reduced the queasiness but did little to ease the throbbing. Once her head cleared enough to function, she grabbed Sintha and unfastened the collar. A scan of it revealed the recording device. Avei's mind whirled in circles until it landed on the only possibility, which shook her to her core.

Sintha jumped to the other bed, and Avei noticed the sheet-draped body for the first time. Zarul must have struck again; someone else had died. It jarred loose what

Eadren had said before she lost consciousness. He warned her to play dead.

With a rush of dread, she gripped the edge of the table and acknowledged how weak she felt. Even so, finding out the victim's identity took priority over discomfort. She rolled off in one quick motion. When her feet hit the floor, her legs shook and threatened to give way. Lightheaded and shaky, she held onto the table until her equilibrium came back.

Avei stumbled to the other table and leaned against it as a brace. Sintha headbutted her and she petted the animal again, while her mind raced. Could it be Eadren who was the greatest threat to the killer? It made sense to eliminate him. Given their rocky start and the short time they had worked together, the deep regret that he might be dead came as a surprise.

She pulled back the sheet and Dr. Hueson stared back at her through lifeless eyes, his face frozen in agony. The large bite on his neck left little doubt as to what had killed him. On the floor, a crushed dispenser, surrounded by liquid, told the full story. Eadren had tried to save the doctor by giving him the antidote, and Zarul had stopped him.

Anger ripped through Avei. The doctor was innocent, no threat to anyone. Avei closed his eyes and pulled the sheet over his head.

Zarul must have been in the medical bay when Eadren whispered to her to stay still. He had saved her at grave personal risk.

She limped to the six mortuary drawers on the back wall and scanned the names on four of the drawers: Caerson Mercer, Ocia Doni, Imara Tiniba, and Marsa Baako.

One of the four drawers was missing a body, and she knew which one. She tapped the green pulsing button next to the far-right drawer. It slid open. Empty.

Avei slammed her hand on the metal shelf. The loud boom spooked Sintha, who sat nearby. "I've been an idiot."

Marsa Baako was Zarul. Avei knew better than most how much Marsa lacked morals. But murder? Avei shook her head in disbelief. *What caused Marsa to take such a dark path?*

"It's the damn money." Avei smashed the green button, and the shelf slid closed. "It's always been about the damn money." Avei had been Marsa's meal ticket for the last nine years, and the woman must have panicked when she went on medical leave. The author published a book or a screenplay almost every month based on Avei's latest case. Given Marsa's affluent lifestyle, those lost months would have put a sizable dent in her income. *Did she orchestrate all this just to get me back to work?*

Marsa knew every detail about Avei's life, including her love of arachnids. *What better way to push me out of retirement than a serial killer who used spiders as a weapon?* The only problem was that she didn't take the bait. Not initially, anyway. It had taken D.I. Skora, forcing her onto the *Delphi* to investigate Caerson Mercer's death.

That brought up Caerson's and Ocia's murders. Their deaths appeared rushed and ill-thought-out. Nothing like the first victims. As she thought about it, the more certain she became. Marsa had crafted the first six killings to get her working again and had planned to stop. The *Delphi* deaths were spontaneous. Somehow, Caerson and Imara had figured out Marsa was Zarul and blackmailed her. Marsa needed to silence the couple before they could expose her as Zarul. *How did Ocia fit in?* Most likely in the wrong place at the wrong time. Marsa must have been worried Imara might have said something during her ravings in the corridor and Ocia had overheard them.

The double bites now made sense. Marsa had experimented on the victims until she found the right dosage of venom and antidote to fake her own death should the need arise. Avei flashed back to the Solarium. Marsa had blood on her arm. She had given herself the antidote before they arrived.

First order of business, find Marsa before she killed again.

Avei headed through the hatch and into the medical laboratory and stumbled to a stop. It looked like someone had turned the room upside down and shaken it. Medical supplies pulled from cabinets lay scattered across the floor, including smashed medicine bottles. The container that had held the grenwal lay empty on the floor, half covered with packages of gauze bandages. Smoke poured from a large hole in the synthesizer and filled the room with the smell of burnt electronics. Avei's hand shot to her belt. Her holster was empty, and the knife was missing. She remembered Eadren placing them on the tray next to her bed before she passed out. *Great. Just great.* Marsa had a gun, a knife, and the grenwal at her disposal.

Avei scanned the walls and landed on the comm display next to the hatch. She stumbled toward it. The captain needed to know the identity of Zarul, and that Marsa had her weapons. Sweat beads covered her forehead and breaths came fast and labored. The headache intensified and bile rose in her throat. She forced it back down. The lives of everyone on the ship depended on her, and she had to keep going. Leaning her forehead against the wall next to the display, she took several deep breaths and willed her stomach to settle.

Sintha picked a way through the mess until she reached her side. Avei stared at the animal with pity. No matter what one thought of Marsa, there wasn't any doubt the woman loved her pet. Atiza were prized for their intelligence. Avei's father longed to own one, but her mother always said no and was steadfast in her convictions. The Atiza were natural predators of their beloved arachnids and had no place in their lives. "I will find a wonderful home for you. I promise," Avei told the cat, then she turned her attention back to the screen and tapped it. "Secure channel to Captain Dimphi."

The captain's face appeared on the display. "Thank the Goddess Mima, you're alive. Doc didn't think you'd survive."

Captain looked behind him. "The inspector is alive."

The bridge crew behind the captain cheered. Sezin leaned over Dimphi and smiled. "Inspector, you are a sight for sore eyes. You look half dead. Shouldn't you be in bed?"

"No time for that." The sight of her old friend brought with it a rush of strength and determination.

Captain Dimphi leaned closer. "The cameras will be online at any moment. Sezin's been a tremendous help."

"We've isolated the subroutine that shut off the camera systems. Quite ingenious, actually," Sezin said.

"Good. Where's Eadren?" Avei asked, hoping to hear good news.

"I can't raise him or Dr. Hueson." Captain Dimphi crushed her last vestiges of hope.

"The doctor's dead."

"Sweet Mima, this is terrible news." The captain blinked back tears. "He was so young. And so kind. Had his whole life ahead of him."

"Marsa Baako is Zarul. She killed the Doctor, Caerson, Ocia, and Imara."

"How can that be? Ms. Baako's dead."

If Sezin had a solid body, the captain would be on the ground. Sezin leaned through him and stared at Avei with intensity. "The double bites. She discovered a way to fake her death using venom."

"Yes, and now she has my gun and knife. Lock the bridge down until I find and restrain her. And don't stop working on those cameras. I'm going to need them."

Captain Dimphi shook his head, his eyes wide with fear. "Do you think Eadren—?"

"There was a struggle, and his... he isn't here. Marsa destroyed the synthesizer and all the ingredients for the antidote." A wave of dizziness hit, and Avei closed her eyes for a moment.

"Inspector, are you okay?" Captain Dimphi and Sezin both leaned closer, their faces filling the screen.

She braced herself and opened her eyes to a strange sight. Sezin's face superimposed over the captain's. "I'm fine. When do we reach Charnos?"

"Two hours." Dimphi didn't disguise his relief. "We exited the wormhole a few minutes ago."

"Get a message to Mernin and Charnos Security Forces, alerting them of the situation."

"They're already informed. I alerted them of the deaths the moment we were free of the event horizon," Sezin said. "I'll send an addendum letting them know of the doctor's death and Zarul's identity."

"Good." Avei needed to find Marsa, and fast. She thought through everything she knew about the woman. Trapped on a ship on its way to Charnos, Marsa needed to leave before arrival. Cybernetic shuttles were designed so anyone could fly them in an emergency. All Marsa needed to do was tell the navigation system her destination. "Sezin, can you lock down the two shuttles from the bridge?"

Sezin stilled and then nodded. "Done. No one appears to be aboard."

"I'm headed there now. Keep working on those cameras just in case I'm mistaken, and Marsa isn't headed to the shuttle bay."

"You got it, Inspector." Sezin straightened, to the captain's relief. Even though he could feel nothing, it was unnerving to see a head sticking out of his chest. "Watch your back. As soon as those cameras are online, I'm coming to you with a security team."

"Thank you, Sezin. I'd appreciate that."

"Let me echo your partner's words. Be careful, Inspector." The captain's face was full of fear and worry while Sezin beamed with delight at being called Avei's partner.

Avei turned off the display and took a moment to scan the laboratory for anything that might make a useful weapon. The medicine cabinet caught her attention. A quick search through the vials still on the shelves netted an ampoule of zasapam. Finally, a bit of luck. She combed through the debris on the floor and found an empty dispenser. She slid the vial inside and jammed it into her pocket.

Time to face Zarul and bring the killing to an end. Avei kissed her necklace, then ran out of the lab, Sintha hot on her heels.

36

The massive hangar door reflected the bright lights that blazed down on the shuttle bay and made the small space feel cavernous. Steel cables anchored the three hover workbenches to the bulkhead. The engineering shop ran the length of the back wall and held racks of spare parts, all housed behind webbed netting. A row of lockers, along with a table and four chairs bolted to the deck, sat in the bay's corner, behind a thick glass wall.

Docked next to each other, the shuttles filled the bay. The large ship could transport up to sixty passengers and the small one carried up to ten people. In the unlikely event of a catastrophic incident, the crew would leave the ship in escape pods scattered around the outer edges of the ship. This left the shuttles for the guests, and the ship's officers as the pilots.

Avei limped into the hangar through a hatch in the far wall. Loud banging echoed throughout the bay as Marsa hammered the side of the small shuttle. Sezin had locked down the ships in the nick of time.

Marsa wore a long, bright pink coat that flowed to her ankles and had a high collar that clashed with her tangerine hair. A suitcase floated several inches off the floor. Eadren stood next to her, his back to Avei. Relief at seeing him alive was tempered by his ramrod posture. *Something's wrong.* Sintha ran past her and made a beeline for Marsa. So much for sneaking up on them.

With discovery imminent, Avei stumbled across the hangar toward them. Her whole body ached with a deep, burning pain that brought on waves of cold sweat, and she embraced it. That she had survived was a miracle and the discomfort a small price to pay for being alive.

Gods, she hated Marsa Baako. She'd make sure the woman spent the rest of her life confined to Meflogun, a notorious underground prison on a barren moon. Marsa needed to suffer every day that was left of her miserable life to make up for the horrifying deaths her victims had endured. All because this monster wanted to maintain her affluent lifestyle.

"Why won't this damn door open?" Marsa bellowed as she pounded on the shuttle door. The sound ricocheted off the walls like a battering ram.

Sintha reached her and rubbed against her owner's legs. Marsha glanced at Sintha and froze. She whirled around, Avei's gun in her hand.

"You! Why aren't you dead?" Marsa stared, flabbergasted. Her shock caused the gun to droop. This allowed Avei to move closer than she expected.

"Right back at you." Avei glanced at Eadren, who hadn't turned to face her. Something was definitely wrong.

Marsa raised the gun and held it steady. "Don't come any closer or I will shoot you."

Avei stumbled to a stop. Her legs turned rubbery, causing a moment of fear. Not being particularly religious didn't stop her from saying a silent prayer to whichever deity might be listening to keep her upright. "Eadren, are you alright?"

Eadren turned slowly to face her. The grenwal clung to his chest. Its upper legs hooked around his neck in a terrifying embrace. "Did I mention how much I loathe spiders?"

Dread settled on Avei. Marsa had destroyed the remaining antidote and the synthesizer. Even with Lorestal, he wouldn't last the two hours it took to reach Charnos. Avei took a few steps closer. "Eadren, no sudden movements."

Marsa tapped once on the small device on her wrist. The spider jumped to Eadren's neck and molded itself around the side of his head, its fangs positioned just under his chin. Eadren shuddered and closed his eyes.

Marsa gloated at her and held up her wrist. "You're not the only expert on spiders. Two taps on this here device and Fergus bites the chief."

Avei stared at Eadren, horrified. If she tried to remove the spider, it would bite him. Little chance she could convince Marsa to do the right thing and remove the grenwal. The author was arrogant, deceitful, intelligent, and impervious to shame. Avei needed to play to the woman's ego and buy time until a plan presented itself. A difficult balancing act. Overplay the obsequiousness and she risked Marsa catching on. The wrong word or phrase could end both her and Eadren's lives.

He stared at her with terror-filled eyes, and her own fear rose. It required a level head to get them out of this predicament, being afraid did no one any good. Time to have her suspicions confirmed. "I saw you die. How did you do it?"

"It was my – if everything goes to hell plot. My last resort, if you will." Marsa waved the gun around, looking none too pleased. "And I'd say everything has gone completely to hell." She emphasized each word by jabbing the gun at Avei. "Do you know how much experimenting it took to make it look like I died and not actually kill myself? And do you really think I wanted to poison myself and go through that torturous pain? Of course not. And yet, here we are, with you ruining everything. Again. You forced me to accelerate my plan F."

The first confirmation. Avei flashed back to the two bites on five of the six of the Zarul victims. Time to stroke the ego. "You did your experimenting on the Zarul victims. I've never heard of anyone attempting what you did. It's a unique approach. I'll give you that."

Marsa shrugged her agreement. "Pushing boundaries is how you advance science."

Avei felt her ire rise. Not in any reputable school or laboratory.

"Dr. Hueson helped you, didn't he?" Avei never thought he did, but keeping Marsa engaged in conversation bought them precious seconds.

"That imbecile? He had no idea he killed that cleaning woman with the venom-laced sleeping pills I put in his medicine cabinet." Marsa giggled and looked pleased. "You should have seen his face when I rose from the dead."

Eadren sucked in his breath when Fergus probed his face. He trembled from head to toe.

Avei needed to pick up the pace. Given his fear of spiders, Eadren could very well panic and try to pull the spider off, causing it to bite. "I'm curious about something. How did Caerson and Imara figure out you were Zarul?"

Marsa stopped giggling and became angry. "I wore a disguise while doing my research on Celethe. Imara still recognized me. Those idiots thought they'd be safe confronting me on a ship." Marsa shook her head in disgust. "They wanted to extort my hard-earned money. They deserved to die."

Avei glanced at Eadren, who closed his eyes and stood rigid, which soothed the spider, causing it to settle down. She turned back to Marsa. "You planned to frame Wilm for the Zarul murders."

"I selected him to be the antagonist in my story. He was perfect. The loving husband avenging the wrongs done to his beautiful wife. Then he got into bed with MSF and agreed to rat out his Iscun buddies. What a fool. He'd bring attention to my little enterprise, so I had to drop him."

"What's this really about?"

"Don't you get it? You were my muse, and I thought I couldn't write without you. In desperation to get you solving crimes again, I paired your spider obsession with Celethe's sad story." She glared at Avei. "Despite all that effort, time and money, you wallowed in your depression and never once lifted your head to see what was going on. Unbelievable."

"People died, so you can write more stories?" Fists clenched, Avei advanced on Marsa, seething with disgust at this woman who put her financial well-being over the lives of innocent people.

"I destroyed the antidote. Come any closer, and he dies." Marsa lifted her jaw and scowled. "And stop being so overdramatic. The first six people I killed were not what you'd call model citizens. They did terrible things to innocent people and deserved to die."

Avei slowed to a stop. Eadren caught her attention when he pinched his fingers together a few times. What he proposed came with extreme danger and might also be the only chance they had. She gave a discreet nod before turning her fury on Marsa.

"All this is about money. Isn't it?"

Marsa shrugged. "My lifestyle and wealth are bound to you. I didn't realize how much until you stopped working cases. Nobody wants a Marsa Baako novel without the remarkable Inspector Savei Demis, and her latest case."

Avei risked a quick glance and saw Eadren's hand inch closer to the spider. She needed to keep Marsa distracted, and that meant being provocative. "You're insane."

Marsa shot an angry glare her way. "That's harsh. Psychopaths murder for the thrill of it. I'm more of a means-to-an-end person. I'm not crazy. I'm pragmatic."

Avei watched Eadren out of the corner of her eye as his hand approached the spider's midsection.

"Stop wasting my time and unlock this hatch, or you both die." Marsa jabbed the gun at Avei.

When Eadren's hand came within an inch of it, the spider pulled back and jittered in warning. He lowered his hand.

Avei met Marsa's eyes and held them. "There's no place in the galaxy where you can hide from me or the MSF. We'll turn over every rock you might slither under until we find you."

"I have no plans on disappearing, Ms. Hoity-Toity." Marsa smirked. "When you came aboard the *Delphi*, I implemented plan C. I turn myself in to the warden at Yapho Penitentiary, where he has a luxury suite waiting. In return, he gets twenty-five percent of the proceeds from my future books. After the success of this little venture, I realized I can come up with my own storylines. So, as of this moment, consider yourself fired as my muse. I no longer need you." Marsa tapped the side of her head. "Not when I have this fertile imagination going for me."

As she smiled and leaned against the shuttle, the gun drooped. "Serial killer writing murder mysteries. First time that's ever been done. I'll be the most famous novelist in the history of our galaxy. And the richest. It'll mean serving a little time, then bribing the Tribunal to drop all charges." Marsa let out a satisfied sigh. "My fans will love this new direction and, best of all, I'm finally free of you."

Sintha jumped on Marsa's leg, distracting her. "No, my love. Not now."

Avei took advantage of the situation and closed the distance between them, the cylinder gripped in her right hand.

Marsa startled when she looked up and saw Avei was only a few feet away. She aimed the gun and fired. The shot went wide, missing by a few inches.

Avei reached Marsa before she could shoot again. She slammed the cylinder on her neck. With her other hand, she grabbed the author's arm and pushed the gun away from Eadren.

Marsa faltered as her pupils dilated. "What did you... what did you give me?"

"Something to knock you out."

"You conniving... You—" Marsa collapsed on the ground.

Avei seized the gun and turned to Eadren, who held Fergus with both hands. Her smile disappeared when she caught sight of the large bite on his neck, oozing orange venom.

"Take it. Please." Eadren sucked in a quivering breath as the spider bucked and tried to break free.

Avei needed no convincing. Ordinarily, killing such a beautiful creature went against everything she believed in. Not this time. Marsa had trained it to be a killer, and Avei couldn't risk it harming someone else. MSF rules be damned. She snatched it with one hand and tossed it, then fired her gun and blasted it into tiny, smoking bits.

Eadren wavered, tried to smile, and failed. "This is not how I expected to die."

Avei helped him sit on the ground as her mind raced for a way out of the inevitable. "Spiders are unpredictable. She'd have brought the antidote with her."

"Marsa destroyed the only other vial when I tried to give it to the doc."

Avei turned her attention to the floating suitcase. "Marsa injected herself with the antidote right before she drank the brandy. It's how she survived. She'd have her own supply."

"You said three minutes, right?" Eadren touched the bite, then scoured the venom from his fingers, using the bottom of his tunic.

Avei couldn't meet his eyes. "Maybe ten. There will be hallucinations."

Eadren let out a long sigh and stopped scrubbing his fingers. "Bind my hands and feet so I don't hurt you or anyone else."

"We're not there yet." Avei jerked Marsa's suitcase open and tipped it on its side. A pile of garish cat suits spilled out and Avei dug through them, looking for a vial or a dispenser of some kind. She sat back on her heels, frustrated. "Nothing."

"My parents already lost one son." He closed his eyes. "Now, they'll lose another.

"We're not giving up." She squatted next to Marsa, who lay on the ground unconscious. A quick check of her coat pockets and interior lining turned up nothing. Avei tried to slow her rattled mind and think of a solution.

"On the observation deck, she had blood on her arm."

Eadren grabbed his head and hunched over, moaning. Sweat slid down his face. He sucked in a few breaths. "We would have found a dispenser."

"Unless she disguised it." Avei checked through the many rings on Marsa's hand and rejected them. The glint of the gaudy star-shaped pendant necklace caught her eye, and she yanked it free. Her fingers slid along the edges of the heavy medallion and across the surface, searching for anything unusual. The catch at the top seemed a likely activation mechanism. She pushed it. Nothing happened. Her fingers worked their way around the pendant again.

Eadren jerked around and hunched over to gape under the shuttle. "Avei! Avei! There are more of them."

To hallucinate so soon meant the venom was taking hold faster than normal. Eadren's fear of the grenwal had caused his pulse rate to increase, which sent the venom surging through his body. Death was imminent. Avei shoved the necklace into her pocket and rushed to Eadren, who struggled to stand.

"There's nothing there." She forced him back down and grabbed his face. "Look at me."

Eadren fought her grip with brute force, brought on by sheer terror. It took every ounce of strength to keep him on the ground. "Eadren, there's nothing there. Please. You need to trust me."

He trembled violently. "Don't lie to me, Avei. Tell me the truth, no matter how bad it is."

Avei smiled at him. "I'm telling you the truth. I killed the only grenwal in this shuttle bay. Close your eyes. That will help." When Eadren shut his eyes, she grabbed his hand and squeezed. "I'm not leaving you."

Eadren curled up on the floor. "Marsa killed the doctor. I tried. I had the antidote in my hand and that monster knocked it away. Smashed it before...." He groaned in pain as the venom cramped his muscles.

Avei squeezed his hand again. "You saved me, Eadren. You told me to stay still, so Marsa didn't know I was alive. If you hadn't done that, I would be dead too."

She sat next to him and pulled the pendant from her pocket. "The delivery system needs to be easy to use." Another careful check of the prongs of the star showed a small dimple on the bottom one.

Eadren cried out as muscle spasms consumed his body.

Avei gripped the pendant, dimpled side down, and slammed it on his arm. When she pulled it away, she saw a needle retract into the pendant, leaving behind a small drop of blood.

Avei grabbed Eadren's hand while he fought to stay conscious. She didn't know if the pendant was empty or if it even held the antidote. Eadren needed hope, so she'd keep worries to herself. "The pendent contained the antidote, and we need time for it to work. Fight, Eadren. Fight hard. For your family. For yourself."

Eadren turned to her, his face rigid with pain. "Don't know... if... I..." His body contorted, and he wrenched his hand away.

The hatch opened and Captain Dimphi rushed in with three security officers and two medical staff, who brought a floating gurney.

Sezin zoomed around them wearing an exterminator suit with a chemical pack on their back, a long rubber hose, and tan-colored coveralls. Their holoball trailed behind them as they raced to Avei.

“We got the cameras working and saw the situation,” Captain Dimphi shouted behind Sezin, as they raced across the deck.

Sezin slid to a stop in front of her. “You don’t look so good. Are you okay?”

“I’ll be fine once I know Eadren will live.” Avei struggled to stand. Her legs shook, threatening to collapse. She had reached the end of her endurance. “I gave Eadren a shot of something Marsa had on her, and I’m hoping it’s the antidote. Do you have Lorestal on you?”

One of the technicians reached into a small bag attached to his belt and pulled out a silver canister.

“Give it to him. It can’t hurt, and might buy him enough time for the antidote to work.”

After the technician gave Eadren the shot, the medical personnel crowded around him. They lifted him onto the gurney. Sezin hovered next to Avei, concern etched on their face.

The captain stood with the security officers, who circled Marsa.

Once the techs had Eadren secured to the gurney, they rushed him out of the hangar with Captain Dimphi following.

Avei took in Sezin’s attire. “Exterminator? Really?”

“A killer bug is on the loose. How else would I dress?”

“I killed it.”

Sezin nodded. “Something we should have done earlier. Rules be damned.”

“Yeah. Another regret I’ll need to live with.” Avei turned her attention to Marsa, who moaned as she came awake.

"Hmmm. We have one more killer pest that needs exterminating." Sezin pointed their rubber hose at Marsa and a holographic stream of green chemicals spewed from the end and covered the author.

"Sezin, not now." Avei waited until the hologram dissipated and revealed Marsa Baako, struggling to open her eyes. "Can I borrow a pair of handcuffs?"

One of the security officers handed Avei a thick green band. She crouched next to Marsa, who finally got her eyes open. "Nod if you can hear and understand me."

Marsa took in the security officers, who towered over her, and nodded.

"Marsa Baako, you're under arrest for the murders of Caerson Mercer, Imara Tiniba, Ocia Doni and Dr. Rymond Hueson, as well as for your first six victims. Also, for the attempted murder of me, and Eadren Omu."

Sezin's persona changed to a beefy security guard, seven feet tall, when Avei mentioned the attempted murder charge. They glared over Avei's head at Marsa, who smirked back at them.

"Tell your AI to back off. They don't scare me. Now, get me off this cold floor." Avei stood and nodded to one of the security officers, who held out his hand. Marsa grabbed it and he pulled her to a standing position.

Sezin maintained their appearance as they settled in next to Avei.

"Take me to Yapho Penitentiary. They're waiting for me." Marsa wobbled as she straightened her coat.

Avei spun Marsa around and wrapped the tie around her wrists. They molded into place. She turned the woman back around and looked her in the eye. “You, of all people, should know what I do with serial killers.”

“I made you famous, Avei Themis.” Marsa paled and for the first time had the decency to appear afraid. “You owe me, big time. Repay your debt by taking me to Yapho.”

Anger and disbelief surged at the audacity of this woman. “I owe you nothing. You stole my life and never once asked if I was okay with it. You did it all for your own self-aggrandizement and wealth. Fame is something I never asked for or wanted. When you usurped my identity, you did it without a thought or care about how it negatively affected me.”

Marsa leaned back from the heat of Avei’s rage. “You don’t understand, it’s already arranged. Take me to Yapho. I insist upon it.”

“No, Ms. Baako. I will not. You will spend the rest of your miserable life in a maximum-security prison of my choosing. And I choose Meflogun.”

Sezin whooped and danced around, distracting everyone.

Marsa teetered and landed on her knees. “Please, I beg of you, don’t send me there. I won’t last a week, and you know it.”

“You’re scrappy. I’m sure you will figure out a way to survive.” Avei nodded at the security officers, who each took an arm and pulled Marsa upright. They escorted her from the hangar.

Avei watched Sintha dart after them. She needed to find a home for the animal.

Sezin held their hand in the air. “High five, Inspector. I got goosebumps when you told her she was going to Meflogun. Literal goosebumps. Come on. Bring it.”

Avei stared at her AI, who continued to stand there with their hands up. She knew Sezin wouldn’t move until she complied. Her AI towered over her, and she had to stand on her tiptoes to fake-slap their holo-hand.

Her elation at ridding Marsa Baako from her life dimmed, knowing Eadren may die. She had to get to medical, but her feet wouldn’t work. The adrenaline was wearing off, her legs turning to rubber. She sagged against the shuttle. “I don’t think I can walk.”

Sezin froze for a moment and then settled in next to her. “Medical reports Eadren has stabilized, and they’ll send along a hover-chair.”

Avei studied her massive AI and felt a wave of gratitude. “Thank you, Sezin. For everything. Your support means the world to me.”

Sezin smiled. “We’re partners, and partners are always there for each other. No matter what.”

Avei smiled and nodded. “Yes. Yes, we are.”

37

Avei stood next to Eadren in the shuttle bay. The fact they were both out of bed after nearly dying, and upright just hours later, was a medical marvel. Bright lights crisscrossed the ceiling and shone down on them, highlighting how pale they were. Both looked like they might keel over at any moment. Two hover chairs sat in the tool cage, along with medical personnel, just in case one of them did a face-plant before the handoff.

AI Sezin stood behind them, wearing an MSF dress uniform, arms behind their back. Avei was relieved her AI had chosen proper attire for the handoff. One never knew what they'd turn up in throughout an investigation, and Avei wouldn't have it any other way. Chasing serial killers meant having to walk on the dark side for a significant portion of her life. Sezin kept things light, even when evil beckoned to the shadows.

Marsa sat in a chair in front of them. Metal bands wrapped around her hands and ankles, making escape impossible. Two security officers waited nearby. She rocked back and forth, moaning. Her tangerine hair draped over her face in a tangled mess.

Avei felt nothing but disgust for the woman as she watched her histrionics. Ten people had died so that she could keep her wealthy lifestyle. Given the plethora of evidence and Marsa's own confession earlier in the hangar, the trial should be blessedly short.

Avei wanted Marsa off the ship before the guests started offboarding. Given the author's ego, the woman would revel in the notoriety of being Zarul, so Avei kept the greeting party to just herself, Sezin and Eadren. She got confirmation she'd made the right decision when Marsa asked why the guests weren't there, becoming angry when she learned no one else was coming.

The head of Charnos Security Forces assured Avei that Ms. Baako would not go to Yapho Penitentiary. When she returned to Mernin, Avei planned to petition the Tribunal to send Marsa to Meflogun Prison. Located underground and impenetrable, it housed the most violent offenders in their sector of the galaxy. Every time Avei had brought a serial killer before the Tribunal, they had agreed to her request to send them to Meflogun. She hoped to continue that record.

Having Marsa permanently out of her life brought mixed feelings. The woman had made life hell by chronicling every detail of her personal and work life. Billions of strangers knew everything about her, and Avei found that frightening. Not only did it make her job as a homicide investigator harder, it gave ammunition to the serial killers she tracked. Thanks to Marsa and the Nexus, they knew where she lived, what businesses she frequented, and her patterns of behavior. This meant she had to be methodical in changing how she lived her life every day. Relief came with the realization she never had to do that again.

The money from the sale of Marsa's books and movies had lessened the loss of her privacy but funding the Themis Institute for Arachnology made it bearable. Her parents' work creating lifesaving antidotes and medicines had made the institute solvent so that they no longer needed the cash infusions from the books. Given Marsa's current notoriety as Zarul, the sale of her works would skyrocket and bring in even more money. That meant finding new charities and also giving a large portion to the families of the Zarul and Apollyona victims.

Avei looked up at Eadren, amazed he had the strength to even get out of bed. The medical staff had concealed the bite on his neck with a large bandage. It had been touch and go for a while. "You really should be in the medical bay."

Eadren smiled. "I remember telling someone else that recently and having them completely ignore me."

Sezin leaned between them and smiled. "Do you see what I have to put up with? I say something, and I'm ignored. Say something else, still ignored."

Avei chuckled. "Point taken and I'll do better in the future."

Sezin snorted their disbelief and Avei shot an exasperated look at them both.

A shudder rippled through the ship as it slowed to a stop, followed by a gentle bump. They had docked at the Charnos spacehub.

Avei and Eadren shared a long gaze. She had a good idea what was going through his mind. The same thing that was going through hers. Gratitude for being alive and glad to see the nightmare end. She touched her chest, where the necklace of Anastasia lay, and felt a surge of relief that her parents hadn't lost another daughter. Avei saw Eadren's hand go to his right pocket and she smiled. They had much in common and she looked forward to getting to know him better. Maybe later their friendship would evolve into something more. Right now, friends felt right.

A large hatch on the side of the hangar door opened. Seven Charnos Security Force officers filed in from the station. D.I. Henra Rico, a powerhouse of a woman in both stature and reputation, led them across the floor.

Marsa's head shot up when they entered. She sprung to her feet and stumbled. The metal bands on her ankles reduced movement and she landed on her knees. No one lent a hand as she tried to get back on her feet and failed. "No, this can't be happening. I can't go to prison." She turned around to beseech Avei and fell forward. Marsa caught herself with her cuffed hands and pushed herself to back to her knees. "Avei, please. Send me to Yapho like I planned. Do this one thing for me. You know you owe me."

Avei walked around Marsa until she could look her in the eyes. "This is the last time you will ever see me." She watched Marsa stiffen and headed her off before she said anything. "You say I owe you. I don't. You enriched your life at my personal and professional expense. Every bit of the money I received from the sale of your books and movies went to charities and into building the Themis Institute of Arachnology. That money has saved countless lives and I'm forever grateful for it, even at the cost of my privacy."

Marsa brightened. “As you said, I’m the reason for all of that money. The least you can do is put in a good word for me.”

“That money came to me because the Tribunal forced you to pay it. If I hadn’t sued, you’d have kept it all for yourself. I will petition the court to send you to Meflogun, where you belong. Ocia and Dr. Hueson did nothing to you, and you killed them anyway. They were innocent and for that alone, I’ll do everything in my power to stop you from going to some luxury prison.”

Marsa slumped at her words and lowered her head. “I hate ungrateful people.”

Avei turned to face the Charnos contingent, who stopped in front of them. She knew of Henra Rico by her stellar reputation. “D.I. Rico, it’s wonderful to meet you. I’m Inspector Avei Themis of the Mernin Security Forces. Behind me is Eadren Omu, MSF drug enforcement, and Sezin Watson, my AI partner. Welcome aboard the *Delphi*.”

D.I. Rico smiled and held out her meaty hand. “A pleasure to meet you, Inspector. Your methods for catching serial killers are a key part of our rookie training classes. You are quite the legend among my people.” The six officers standing around her nodded vigorously.

Avei’s cheeks glowed with embarrassment as she shook Rico’s hand. “Thank you. I appreciate that.”

D.I. Rico smiled over Avei’s head at Sezin. “We’ve heard wonderful things about your Sezin Watson as well.”

Avei looked back at Sezin, who puffed up with pride. Gods, there would be no living with them now. *Now? There is no now, Themis. Right?* For the first time in three months,

Avei felt a strong resistance to leaving the Mernin Security Forces. She thought back to something Eadren had said in Marsa's room. *The trick to surviving this job is to focus on the good we do, which far exceeds the times we get it wrong.* He was right. Even though her mistake cost many lives, she didn't make it in a vacuum. Her mother had been right to point out that she'd gone through proper channels and vetted her findings with people smarter than her. Skora and four senior colleagues had reviewed her notes and watched her interview with the woman. They agreed with her assessment to release Apollyona. That and the Navra royal family's complicit role in the murders lifted the suffocating cloud of guilt and self-loathing that came with carrying the shame alone. A surge of excitement coursed through her at the possibility of staying at MSF. The journey home would provide the time she needed to make the best decision about her future. Right now, the handoff required her full attention.

D.I. Rico held out a hand to Eadren, who shook it. "Drug Enforcement? Undercover?"

Eadren nodded. "Yes, ma'am."

"One of our most dangerous assignments on the force. I thank you for your service."

Eadren stood straighter. "Thank you. That means a lot to me."

Avei felt a warm glow from the kindness D.I. Rico showed toward them. An equal to D.I. Skora in every way. They both cared deeply about their people.

Still on her knees, Marsa cut into the conversation. “Take me to Yapho. I’ve made arrangements and they’re waiting for me. I’ll make it worth your while.”

D.I. Rico stared at the woman. “Ms. Baako, you will remain in our custody until the Tribunal decides where you will go. And for your information, Yapho doesn’t take serial killers. So, whatever plans you made with them became moot when the body count piled up.” She motioned to three of her officers, who pulled Marsa to her feet. “Get her out of my sight.”

Avei watched Marsa shuffle her way across the hangar floor, supported by two of the three Charnos officers who accompanied her. She struggled to wrap her head around the fact the woman had committed ten murders. Something else to ponder on the way back home. The darkness that consumed her was dissipating. Almost dying for the second time in as many months forced a full reboot of her priorities and expectations. When Marsa disappeared through the hatch, she felt relief. The Zarul nightmare was at an end.

D.I. Rico turned back to Avei and studied her for a moment. “While I can’t speak for the Tribunal, I can speak for Charnos Security Forces. You have my personal guarantee Ms. Baako will not spend one day in Yapho while in my custody.”

“I am relieved to hear that. Thank you.”

D.I. Rico smiled at Eadren and motioned to Captain Dimphi, who stood in the hatch. He nodded and led the first of the guests through the hatch from the *Delphi* promenade. “Time for phase two of this little adventure.”

The captain smiled at them as he passed by, subdued guests shuffling behind him. Word had gotten out about the deaths on the *Delphi* and the arrest of Marsa Baako. Finding out a serial killer had been on board would put anyone into a contemplative funk. Grateful to have survived but rattled; any one of them might have died in a horrifying way.

Avei watched the Sycardian couple, who brought up the rear and towered over the other guests. The two had been the last to enter the elevator on the promenade when she and Eadren were on their way to Marsa's room. They had allowed the other guests to go before them even though the killer was still on the loose. The role of protector came naturally to them. She had deep respect for anyone who put the safety of others above their own. That kind of courage was uncommon in the civilian population, for a good reason. It takes a supreme effort for someone to overcome their instinctual urge to fight, flee, or freeze when confronted with danger.

Avei smiled at the couple as they passed by. They nodded at her and continued to Captain Dimphi, who stood by the hatch into the Charnos spacehub. He greeted each guest as they passed by with a smile and the occasional handshake as they exited the hangar.

"It's unfortunate we got nothing useful from the collar." Eadren touched the bandage on his neck and winced.

"Nothing we didn't already know or suspect," Sezin said behind them.

"Marsa was careful to never speak of her actions around Sintha. I can't believe she would risk that kind of incrimination should she fall under suspicion for the murders. I'm still having a hard time wrapping my head around the fact she is Zarul." Avei watched the Sycardian couple disappear through the hatch.

"The case against her is solid. We don't need the recordings," Sezin said.

"I read your report. You have her dead to rights. I wouldn't worry." D.I. Rico motioned the remaining three officers over to her side. "Okay, folks. Here we go. Pull up your big girl panties because this might get heated."

The Breckins entered the hangar and headed to the spacehub hatch. Wilm trailed behind Julisa and Celethe. Avei looked up at Eadren. "Are you sure about this?"

Eadren nodded and squared his shoulders. "He's squirmed his way out of every battery charge over the years. I'm not letting him walk again."

"It's a risky move." She admired his determination to bring Wilm to justice. Given she felt the same way about Wilm, she had no desire to dissuade him, but it had the potential to backfire.

"He'll spill his guts to avoid a longer prison sentence. I'm certain of it." Eadren appeared confident and that settled her nerves.

When Julisa and Celethe passed by, Eadren stepped in front of Wilm, who pulled up in surprise. Equal in height, the two men locked eyes.

Julisa and Celethe returned to Wilm's side. Both women appeared shaken by the events on the *Delphi*.

"What is the meaning of this?" Julisa asked, her voice thick with fatigue.

Julisa Breckin had one hell of a shitstorm headed her way once Nexus learned of the Zarul killings on the *Delphi* and Wilm's arrest for battery. If Julisa managed the sensational news in her straightforward manner, she might lessen the attention. If she downplayed the incident, she would never escape the tabloid press hysteria. It could cost her the company she had worked so hard at making the success it was today.

"Wilm Breckin, you are under arrest for the assault and battery of an employee on the *Delphi*." Eadren met Wilm's glare with one of his own, daring the man to try something.

Wilm puffed up and took a step toward Eadren, who held his ground. "We had a deal. No prison time. A deal you brokered for me with Mernin Security Forces."

"I've rescinded that offer. You are going to spend the next five years in a prison of my choosing."

Wilm smiled in a sleazy, con-man way. He thought he had Eadren over a barrel. Avei and Sezin shared a smirk.

"Fine, I'm not telling you people anything about my Iscun contacts. Not one damn word." Wilm jabbed Eadren with his finger to emphasize his words. "What do you think about that?"

Eadren maintained his cool. "It's not what I think. It's what I know. And I know you'll go to prison for twenty-five years. Five for the battery and twenty for drug smuggling." Eadren smiled at Wilm. "Tell me what you think about that?"

"You can't do that." Wilm stepped back, shaken.

Avei watched Celethe with interest. Would she continue to stand by her man and accept his behavior? Or has she had enough?

“Sis, do something.” Wilm implored.

Julisa had bailed him out all the other times. Would she do it again? She turned to Celethe, and something unspoken passed between the women. Without saying a word, Celethe shook her head. Julisa studied Wilm for a long moment, then locked arms with Celethe. The women continued to the exit leading into the Charnos spacehub, where Captain Dimphi waited for them.

Wilm tried to run after them, and Eadren grabbed his arm. “The only place you’re going is to a cell.”

“You can’t leave me here. I can’t… I can’t go to prison.” Wilm yelled after his sister, “Julisa, please. I promise I’ll do better this time. You have my word on it.”

The women ignored him and disappeared through the spacehub hatch.

Eadren turned Wilm around and cuffed him. “Wilm Breckin, I am arresting you for the battery of Mesit Urtin. An employee of Breckin Starliners.” He handed Wilm off to D.I. Rico and her officers.

D.I. Rico shook hands with Avei and Eadren. “I’ll be seeing you both at the Tribunal hearings for these two miscreants. Until then, stay safe.”

“Thank you, ma’am. You as well.” Avei watched Rico and her officers walk Wilm through the exit hatch. Two more violent offenders off the street. At that moment, she knew she wanted to keep working, even at the risk of making another mistake. She loved her job, and quitting now meant leaving unfinished business on the table. Anastasia's killer was still out there, along with all the other serial killers who thought they had a right to take an innocent life. She didn't need the trip back to Mernin to decide. An immense weight lifted off her at that moment. She looked up to find Sezin and Eadren grinning at her. Avei smiled back at them.

"Thank the gods and goddesses and all other manner of religious figures out there. I no longer need to break in a new partner," Sezin said.

"It appears that way." Avei smiled back.

"It's been an honor working with you," Eadren said. "I hope our paths cross again one day."

"I hope so too." She meant it.

38

Shifting colors from the holographic ads outside her window slid across the spotless apartment. Avei slept curled up under a soft pink blanket on a plush green couch that had replaced the old scratchy one. A half-full glass of water sat on the new coffee table, along with a bowl of tiny purple conch shells from her vacation on Colea. Beside it, a vase stuffed with vivid yellow flowers added a pop of color.

A floating monitor drifted near the corner of the room, tuned to a Nexus news show, the sound muted. Images of Imara, Caerson, Ocia and Dr. Hueson appeared. A chyron below the pictures flashed – ***Avei Themis catches the Zarul Serial Killer!*** A mug shot of Marsa Baako popped up next to the victims. Her frightened eyes stared straight ahead, as if imploring someone to rescue her. Dread replaced her usual smirk. The fantasy cocoon the author had lived in over the last few months had finally disintegrated, the stark reality of her situation setting in.

A knock on the door startled Avei awake, and she threw off the blanket. She spotted the chyron and frowned. This should be the last time Nexus reported on one of her cases. With Marsa out of the picture and the *Delphi* case wrapped up, she could reclaim her anonymity.

Another knock reminded her of why she had woken. "Lights on. Monitor off." The room brightened and the monitor darkened. The windows frosted over, providing privacy.

Avei jumped up. Her face was a rosy pink from two weeks in the sun on a much needed and long overdue vacation. A retirement present her parents had insisted on paying for, even though she had decided to remain with MSF. After a long conversation with Albert and Iveila when she returned from Charnos, they had both agreed she should follow her heart and they would support her no matter what. In between cases, she would continue her work at the Institute, just like she had in the past. Knowing they were okay with everything had allowed her to really relax and enjoy vital healing time on the beach, physically and mentally.

She ran her fingers through her wild purple hair in a vain attempt to smooth it down. After a few moments, she gave up and hurried to open the door. She had an idea who was on the other side.

Eadren smiled at her, his green cat eyes sparkling. "D.I. Skora said you had returned from vacation. Is this a good time to talk?"

"Come in." Avei stepped back and waved him into her home. "You're looking better." His skin color had returned to light blue, replacing the pallid gray when they thought they had lost him. The puncture marks on his neck had turned a bright purple. She wondered if he would keep his scars. Her fingers found the burn on the back of her hand and traced it.

"Right back at you," Eadren said as he entered the apartment. "Two weeks on Colea did you good."

Avei closed the door behind him. "My favorite place in all the worlds. I've been going there my whole life. Some of my best memories of my sister and my parents are from there."

"I've never been." Eadren moved to the center of the room and remained standing. "It's been on my travel wish list for ages."

"When you decide to go, I'll give you a list of places to stay and what to do while you're there. Can I get you anything? Coffee? Water? I'd offer you alcohol, but I'm on a dry spell."

"I'm here for just a minute to update you on the case. Wilm gave us all of his Iscun contacts. He's not going to prison for the drugs, but he will do five years for the assault." Eadren's relief was palpable. "Multiple agencies across the worlds are rounding up the Iscun scum as we speak. In a matter of days, that group of psychopaths will no longer exist."

Avei understood the risk Eadren had taken in arresting Wilm for assault, and she respected him for it. If Wilm had retracted his agreement to cooperate on the Iscun case, Eadren would have lost his best chance at getting Zenith off the streets. "Getting Wilm, the Iscun Crime Syndicate, and that drug off the streets, is a major win. Well, done, Eadren."

"Thank you. I appreciate that."

"Uma took over wrapping up the Zarul case while I was on vacation. As much as she gets on my nerves sometimes, she is an exceptional inspector. Skora said the case against Marsa Baako is so airtight there's zero chance of her overturning the murder charges. Uma and I appear in front of the Tribunal in three weeks to address any questions they have, and I will ask them to send Marsa to the Meflogun prison colony. The Tribunal has never turned down my request in the past, and I have no reason to think they will now."

Eadren nodded with a smile. "Good. Meflogun is a dismal, dangerous place, and the perfect prison for someone as depraved as Marsa Baako."

"Hey, I found a good home for her pet, Sintha. One of scientists at the Institute owns a male Atiza and has wanted a breeding pair for a while. Garan said Sintha is settling in and doing well. Although she is currently ignoring him and Titus. Acting like they don't exist." Avei laughed. "Garan's in it for the long haul and is happy to give Sintha the time she needs to adjust to her home."

"While I have no love for that animal, I'm glad she is safe. And I have news you might be interested in. During one of our interrogations, Wilm groused about how his sister and wife were conspiring behind his back. Apparently, Julisa is training Celethe to be her eventual successor at Breckin Starliners. That holds even if she decides to divorce Wilm."

Avei nodded, genuinely pleased. The life Celethe had experienced in her younger years could have destroyed her or made her stronger. It was clear which side she fell on. "I'm truly happy for Celethe. Her story is inspirational, and I hope one day she is brave enough to share it."

"As you know, my cover's blown, and I can't work drug enforcement anymore. Skora moved me to homicide as of today." Eadren appeared delighted with his new role.

"He told me." Avei felt the same. Eadren had shown his mettle and his willingness to do whatever it took to bring a case to a successful conclusion; something homicide victims deserved from the investigators hunting their killers.

"Looks like we're partners while I go through homicide training. Your doing?"

Avei shrugged. It had taken very little effort to convince D.I. Skora to bring Eadren on. He agreed Eadren would make an excellent addition to their team. "Skora's sending us to L'reus tomorrow. They have four victims that might be the work of a serial killer."

Eadren rubbed his hands together. "We better get some sleep then."

"Shuttle bay two. Zero 800," Avei said as Eadren opened the door and walked into the hall.

"I'll be there. Boss." Eadren grinned as he closed the door.

Avei smiled. It had been eight years since she'd had a partner other than Sezin, and she looked forward to working with Eadren. After two close calls with death in three months, it felt right knowing someone had her back. Eadren would bring his Marmereck, who seemed every bit as eccentric as her Sezin. She chuckled. Those two would certainly keep things interesting.

Knowing how quickly things could take a turn for the worse, she embraced the moment. For the first time in a long while, Avei felt eager for her future and looked forward to it with gratitude.

Acknowledgements

To my family, who have been with me from launch to landing – thank you. Taryn, my daughter and co-pilot through life, your unwavering support has kept me grounded while I reached for the stars. To my parents, Ray, and Dorothy, who set their ten-year-old daughter's imagination ablaze when they moved us from the bright lights of San Francisco to the vast, star-filled skies of a Montana farm. Your courage and deep sense of adventure gave me the universe. And to my neighbor, whose horse barn roof became my starship, thank you for letting a dreamer chart her course to distant worlds night after night.

A special thank you goes to my brilliant editor, Katharine E. Smith at Heddon Publishing. Your sharp eye and insightful guidance helped refine *The Starliner Murders* into something truly stellar.

To all of my friends over the years, both new allies and long-time crew, thank you for being there throughout this sixteen-year writing odyssey. Your support kept my energy reserves full and my journey on course, even when the path ahead seemed uncharted and endless.

To Rafael Andres Pio and the talented team at CoverKitchen—your exceptional cover design has given *The Starliner Murders* a striking visual identity that perfectly complements the story.

Finally, to you, the reader, intrepid explorer of the written cosmos—thank you for stepping aboard *The Starliner Murders*. Your imagination is the ultimate destination for this story, and I'm so grateful you've joined me on this voyage.

About the author

Kari Charsper grew up on a small farm in Montana, mesmerized by the night skies blanketed with stars and the Milky Way, and dreaming of distant worlds and their inhabitants. This sparked her lifelong love of science fiction and fantasy.

Kari spent 15 years as a screenwriter, sharpening her storytelling skills and bringing stories to life. Now, she channels her passion into writing novels, embracing the creative freedom to build extraordinary worlds without the limits of a film's budget.

Through her vivid imagination and love of adventure, she invites readers to embark on unforgettable journeys into the extraordinary.

Printed in Great Britain
by Amazon

62281167R00180